A HARVEST OF SOULS

BOOK 5 IN THE JOSEPH STONE CRIME THRILLER SERIES

J R SINCLAIR

Copyright 2024 © J R Sinclair

All rights reserved. This book or any portion thereof may not be reproduced or used in any manner whatsoever without the express written permission of the publisher except for the use of brief quotations in a book review.

This is a work of fiction. Any names or characters are fictitious. Any resemblance to actual persons, living or dead, or actual events, or organisations, is purely coincidental.

Published worldwide by Voice from the Clouds Ltd.

www.voicefromtheclouds.com

In memory of my chemo buddy, Dave Ashman. You faced the toughest battle with humour, heart, and laughter. A real friend who I'll never ever forget. This book's for you.

CHAPTER ONE

THURSDAY, 2ND JUNE, 1966

IN THE FADING LIGHT, despite night starting to take hold, the summer hedgerows seemed to be alive with birdsong. As Sally cycled home, everything in the world around her echoed the sense of lightness she felt inside.

Despite all the odds stacked against the young teacher, her children's play of *Wind in the Willows* had gone off without a hitch. By all rights, the responsibility for this should have fallen on the shoulders of an experienced member of staff. But for reasons best known to the headmistress—probably because of some warped sense of humour—this job always fell upon the shoulders of the newest teacher, namely in this instance, the freshly minted Sally Blanchard.

In the staff room, the other members of staff had seemed to delight in recounting their battle-scar stories to Sally about their own experiences running the school's end-of-term summer play. One infamous tale, retold in hushed tones by a colleague, involved one of the children being caught short on stage and relieving themselves in front of all the parents and staff. Thanks to that and other similar tales, Sally had braced herself for the worst. Thankfully, fate had other plans for her, and tonight's performance had been anything but a career-ending nightmare, no sign of a toilet-related mishap in sight.

As she rode through the gathering darkness, she smiled to herself. There were so many highlights from the performance, but the one that stood out was little Stevie Wight, the very definition of wide-eyed enthusiasm. He'd stolen the show with his portrayal of Mole. The role could have been written for the boy.

But the play wasn't the only reason for Sally's happiness. Everyone at school had her pegged as such an innocent. If only they knew the truth.

For well over a month now, Sally had been having a discreet affair with Mike Clifford, a married man, who also happened to be the son of the headmistress at Bambleford. Thanks to that, he'd always helped out with the village school plays. That was how the two of them had met.

Every night for the last four weeks, Mike had been with her through all of the rehearsals. He'd helped to paint sets and all the hundred-and-one jobs it took to put on a children's play. Mike had even been something of a dab hand, helping to sew the costumes for the ensemble of characters for the play. In fact, whatever the project at school, or job that needed doing, he was there to help whenever he could. It seemed nothing was too much for Mike to do for her.

It was little wonder Sally had fallen for him, so when he'd made the first move, going in for a kiss one night when they'd been locking up, she hadn't resisted. That had led to a very memorable encounter behind the stage curtain. Things had only grown in intensity from there, and the illicit nature of their rendevous made it all the more exciting.

The last thing Mike had whispered to her tonight was still echoing through her mind, *'I'll slip away in the early hours, and then we can really celebrate.'*

Now it felt like Sally was riding on air, potholes and all, as she made her way back to her digs with the spinster, Ms Rogers, who was also her landlady, out at Willowcombe. It might be the Swinging Sixties, but Ms Rogers and her moral code were still stuck somewhere in the previous century. She was certainly going to be scandalised when Sally broke the news to her that she would be moving out to *shack up* with her boyfriend, someone who'd already promised he was going to leave his wife. No doubt the look on her landlady's face would be a picture, and how it would set the tongues of the local gossips wagging.

As Sally cycled down the hill, she was so lost in these amusing thoughts, she didn't hear the vehicle until it was almost on top of her. Hearing the crunch of tyres, Sally steered her bike as close to the verge as she dared, so that the driver had plenty of room to get past.

When she didn't hear the vehicle accelerate past, Sally glanced back to see a green flatbed Land Rover keeping pace and making no effort to overtake her. If it belonged to one of the local farmers, this really wasn't like them. Usually, they used the narrowest of gaps to squeeze past at speed. More than once they'd got dangerously close to clipping her handlebars with little thought for her safety.

The young teacher glanced back to see who the driver was, but any view of them was lost behind their headlights. Despite the narrowness of the lane, there was still plenty of room for the vehicle to get past.

Maybe a slightly nervous driver, Sally thought. It was probably one of the young farm lads who'd illegally learned to drive in the fields around the village before they'd even reached sixteen.

Sally pulled up and waved for the driver to go past. This time, she heard the vehicle accelerating. The Land Rover swerved towards her. The vehicle's front bumper smashed into her bike's rear wheel, sending it and her tumbling sideways into the hedge.

It had all happened so quickly that Sally didn't fully realise what had transpired until she found herself upside down in a ditch, looking up at the first stars appearing in the evening sky. The good thing was that, as far as Sally could tell, nothing was broken. The same couldn't be said for her bike. It lay next to her in a crumpled heap.

Sally heard a car door opening and the sound of footsteps approaching as the driver came to check on her. At least he hadn't just driven straight off after hitting her, which was something. The teacher was getting ready to give them a piece of her mind about their reckless driving when the figure loomed over her. Of all the things she might have expected to see, it certainly wasn't a person in a long, dark robe, their face hidden in the shadows of a hood.

She took in the length of cord tied around the figure's waist.

A monk? she wondered with considerable confusion. That didn't make sense. She wondered briefly if she'd hit her head.

Then the teacher's gaze fell upon the silver pendant hanging from the person's neck. It wasn't a crucifix. Instead, it had three interlinked spirals. She'd seen a similar design somewhere before, but couldn't quite place it.

Sally tried to sit up, but a stab of pain made her wince and brought her to an abrupt stop. 'Look, I could do with some help here.'

But the silent figure stood motionless before her.

Anger started to build within Sally. What did this idiot think they were doing? Knocking her off her bike and then deliberately trying to freak her out?

'Will you bloody give me a hand?' she asked more firmly this time.

In a decisive move, the figure leaned down. But any sense of relief Sally might have had was swept away as the figure clamped a piece of cloth over her nose and mouth.

The teacher immediately registered the intensely sweet smell stinging the back of her nose, but her survival instinct was already kicking in. Desperately, she kicked and struck out, trying to dislodge her assailant's grip. But the figure's hands were like iron and, even as she struggled, the world swirled around her.

Sally's vision began to blur, reducing the hooded assailant to nothing more than a silhouette at the end of a growing tunnel. Her arms dropped limply to her sides as a ringing sound filled her ears. Then, finally, her consciousness slipped away and the world around her vanished, and the trajectory of her life changed forever.

CHAPTER TWO

CURRENT DAY

DI JOSEPH STONE sat nursing his half of Guinness in the corner of The Wren and Rose pub in Little Hampton. As he'd done ever since first entering the pub, he surreptitiously let his gaze travel over the patrons. Much to his relief, no one appeared to be paying attention to him.

Joseph took a mental breath, trying to keep his anxiety in check. He had to remind himself that the whole reason for choosing this pub was that it was far away from work, where no one would recognise an Oxford-based DI. More importantly, it was somewhere they could hold their clandestine meeting without word of it getting back to the Night Watchmen.

As the door to the outside opened, Joseph's attention snapped to it, and his heart lifted as he saw his ex-wife, Kate, enter. The moment she spotted him in the corner, a smile filled her face.

She headed straight over and kissed him on the cheek, before glancing around. 'No Derrick yet?'

'I thought you would have come together,' Joseph replied.

'Not much chance of that at the moment,' Kate replied with

a forced brightness as she slipped off her blue wool coat. 'Can I get you another?' She gestured to his drink.

'I cycled here, so I'm grand,' Joseph said, tapping his still very full half of Guinness.

Kate nodded, but her expression stiffened as the outside door opened and DSU Derrick Walker walked in.

'How's it going between you two?' Joseph whispered under his breath.

'As badly as you might expect,' Kate replied, before heading off to the bar, where Derrick joined her to buy a drink.

Joseph couldn't help but notice that this time there wasn't a kiss on the cheek, just a dip of Kate's chin towards her husband.

A few moments later, the two of them joined Joseph, Kate's usual lime and soda in hand, a double whisky by the look of it, in Derrick's. The big man certainly looked haunted as he joined the DI at the table.

For this meeting to be happening at all indicated better than anything else just how dramatically Joseph's life had shifted course over the last month, since the culmination of the Hidden Hand case. Before then, the DI could never have imagined getting together with Derrick in any situation outside work. But now here they were.

'Look, I don't think we should be here any longer than absolutely necessary,' the superintendent said as he sat down, casting a cautious look around him, just as Joseph had done when he'd first arrived. 'If it were down to me, we would have held this meeting over Zoom.'

Kate scowled at him. 'How many times, Derrick? We're playing with the big boys here. There's every chance that any computers and phones we use have already been hacked by the Night Watchmen.'

Derrick's expression flattened. 'If you say so.'

Kate rolled her eyes, took out the photo of her and Joseph's daughter, Ellie, and put it on the table for them all to see. It was the same photo that had been left for the DI to discover on his boat—a not-very-subtle message from the crime syndicate that Joseph and Kate's daughter had fallen into their sights.

'When it comes to protecting my daughter's life, I bloody do *say so*,' she said. But any hardness in her expression was reserved entirely for Derrick and melted away as she turned her attention to Joseph. 'I'm starting to think we should seriously consider telling the National Crime Agency about this,' she said.

The DI shook his head. 'I understand the appeal of that, Kate. The problem is it's difficult to know who can be trusted. Don't forget we're talking about an organisation with a very long reach. If they can get to someone like Chief Superintendent Kennan, not to mention Derrick here, they can get to anyone.'

She stared at him. 'Sorry, you're not seriously suggesting that someone at the NCA could be compromised?'

'I honestly wouldn't put it past them. Think how quickly the NCA stopped their investigation into the prisoner transfer assassination. They must have strongly suspected someone on the inside tipped the syndicate off about Darryl Manning's plea bargain. But suddenly, just like that, their investigation melted away, and they pinned the suspicion on his solicitor instead.'

Kate's jaw clenched as she glared at Derrick. 'Which I suppose was just as well for you.'

Derrick took a long gulp of his whisky. 'Look, how many times do I have to tell you that I was only protecting you?'

Kate visibly bristled. 'Which you should have discussed with me. But no, you acted unilaterally, and thanks to that, dragged Ellie into the firing line. If only you'd had the balls to tell me back then, we could have worked out what to do together. Instead, you gave in to their bloody blackmail.'

The DSU dropped his gaze back to his whisky. 'Maybe I

should have, but when they threatened your life, what choice did I have?'

Her eyes narrowed on him. 'If only you had, maybe we wouldn't be sitting here now, trying to work out what the hell we're going to do about the mess you landed us all in.'

Not for the first time, Joseph felt like he was caught in the middle of a private conversation. The thing was, Kate wasn't exaggerating. His suspicions about Derrick had led to his off-the-books investigation into the DSU's involvement with the Night Watchmen. But things had really gone south when he'd eventually told Kate, who'd reopened her research into the crime syndicate as part of an exposé she'd been intending to write.

That had directly led to her being abducted by the crime syndicate after staking out a people-smuggling operation they ran. Before she'd eventually been released, there'd been one major caveat for both her and Joseph—the threat to Ellie's life if they didn't bend the knee, just like the DSU had been forced to.

Derrick took another long swig of his whisky, before meeting Kate's burning gaze. 'Look, Kate, if I could go back and reverse that decision, I'd do it in a heartbeat. I know you will never be able to forgive me for what I did, but at least try to understand the impossible situation those bastards put me in.'

This stirred more than a modicum of sympathy in the DI, not least because that was exactly the same situation he found himself in with Ellie. Although there was a lot of bad blood between him and Derrick, that didn't mean he would let the man drown.

Joseph looked at Kate. 'Look, this is ancient history, and we have to start looking forward, not backwards—not least for the sake of our daughter, Kate.'

She met his gaze, and once again the fire in her eyes flickered out. 'I know, I know. Sorry, I didn't mean to hijack things.'

The DI nodded and he seized the opportunity to steer the discussion to what they needed to discuss. 'So, moving on, Derrick, did you manage to dig anything up about Chris Faulkner?'

The big man looked visibly relieved at the change of topic. 'I looked back into the DCI's files and, despite your suspicion, Joseph, his promotion doesn't seem to have been authorised by Chief Kennan.'

At hearing that, the DI felt a brief spark of hope. He'd never felt great about suspecting someone he'd considered a friend, at least until he realised the man might actually worked for the Night Watchmen. 'That sounds like good news, then?'

Derrick pulled a face. 'I wouldn't be so quick to assume anything. I wasn't able to find out much, other than that he was put on a fast-track programme, and that brought him to St Aldates. The strange thing is, there isn't exactly a lot in his files either. It's almost like someone has gone out of their way to slim down his profile.'

'Like deliberately removing anything compromising?' Kate asked.

'Precisely. For all we know, there's a senior officer over in Bristol who's been compromised. Maybe they pulled similar strings for Faulkner like Kennan has done for her chosen people across the Thames Valley force.'

'In other words, we still don't know if Chris can be trusted,' Joseph said.

Derrick made a clicking sound with his tongue. 'Afraid not. For now, we have to assume he's the Night Watchmen's inside man at St Aldates, keeping an eye on the two of us.'

'In that case, we need to find out more,' Kate said. She gave Joseph a pointed look.

The DI understood what she was getting at. 'In other words,

I need to maintain my friendship with Chris and keep him close?'

Kate nodded. 'I realise what a difficult situation that puts you in, but it's important that if Chris really is working for the Night Watchmen, he doesn't suspect we might be on to him.'

'Easier said than done, but I'll try my best.'

Joseph wasn't at all happy with this tactic. Part of him didn't want to believe that Chris had crossed the line into corruption. But the DI knew that, in this instance, he had to assume guilt until proven otherwise.

'Just do what you have to do to avoid raising suspicion, Joseph,' Derrick said, sensing the DI's internal conflict. 'Meanwhile, I'll keep digging into the files to see if I can find out anything else. Also, I'm going to go through all the fast-track promotions Kennan authorised. That way, we might be able to build up a clearer picture of who might have been compromised.'

'And once we have that list, then what?' Kate asked.

'That's where you and your paper come in,' Joseph suggested. 'We choose our moment. You go public, blowing the whistle with an article about that cesspool of a criminal organisation. Once the genie is out of the bottle, nobody will be able to turn a blind eye to what they've been up to.'

'That sounds as good a plan as any,' Derrick replied. 'So, are we all in agreement?'

Joseph and Kate both nodded.

'In that case, I'd better get going. I need to get back to my flat and unpack the rest of my things.'

Lines spidered out from the corners of Kate's eyes. 'Do you have everything you need from home?'

'Just a few bits and pieces I still need to pick up. I'll pop over tomorrow, if that's okay?'

'No problem. I'll be at work anyway, so you'll have the house to yourself.'

'Good...' Derrick's gaze slid away from Kate's.

It was hard for Joseph not to recognise the pain in the man's eyes as he nodded at him before heading out of the pub.

Joseph then focused on his ex-wife, who was staring at her drink. 'So, still separated then?'

Kate raised her eyes to his. 'Very much so. It's for the best, for both of us,' Kate replied, for the first time with a sad look.

'Surely, you and Derrick will be able to get past this.'

'I wish I could believe that, Joseph. But it's hard not to feel betrayed by his actions, especially when he didn't feel he could confide in me about what was going on.'

Joseph grimaced. 'He wasn't the only one who held things back from you, Kate.'

'Don't you worry, I know. But to your credit, you did eventually come out and tell me, which is what really matters.'

The DI mentally thanked his good friend, Professor Dylan Shaw, who had nudged him to do exactly that. 'Maybe I did, but I still think you're being a bit hard on your husband.'

Kate raised a shoulder. 'Possibly, but we both know that's not the only reason this happened.'

Joseph felt his heart contract inside his chest. Of course he knew exactly what she was talking about, because it had been the same thing that had been keeping him up at night.

Only a month ago, Kate, in a moment of extreme vulnerability, had confessed she was still in love with Joseph. Just as he was very much in love with her. Not that Kate had allowed him to tell her that, even though he was absolutely certain she already knew. And the reason she hadn't wanted to hear it, apart from the fact she was married to someone else?

The major fly in the ointment, which neither one could overlook, was that Joseph was currently dating Amy Fischer, the chief SOC officer. Yes, what with that and now Kate's separation from Derrick, it was the very definition of a landmine-filled situation.

'Can I tempt you with another drink?' Kate asked. 'I can always pop your bike into the back of my car.'

'Actually, I'd better not. I've got an early start tomorrow.'

'I thought you had the weekend off?'

'Indeed, I have. But somehow, Megan managed to persuade me and Dylan to join her on an archaeological dig over near Fernbridge Village.'

'That's seriously what you're going to do for fun during your time off?'

'Aye, tell me about it, but you try saying no to Megan.'

'Well, I'm sure the experience of digging through frozen mud in the middle of winter will be good for you.'

He gave her a sardonic look. 'The very definition of character building.'

His ex-wife smiled at him. 'Well, if you do find anything interesting on your dig, please let me know. A local interest piece is always good for the Oxford Chronicle.'

'If we dig up the equivalent of the Sutton Hoo treasures, I'll certainly keep you in mind.'

Her smile broadened. 'Make sure you do. Anyway, if you're going, I will too. I have to say, though, the idea of heading back to an empty house hasn't got much appeal.'

Was Kate fishing? Joseph had to mentally force himself not to invite her back to his narrowboat, *Tús Nua*, there and then. His willpower only went so far, and that wouldn't be the right thing for either of them. It certainly wouldn't be fair to Amy. So instead, he went for deflection.

'Maybe we should organise a family Sunday meal at yours. Ellie could bring John.'

'That's a great idea. Although, for obvious reasons, I'm not about to invite Derrick. Anyway, it would be a great opportunity to catch up with our daughter. It feels like I've hardly seen her recently.'

'You're not the only one.'

Kate spread her hands. 'Well, we did teach her to be independent in the first place. Anyway, let's do it this Sunday, and you should invite Dylan as he practically counts as family.' Kate gave Joseph her brightest forced smile. 'And Amy, of course. Let's make a real occasion of it.'

Joseph matched her false smile with his own. 'That sounds grand. Although, if Dylan is coming, he'll insist on helping you in the kitchen.'

Kate grinned. 'Why do you think I'm inviting him?'

Joseph chuckled. 'Good plan. Anyway, I must be away. I'll have to love you and leave you.'

'Yes...' Kate replied with a small voice.

Their eyes met, and there was a whole other conversation without any words that pulled at the depths of Joseph's soul. But then he blinked, as though waking from an impossible dream, stood, and leaned over to kiss her on the forehead. With a sad look, she raised her hand in farewell.

Before Joseph's resolve crumpled, and without a backward glance, he walked away from the woman who would always occupy a special place in his heart.

CHAPTER THREE

The next morning, the *freeze-your-nads-off* wind was blowing across the ploughed field, and had been since Joseph first arrived at the archaeological dig site. He was starting to suspect the wind never stopped in the rolling hills of the Chilterns, where there was little to block its path. The rooks and jackdaws certainly seemed to appreciate the constant blow of air. They wheeled in its currents over the dig team's heads, keeping an eye out for any juicy worms they might dig up.

But there was something beyond the desolate atmosphere that the DI found disturbing about this place. The shivers that kept sweeping through him weren't just down to the winter cold. Even though he couldn't explain why, part of him felt distinctly uneasy about working here. It was almost like some part of his buried animal instinct was telling him to walk away and not look back. He had no idea why.

Trying to ignore the irrational part of his brain, especially as no one else looked freaked out, trowel in hand, Joseph was doing his best to scrape away at the frozen earth. He was starting to seriously suspect a jackhammer might be a more suitable tool for this particular excavation. Despite the thickness of his winter-insulated jacket, not to mention his Merino wool skiing thermals he'd dug out from the bottom of a drawer, the DI still felt frozen to his marrow.

The thing Joseph couldn't quite get his head around was that this was apparently Megan's idea of fun when she was off duty. The last dig he'd accompanied her on had been during the summer. In his humble opinion, that was a far more civilised time of year to muck around in the earth. On a winter's day like this, less so.

Then he heard the DC's laugh drift across to him from the other excavation trench, where she was working with the pathologist, Doctor Rob Jacobs, who she'd also persuaded to join them. They were obviously sharing some joke, as Rob was grinning at her like a right eejit.

Just friends—right, Joseph thought.

Megan might insist it was purely platonic between herself and the good doctor, but the DI had become increasingly certain Rob had a thing for her. Certainly, any sane person who could be persuaded to join her on an archaeological dig in the depth of winter indicated something more than a passing infatuation.

As for why Joseph was here... That had everything to do with the man currently crouched over an iron pot hanging from a tripod over a fire next to the dig site—the one and only, Professor Dylan Shaw. It was Dylan who'd persuaded Joseph, despite his better judgment, to join them on this archaeological excavation in perishing weather. But there had also been bait in the form of one of Dylan's culinary creations—namely, a stew of Boston beans.

The professor had seized the chance to try out his new Dutch oven and cook alfresco. The way the scent of sweet molasses, earthy beans, and savoury salted pork was wafting over the dig site, it was little wonder that his latest culinary creation had been getting him a lot of attention from the dig team. Now everybody wanted to be his friend.

After several stirs of the pot, steam curling around his head like a wizard brewing up a magic elixir, Dylan turned and headed back towards the DI, thermos in hand. Rather than being dressed like an Arctic explorer as Joseph was, his friend was wearing a simple ancient brown duffle coat, with a scarf and a bobble hat. Despite the lack of serious outdoor clothing, the professor still somehow managed to look toasty warm.

Dylan held up the thermos as he neared Joseph. 'What do you say, my friend? Fancy a cup of coffee to warm up?'

Joseph put down his trowel. 'God, yes. If I get any colder, penguins will start following me around, thinking I'm one of their own.'

Dylan snorted as he unscrewed the flask and poured them two generous mugfuls.

On his first sip, Joseph instantly recognised a strong Java brew, but then he picked up the fragrant smell of peat, not to mention the nip of alcohol on his tonsils.

The DI gave his friend a knowing look. 'What's your secret ingredient? Whatever it is, it's a welcome addition.'

'A drop of Talisker. I thought you'd appreciate the extra kick to keep you going until the beans are ready.'

'Well, I certainly approve of this as a way to hold off the frostbite in the meantime,' Joseph said, raising his tin mug and clanking it against Dylan's. He climbed out of the trench to join his friend, taking a break from the backbreaking work.

Along the dig's two trenches, despite the inhospitable conditions, dozens of volunteers were carefully scraping away the soil, trying to pick up any clues of the Celtic settlement believed to have once been there. Aerial drone photos had revealed circular markings in the field, the telltale indicator of buildings that had once stood where wheat was now planted. The two trenches had been dug through the largest of these building footprints.

So far, they'd unearthed fragments of ceramic pots, a selection of iron tools, but the greatest excitement had been reserved for a weight from an ancient loom. That proved that textiles had once been woven there and suggested a certain level of industry.

All Joseph knew was that if the Celts had endured the same sort of bone-chilling weather they currently were having, he hoped they'd woven plenty of blankets to offer better protection from the elements than his modern outdoor jacket could.

His attention was drawn by a burst of applause from the other trench, which seemed to be centred around Megan and Rob.

Joseph and Dylan exchanged a look, before hurrying over to see what all the fuss was about.

Megan and Rob stood next to Professor Amanda Bailey, the chief archaeologist leading the dig, in the middle of a growing ring of people. Professor Bailey was squatting next to something buried in the ground and carefully brushing the dirt from it.

As Megan and Rob headed out of the circle, people patted them both on the back as they squeezed past.

'What's all the excitement about?' Dylan asked as they reached them.

'Megan just unearthed a large stone slab in the entrance to the larger of the two buildings,' Rob said.

'What's so special about a stone slab that makes you two look like you've just won the lottery?' Joseph asked.

'There's a triskelion design on it,' Megan replied.

'Come again?'

'Ah, now that is fascinating,' Dylan said.

Joseph looked over the sea of heads, at an interlocking three-spiral design that Professor Bailey was slowly revealing with her brush.

'And a triskelion is significant because?' he asked.

'It represents the cycle of life, death, and rebirth, and the three realms of land, sea, and sky,' Rob replied.

Megan nodded. 'And there's something else as well. Someone found a fragment of a sun wheel.'

The professor's eyes widened. 'Which represents the sun and, once again, the cyclical nature of the seasons. Has anything else been discovered?'

Rob gave him a knowing look. 'Just animal bones arranged in patterns.'

'Oh my goodness.' The professor shook his head.

The DI looked between the three of them. 'Will someone please let me in on the big secret?'

Megan turned to him. 'Professor Bailey is convinced this was some sort of religious site where animal sacrifices were made, probably to ensure a good harvest.'

Joseph's gaze took in the desolate winter field around them, thinking of the unease he'd felt since first reaching the site. Not that he was about to share that particular titbit of information.

'And there was me, thinking this was just another cold, muddy patch of earth.'

'A muddy patch of earth that's been hiding away a significant archaeological site, just waiting for us to discover it,' Rob said.

Megan nodded. 'It's days like today that underline why I love archaeology so much.'

'I can understand that, but I have to say that right now, I'd be happy to call it a day and head off for a cheeky pint,' Joseph said.

'No knocking off early just yet. We've got at least another

hour's excavation work to do,' Dylan said. 'Besides, my Boston beans will help thaw you out.'

'Which is basically the only reason I'm here,' the DI replied, shrugging with an apologetic look at the others.

Courtesy of Dylan, one incredible meal of Boston beans later, which had more than delivered on its promise of smoky goodness, they'd all been put to work in the single trench where the stone had been found.

At the beginning of the day, Professor Bailey had informed the team that they had until the end of the weekend to conduct their excavation. After that, the field would be ploughed in readiness to sow a crop of winter wheat. Any further digs would have to wait until sometime after the crop was harvested.

That was why Joseph was now working with Rob, helping the man excavate the far end of the trench with shovels. The two men had already exhausted the usual subjects—weather, work, the best tea to drink during a dig—when the doctor turned to him.

'Do you mind if I ask you a question?' Rob whispered, glancing back over his shoulder to check that Megan was a good distance away, where she was working with Dylan at the other end of the trench.

Joseph's instincts warned him that this might have something to do with his colleague. 'Fire away,' he replied.

'I'll just come straight out and say it. Do you happen to know if Megan's seeing anyone right now?'

So there it was. The DI had always suspected Rob was attracted to Megan. But beyond the obvious spark between them during autopsies, the man had done nothing about it. It seemed that might be about to change.

'Not that I know of, Rob. But why are you asking?' Joseph did his best to keep a straight face, but then broke into a broad grin.

Rob's expression briefly tightened before relaxing again. 'Have I been that obvious?'

'Let's just say everyone, including your colleague, Doctor Reece, won't be at all surprised.'

'I see. And there was me thinking I was playing my cards close to my chest.'

'So maybe don't take up poker anytime soon.'

Rob chuckled. 'Probably good advice. But you don't think the age gap between us is too big?'

'That's not for me to say. That's between you and Megan.'

'Would she be interested in dating me, do you think?'

Megan had once told Joseph she saw Rob as nothing more than a friend, even if there was a connection between them. The DI decided he needed to duck that question. It really wasn't any of his business.

'Once again, that's something you and Megan need to talk about,' he said.

'Right...'

Joseph heard the disappointment in the man's voice, no doubt hoping to hear a ringing endorsement. But he was old and wise enough to steer well clear of other people's personal lives whenever possible.

As the silence lingered between them, Joseph's thoughts returned to Chris. The man had gone out of his way to befriend Joseph. The question the DI kept finding himself asking was why. Had it been a way to butter Joseph up so he could eventually be recruited into the Night Watchmen?

Although Joseph realised he needed to carry on as though nothing had happened at work, he didn't know if he could continue being friendly with Chris outside of work.

Chris had even shared his home-brewed stout with Joseph at his home, where they'd worked together on restoring the man's cars—the male equivalent of breaking bread. But like the saying goes, keep your friends close and your enemies closer. The question still in Joseph's mind was whether Chris could really be that enemy. Instinct told him no. Circumstantial evidence said otherwise.

It was then, with the next dig of the spade, that Joseph noticed the banding in the soil in the clod of earth Rob had just deposited on the ground from his shovel. The doctor had noticed it too and stooped for a closer look.

'This is something new,' Rob said.

'Something linked to the Celts who once lived here?' Joseph asked.

'Only one way to find out.' Rob raised his hand. 'Doctor Bailey, have you got a moment?'

The chief archaeologist turned and headed straight over. 'Have you found something interesting?' she asked as she reached them.

'Not sure, but it appears to be some sort of white deposit in the soil,' Rob said.

Amanda nodded and, scooping her dark hair back over her ears, knelt beside the clod and examined the hole that it had come from. She pointed to the layers. 'Okay, you can see that whatever is forming these white streaks has been deposited over many years, hence the layers of strata. So what does that tell us?'

'That it's something that's been deposited on the soil on a regular basis?' Joseph asked.

Amanda smiled at him. 'Just so. And where exactly are we standing?'

'On an ancient Celtic site,' Rob suggested.

'Yes, but much more recently than that?'

'A farmer's field,' Joseph said. 'Ah, you're saying this is probably some sort of fertiliser?'

'Exactly, and based on the colour...' Amanda unhooked the trowel dangling from her belt and scraped away at the section of white, which crumbled onto the ground. 'Yes, as I thought, it looks like bone ash to me.'

Rob frowned and pointed at something shining dully in the powder. 'Hang on, that looks like a shard of a tooth.'

'It will just be an animal tooth that made it through the milling process,' Amanda replied. She picked up the object the doctor was pointing at.

Joseph leaned in for a closer look. The tooth was charred and had been cracked in half. But it was unlike any sort of animal tooth Joseph had ever seen.

Rob and Amanda both frowned at the object.

'What?' Joseph asked, looking at Rob, who was shaking his head.

'That's part of a human molar,' Rob said.

'You mean, from an ancient Celt who once lived here?'

'Not likely. It was found far too close to the surface,' Amanda said.

The archaeologist and pathologist exchanged a tight look and Joseph realised the significance of what they'd said.

'Oh, shite—as in, these could be recent human remains?'

'Until we run some tests, we won't be sure,' Amanda said. 'But if I were a betting woman...'

Joseph nodded, his gaze already sweeping over the two dozen people stomping all over what could be a crime scene. 'Okay, Amanda, if you could ask everyone to stop digging, I'm going to call in the troops.'

'Of course.' She nodded and headed off to speak to the rest of the team.

'Some sort of problem?' Megan asked, reaching them, with Dylan not far behind.

'Let's just say I think we're going to have to cancel any more plans we might have had for our weekend,' Joseph replied grimly.

His gaze swept over the field again, and it was hard to ignore the shiver that ran up his spine. Could he have really sensed that this place was what—haunted? Pulling out his phone, he made a vow never to say anything about that to anyone, as he would never be able to cope with all the piss-taking it would bring.

CHAPTER FOUR

Amy and the rest of the SOC forensic team were hard at work less than a couple of hours after the discovery of the tooth shard. The whole archaeological dig had been cordoned off and patrol cars had been positioned in the gates.

Banks of arc lights illuminated the site as the winter sun tipped towards the horizon, turning the scudding clouds slate grey. Whilst Joseph and Megan had stayed behind, Dylan had caught a lift with Rob. Most of the rest of the dig team had already headed off to a local pub for a quick pint.

As the never-ending wind worried the edges of the tent flap, Joseph and Megan were doing their best to warm up inside the forensic shelter that had been set up over the scene. Through the gap, the DI could see a small crowd of local onlookers from the nearby village of Fernbridge, who'd gathered to see what this *grand craic* with the police was all about. It seemed, thanks to the dog-walking mafia, word had quickly spread across the area. Certainly, based on the number of phones taking videos and photos, there would be no keeping this story out of the papers.

Because of her significant expertise in forensic archaeology, Professor Bailey had stayed behind to assist with the investigation. Amy, who'd been working closely with her, headed over to the archaeologist with yet another sample bag from the scene, where the SOC team had concentrated their efforts.

'Another tooth?' Joseph asked, as he and Megan went to join them.

'Yes, that's the twentieth so far, and all from different levels in the soil,' Amy said.

'Is that significant?' Chris asked, having just arrived from a classic car meet-up over in Chepstow.

Joseph had to mentally check himself at the appearance of his boss. This was going to be the first real test of his ability to keep up the pretence that he didn't suspect the DCI was a potentially corrupt police officer. Thankfully, the others were there to take up the slack as the DI got himself into the right headspace for his coming performance.

'The difference in depth indicates the tooth fragments come from over a long period of time,' Amanda said to Chris. 'Although we've discovered them at multiple layers, and there's been a fair bit of churning together thanks to ploughing over the years, my estimate is the earliest human remains among them are reasonably old.'

'And you are?' the DCI asked.

'Sorry, I'm Professor Amanda Bailey, and this is—or maybe I should now say, *was*—my dig. I'm just here to add my expertise to your investigation.'

'And I'm glad to have you here,' Amy quickly added.

Chris dipped his chin towards Amanda. 'Then thank you. But when you say some of the human remains are old, we're obviously not talking as far back as the Celtic era, are we?'

'Sadly not. Based on the distribution, the earliest tooth fragments we've found so far, and taking into account their depth in the soil, date back roughly sixty years.'

Joseph realised this was his moment to get his head in the

game. 'So you're saying we could be dealing with multiple bodies?'

'That's not for me to say,' Amanda replied. 'All I can do is assist Amy in coming up with enough information so she can make an assessment.'

'Well, you've already been a great help,' Amy said.

Chris gazed out at the field stretching away around them. 'So, what are your collective thoughts? Are we going to end up having to dig up this entire field to know exactly how many victims we're dealing with here?'

Thankfully, Amanda shook her head. 'No, the pattern of the ash strata seems to be limited to being scattered around the Celtic building we believe was some sort of temple.'

'Hang on, that can't be just a coincidence, can it?' Megan asked.

'That's exactly what I've been wondering,' Amy said.

Joseph narrowed his eyes. 'Sorry, you're not seriously suggesting that someone deliberately dumped the ashes of their victims on this spot because they somehow knew it was once a Celtic temple where sacrifices were made?'

Amanda frowned. 'I realise how crazy that sounds. Apart from anything else, we've not been able to discover any records that there was even a Celtic settlement here. So how anyone could know there was an ancient temple on this spot is beyond me.'

'But what if someone in the area knew about it?' Megan suggested.

'Well, if they did, they've certainly kept it a very well-kept secret for a long time. There was nothing in any historical records that we could find.'

'What about the farmer who owns this field, Charlotte Harris?' Chris asked. 'Did she really not know anything about the Celtic settlement on her land?'

'She certainly seemed surprised when we approached her for permission to excavate the field, which I suppose in hindsight could have been an act,' Amanda replied.

'Regardless, she's still going to be one of the first people we interview after this,' Joseph said.

'We're going to need to talk to everyone in Fernbridge to see if anyone knew anything about the temple, or if anyone has gone missing from the village dating back to the sixties,' Chris added.

Megan nodded. 'Talking of which, is there any way you and the team can help to identify the victims forensically, Amy?'

The SOCO shook her head. 'Not easily. There won't be any DNA evidence left in the bone ash, and before you ask, that goes for the teeth fragments, too. The high temperature that destroyed the rest of the bones will have wiped out any trace of DNA.'

'What sort of temperatures are we talking about here?' Chris asked.

'Well, we're certainly not talking about your average bonfire. It will have to have been a furnace of some sort.'

'Then we need to draw up a list of any furnaces like that in the area,' Chris said.

'What about checking through dental records of any missing people in the area as well?' Megan asked.

Amy held up the bag and pointed to the shattered tooth fragments inside. 'Not exactly a lot to go on here.'

'But surely we can use carbon dating to get a rough estimate of the time of death?' Joseph asked.

Amy scowled. 'I hate to be the bearer of bad news once again, but unfortunately, the high temperatures used to dispose of these bodies will have also altered the carbon content in the remains, making it difficult to obtain a reliable reading.'

'So that's it, then? We have no way to link these remains to any missing people?' Megan asked.

Amanda held up a hand. 'Don't give up hope just yet. This is where a technique called thermoluminescence might be useful. We sometimes use it in digs when human remains are discovered and where carbon dating isn't good enough.'

'And what's thermoluminescence when it's at home?' Joseph asked.

'If you don't mind a quick science lesson?' Amanda said.

The DI waved a hand. 'Educate away.'

Amanda grinned at him. 'Well, teeth are composed primarily of enamel and dentine. Enamel, the hardest substance in the human body, has a dense, highly mineralised structure, primarily made up of hydroxyapatite, similar to bone. Thanks to the teeth's dense structure, they might still retain some trapped electrons.'

'And that's what the thermoluminescence measures?' Joseph asked.

'That's right. There's a lab I like to use for running the test. They should be able to get some results back within a week or so —maybe sooner, if I lean on them. That will give you a rough estimate for the time of death from the bone fragments we've been able to recover so far.'

'Then please go ahead and with my blessing,' Amy said. 'I'll take all the help you can give us on this case.'

Amanda nodded towards the forensic officer. 'Consider it done.'

'Okay, it sounds to me like we need to have a conversation with the farmer who owns this field,' Chris said. 'Joseph and Megan, if you can handle that?'

'Consider it done,' Joseph replied.

The entrance to the tent was pulled back, and PC John Thorpe stepped inside.

'There's a member of the public who is keen to talk to the lead investigating officer as soon as possible.'

'About?' Chris asked.

'She wouldn't say, other than that it might be relevant to what we've discovered.'

The DCI raised an eyebrow. 'Oh, did she now.' Looking at Joseph and Megan he said, 'Shall we?'

The three detectives headed across the field, following the constable towards the perimeter of the police cordon. A scowling woman wearing a tweed skirt and jacket, and somewhere in her early seventies, was waiting for them among the onlookers.

The woman sniffed as the officers reached her. 'Here you are at last. So which one of you is in charge?'

'That would be me—DCI Faulkner,' Chris said.

'Good, I'd like a quiet word.' She gestured to the rest of the public gathered on the other side of the police cordon. 'Maybe out of earshot of these other people as this is somewhat of a sensitive nature.'

'I see.' Chris raised the cordon to allow the woman to pass beneath it.

As they headed towards a gate a short distance away, they were watched with interest by several members of the public.

'Are the rumours correct? You've found human remains in this field?' the woman asked.

'And where did you hear that exactly?' Chris asked.

'A group of archaeologists were talking about it in the local pub. I'm afraid people do love to gossip.'

Chris raised his eyebrows at Joseph and Megan as they took in the size of the crowd that had already gathered. Even so, the DCI valiantly tried to duck the question. 'As this investigation is still at such an early stage, I'm sure you'll appreciate that I can't really discuss that yet. Mrs...?'

The woman sniffed again, as though the DSI had just wafted a turd under her nose. '*Ms* Trelawney. Apart from running the post office and village shop in Fernbridge, I'm also one of the local parish councillors. In that capacity, you can obviously talk to me in confidence. Besides, as a local citizen, I have every right to know what's happening on my doorstep, especially when it's happening on *this* farm.'

'What do you mean by that, exactly?' Joseph asked.

'I don't want to tell you how to do your job...'

But you're going to do it anyway, Joseph thought.

'However, I suggest you pull in Charlotte Harris for questioning at once. She owns this farm.'

'And is there any particular reason for that?' Chris asked.

Ms Trelawney leaned in, conspiratorially. 'Because that woman's a witch!'

'Sorry?' Megan asked, giving the shopkeeper a confused look.

'There've been stories for years about what she gets up to on Shadowbrook Farm, now that she runs it by herself.' Ms Trelawney gestured towards the gate next to them. 'If you want proof, you don't have to look much further than that.'

For the first time, Joseph noticed the twigs woven into a wreath placed on top of one of the posts like a crown of thorns.

Chris peered at it. 'What exactly is that?'

Ms Trelawney crossed her arms. 'Probably some sort of spell. So, as you can see for yourselves—witchcraft, plain and simple. I wouldn't be at all surprised if Charlotte even had a hand in these murders.' The woman tapped the side of her nose.

Joseph scowled at the woman. 'I'm sorry, but wrapping a few twigs round a post isn't exactly proof of anything.'

The woman gave the DI a sharp look. 'Well, it isn't exactly Christian behaviour, is it? Besides, there have been plenty of rumours swirling around about what Charlotte gets up to on her farm.'

'Such as?' Megan asked.

'Strange goings-on in the middle of the night.'

'Well, we prefer hard evidence rather than rumours, so if you have any of that, we'd be more than happy to hear about it,' Chris replied.

Ms Trelawney sniffed. 'Not as such. Just things people have said over the years. But mark my words, there will be trouble if you don't arrest that woman immediately.'

Joseph narrowed his gaze on the woman. 'What sort of trouble?'

'Mentioning no names, but there are some hotheads in the town who might want to take matters into their own hands.'

With a lot of encouragement from you, no doubt, Joseph thought.

'Then they'll find themselves in a lot of trouble, along with anyone stirring anything up,' Chris said, smiling at the woman.

Despite his suspicions about him, Joseph was struck by how much he actually liked the man.

Ms Trelawney made a harumphing sound, turned, and stalked back to the onlookers whose numbers had increased in the short time they'd been having their conversation.

Chris shook his head at her. 'Jesus, I can already tell that woman's going to be a right royal pain in our arses.'

'I have an unfortunate feeling you might be right there,' Joseph replied.

'You don't actually believe what she said about Charlotte Harris being a witch, do you?' Megan asked.

'Not in the way that she means,' Joseph said. He gestured to the twig wreath on the post. 'But I'm intrigued to know what the significance of this thing is. Thankfully, I know just the person who will know.' He took out his phone to take a photo of the wreath.

'In other words, Dylan?' Megan asked.

'Aye. Apart from being a walking encyclopaedia, he's something of an expert when it comes to the occult.'

'Isn't he your neighbour?' Chris asked.

'That's the man. And with your blessing, boss, I'd like to send this photo to him to see what he thinks.'

'No problem with me,' the DCI replied. 'But, without giving Ms Trelawney too much credit, maybe have that conversation with Charlotte Harris sooner than later. We certainly need to kick the tyres on our local busybody's theory of witchcraft being a factor in these murders.'

'Leave it to us—we'll head over there now,' Joseph replied. 'Besides, we don't want to give that woman too much time to get the village stirred up against the farmer.'

A short while later he was following Megan towards her Mini Cooper, wondering how exactly he was going to go about asking the farmer if she was a witch. One thing was for sure, it was certainly going to be an interesting conversation, especially if the tweed-wearing Miss Marple-wannabe had pointed them in the direction of a potential serial killer.

CHAPTER FIVE

A SCRAPING SOUND CAME from beneath the Mini Cooper as Megan grounded it on another boulder while they bounced down a rutted track filled with glistening puddles.

'Bloody hell, I'm going to end up losing my exhaust at this rate,' the DC complained as she clutched the steering wheel, doing her best to avoid the largest of the potholes.

'Then maybe slow down a bit and stop pretending this is a rally event,' Joseph muttered as his head bumped up into the roof for the fifth time.

Before Megan could respond, they rounded the corner to see any semblance of a track disappear. Instead, spilling across it was a huge pool of glistening slurry. The DC hit the brakes hard, throwing Joseph forward against the seatbelt as the Mini shuddered to a stop. But it was already too late. The vehicle was in the middle of the small lake of effluent.

Scowling, the DC pressed the accelerator, only to be rewarded with the sound of spinning wheels.

Joseph glowered at her. 'For feck's sake, do you make a habit of getting stuck in mud?'

The DC ignored him and pressed her foot harder to the floor, resulting in a geyser of slurry being thrown up from the front wheels and over the sides of the Mini. Within seconds, both side windows were coated in a film of viscous grey-brown material.

Joseph didn't say anything, waiting for it to dawn on his companion that they weren't going anywhere anytime soon. But Megan wasn't anything if not determined, and it took a good two minutes before she finally admitted defeat, slumped back in her seat, and turned the engine off.

'I think we're stuck,' she said.

Joseph arched his eyebrows at her. 'You don't say.'

The DC gave him an apologetic look. 'I think we're probably going to need a tow out of this mess.'

'You think?' The DI sighed. 'Hopefully, Charlotte Harris will have a tractor to tow us out. Maybe we should ask her to do that before we arrest her.'

'Alright, alright, I get the message,' Megan replied.

Shaking his head, Joseph opened the door and looked down at the glistening lake of slurry, shimmering with an oil rainbow stretching out around them. A poet might have seen the beauty in it, but not Joseph, especially as his wellies were stowed in the Mini's boot. He looked down at his clean brown suede boots and sighed. Megan, meanwhile, had no such worries as she was still wearing her walking boots and had already exited the vehicle.

'For feck's sake,' Joseph muttered again as he stepped out into the gloopy, stinking mess that rose around his boots.

Megan, who was already safely back on terra firma, grimaced as she watched her colleague wade towards her. As he stepped onto solid ground, they both looked down at the slick of slime now coating his formerly pristine boots.

Megan opened her mouth to say something, thought better

of it when she saw the look Joseph was giving her, and closed her mouth again.

Without saying a word, the DI turned and stalked away along the track, pausing only briefly to try to wash the worst of the muck off his boots in a rain-filled puddle.

As the two detectives rounded another bend a lone farmhouse came into view, its dark windows reflecting the grey storm clouds scudding overhead. The wind moaned around them, tugging and pushing at them, almost as if the weather itself didn't want them to approach the house. If Joseph had been a superstitious man, something he was starting to wonder about after sensing something at the dig site, he might have been inclined to believe Ms Trelawney's nonsense about the owner being a witch. Maybe Charlotte was able to cast weather spells to keep intruders away.

But footstep by dreary footstep, spell or not, the two officers trudged towards the farm, heads bent down into what was threatening to turn into a gale.

It was Megan who finally broke the silence. 'Nice weather for it.'

Joseph snorted, casting her an amused look. 'Aye.'

Then the DC pointed to a small brick outbuilding with a tall chimney beyond a small woodland situated on a hill behind the farmhouse. 'Does that look like some sort of old incinerator to you?'

Joseph raised his eyebrows at her. 'Shite, you're not wrong. Before you say it, I'm assuming no foul play until we've had a chance to talk to the woman. But if that really is some sort of incinerator, we'll waste no time in having Amy and her team go over it.'

Megan nodded as they neared the farmhouse, with *Shadowbrook Farm* on a battered sign nailed to the gate. Below it was also a *Beware of the Dog* notice. But that wasn't what drew

Joseph's attention. That was reserved for the wreaths sitting atop the posts on either side of the gate.

'Just like the one on the gatepost near the dig site,' Megan said, also noticing them.

'Maybe all this gossip Ms Trelawney is so invested in about Charlotte being a witch actually has some basis in fact.'

'I suppose that depends on your definition of what a witch is,' the DC replied as they headed through the gate into the courtyard.

Joseph shrugged. 'It strikes me that Ms Trelawney probably sets a very low bar for such things. Wearing too much black would probably put you in her bad books.'

'What about the vicar from her church in Fernbridge?'

'Maybe they're one of those trendy vicars who wears a cardigan so they get a pass.'

The DC smiled, then cast a wary look around them. 'About that *Beware of the Dog* sign?'

'I don't normally hold much stock in those things. But the first sign of any snarling teeth and we're out of here.'

'You do remember that I'm faster than you, so any devil hound will likely catch you first?'

The DI sighed. 'Such are the breaks of being the senior officer on a team.'

Megan laughed. 'Remind me not to rush towards getting promoted anytime soon.'

Joseph winked at her. 'Understood.'

An old weathercock squealed as it rotated in the strengthening gale. A flock of rooks raced overhead, carried by the wind towards a small wood in the distance.

For all his humour, a sense of unease was growing in Joseph. That bloody shopkeeper putting ideas in his head. He'd be jumping at shadows next.

The DI's gaze took in the rusty ploughs and other ancient

farm machinery filling the yard. Quite a few of the outbuildings had sections of their roofs missing, their window frames and doors looked rotted through.

A sign over one outbuilding proclaimed *Farm Shop,* written in a flowing script. But based on the boarded-up windows and the door hanging off its hinges, Joseph suspected it hadn't seen any business in a very long time indeed.

'This place doesn't exactly feel like it's thriving,' Megan said.

'I wouldn't be so sure. I've seen plenty of farms back in Ireland that looked just like this but were actually doing just fine. It's just farmers often don't like to throw anything away, based on the *just in case* hoarding principle.'

'That sounds just like my dad. He has hundreds of jam jars in the garage filled with bolts, screws, washers, and the rest.'

'Well, I can guarantee that the moment he threw any of them away, he'd discover he had an urgent need for the thing he'd just got rid of.'

Megan smiled. 'That's exactly what he keeps telling my mum.'

Joseph snorted as they approached the front door, noticing another wreath tied to it.

'Those things seem to be everywhere around here,' Megan said, as the wind howled at their back, propelling them the last few feet towards the house as though it was now deliberately herding them.

So much for a protection spell, Joseph thought, giving the knocker a sharp rap that was immediately answered by a bark.

Megan's hand went to her pocket, where Joseph knew her baton was stowed, and they both took a step back. The DI couldn't help mentally bracing himself to see a woman wearing a pointy hat with a hellhound at her side. He was slightly disappointed by the actual person who opened the door to them.

The woman gazing expectantly at them had a kind oval face and wore nothing more extraordinary than a faded blue denim shirt and jeans. If anything, this woman reminded him of his gran back in the day. Next to the woman was an ancient black-and-white Border Collie with a greying face, doing its best to summon enough energy to wag its tail. Behind them, blues music was playing somewhere in the house.

'Charlotte Harris?' Megan asked uncertainly as she exchanged a look with Joseph.

'Yes, and you are?'

The two detectives showed the farmer their warrant cards.

'Can I ask what this is about?' Charlotte asked.

'It's connected to the archaeological dig you authorised,' Joseph replied. 'We need to ask you a few questions about something that was found there.'

Her brows lifted just a fraction. 'Well, if it's treasure, the archaeology team are welcome to it. I have everything I need in life.' She made an expansive gesture at the farm around her.

'Sadly, it isn't anything like that,' Megan said.

A small crease formed on Charlotte's brow. 'In that case, you'd better come in out of the awful weather before you get blown away. But your timing is perfect. I've just got a pot of tea brewing if you fancy a cuppa and some shortbread—freshly baked and ready to take out of the oven.'

'That sounds grand, and anything to get out of this wind,' Joseph said.

'Yes, it does rather love to make mischief up here,' Charlotte replied, gesturing for the two detectives to enter.

As the farmer closed the door behind them, the wind snarled into silence.

Joseph was already slipping off his ruined suede boots, rather than leave a trail of footprints over the well-polished cobblestones inside.

Charlotte cast a frown at his footwear. 'You really need wellies when walking around here.'

'Oh, trust me, I know. But sadly my wellies are currently in the boot of my colleague's Mini and it's stuck in a pool of slurry that's across your track.'

The corners of the woman's mouth turned down. 'My most sincere apologies. The valve on my muck spreader failed and dumped a full load there when I was towing it to another field. I was going to clear it up, but wasn't expecting visitors anytime soon. I don't get a lot of those up here now.' A sad look filled her face.

'Well, if you could give us a tow out when we go, it would be much appreciated,' Megan said.

'No problem at all. Anyway, if you'd like to follow me, let's sort out that tea and shortbread for you.'

This woman really did remind Joseph of his gran. Her homemade shortbread was exactly the sort of thing his gran would have offered to any visitor to her home in Kilree, one of those villages where time had stood still. Much like it seemed to have for Shadowbrook Farm.

'Okay, lead the way, Fergus,' Charlotte said to her Border Collie.

Tail slowly wagging, the dog and his owner headed down a dark wood corridor, followed by the detectives. Joseph took in the numerous prints of trees, birds, and animals lining the walls. There were illustrations of fairies among them, along with one very striking carving of a man's face made from leaves with his mouth wide open.

As Charlotte opened a door, she glanced back to see the DI gazing at the sculpture. 'I see you're admiring my Green Man, DI Stone.'

'A Green Man?'

'In modern paganism, he's a symbol of rebirth and represents the cycle of growth each spring,' Charlotte replied. 'Rather fitting for a farm, don't you think?'

'I suppose it is,' the DI replied, as they followed the farmer into the kitchen to discover the source of the music—a record spinning on an old-fashioned gramophone with a large funnel speaker.

The kitchen couldn't have been cosier if it had tried—a warm hug of a room on a wind-filled winter's day. An ancient white enamel Aga stove belted out enough heat to melt an iceberg. The dog had already taken up residence in its basket in front of it, next to one of the largest kitchen tables Joseph had ever seen.

'Does anyone else live here with you?' he asked.

'Not now, although I was married years ago. My former husband, Mike Clifford, did a flit one day and I never saw him again. Mind you, I doubt there's anyone on this planet who could put up with me and my idiosyncratic ways these days. I'm far too old to change too.' She winked at them, raising a smile from both officers. Then she slipped on some oven gloves and took out a batch of shortbread that smelled sensationally good to Joseph.

Megan's biscuit radar was already on full alert, her eyes almost as wide as the Border Collie's, who was also watching the passage of the biscuits from Aga to the large serving plate with laser focus. At least, unlike Fergus, his colleague wasn't drooling—yet.

Charlotte set to work pouring three very large mugs of tea and gave Joseph one with *Farmers Do It in the Dirt* emblazoned on its side.

Once her guests were all sorted and settled at the farmhouse table, biscuits and all, Charlotte set her steady gaze on the detectives. 'So what's this all about?'

'There's been a significant discovery in your field,' the DI replied.

Charlotte leaned forward in her seat. 'Anything to do with the ancient Celtic site Professor Bailey was hoping to discover there?'

'Well, she certainly did find that, and it looks like it might have been used for religious purposes.'

The farmer's face lit up as she clapped her hands together. 'I absolutely knew it. I've always sensed an energy in that field when I've been working it, and now I know why.'

Joseph mentally added *sensing energy* to the *possible witch* column. If so, maybe he needed to add himself to that list.

Then Charlotte frowned. 'But that's not why you're here, is it? Something to do with the discovery you mentioned?'

'Yes, I'm afraid some bone ash was found on your field.'

Charlotte's forehead ridged. 'So?'

'You don't sound very surprised,' Megan said, trading a look with Joseph.

'That's because I'm not. I use bonemeal fertiliser all the time on my arable land.'

'I see. And where exactly do you purchase your fertiliser?' Joseph asked, the cogs beginning to turn.

'At my usual farming supplier. Why, have you discovered a problem with it?'

'We'll get to that in a moment. Is that an old incinerator we saw on the hill behind your house?'

'Yes. My father built it, but it hasn't been fired up in years,' Charlotte replied. 'Any reason you're asking about it?'

'You really have no idea?' Joseph replied.

'None at all, so please put me out of my misery.'

'I'm afraid the remains of shattered human teeth were found mixed in with the bone ash in your field.'

The farmer stared at them. 'But I would have spotted anything like that in my fertiliser.'

'It wasn't necessarily in your fertiliser.'

Charlotte gasped. 'Oh my God. You're saying that someone scattered the remains of a person on my field?'

'Not just one person. By the looks of it, quite a few, and over a long period of time, based on the soil depth some of the fragments were discovered at.' Joseph narrowed his eyes at the farmer. 'Any idea how they might have got there, Charlotte?'

Her eyes widened. 'Hang on, you don't seriously think I had anything to do with that?'

Megan didn't even bat an eyelid before asking the question, her notebook already out, ready for the answer. 'Well, did you?'

Charlotte stared back at the DC. 'Of course I bloody didn't. Apart from anything else, if I was the murderer, why would I get rid of the remains on my own land? Oh, and not forgetting it was a field I gave the go-ahead for an archaeological team to excavate. You can't seriously think I would have done that if I had anything to do with this? And what motive could I have to do something so awful?'

Joseph felt embarrassed as he prepared himself to ask the question he knew he had to. 'I don't know quite how to ask you this, Charlotte, but we were told that you're a witch. Is that correct?'

Charlotte's eyebrows twitched as she stared first at Joseph and then at Megan. Of all the reactions the DI might have been expecting, it wasn't the one he got.

The farmer burst out laughing, her chest heaving as she tried to breathe.

'Oh my lord, that's the best thing I've heard in years. Don't tell me—you think I've been cavorting naked through my fields at night, sacrificing people to my land to ensure a good harvest.

Oh, now I see it—I burn my victims in the old animal incinerator? Is that the measure of your theory so far?'

Joseph felt his cheeks grow warm as he shrugged. 'I'm sorry, but I'm sure you understand we have to follow through with any information we're given that might be relevant to our investigation.'

The farmer's eyes widened. 'Don't tell me. Maggie Trelawney sent you to my doorstep. She's always had it in for me. She's never been a fan and loves to stir up the village against me at every opportunity. It probably has everything to do with her having the hots for Mike, who ended up marrying me.'

Joseph filed that valuable piece of information away. It would certainly explain Ms Trelawney's hostile attitude towards the farmer.

'It really doesn't matter who told us, but could you please answer the question,' Megan said. 'Are you a practising witch or not?'

Charlotte sighed. 'Well, if you want to peg this as confirmation of witchcraft, I do believe in Gaia.'

'Gaia?' Joseph replied.

But Megan was already nodding. 'You know, the theory that the Earth and all life on it are a single living organism.'

Charlotte smiled at her. 'That's right. That's why I'm a keen organic farmer, using old-school farming methods, and avoiding modern fertilisers that are slowly but surely killing the soil.'

'I see. And what about the twig wreaths that we've seen scattered around your property?' Joseph asked.

The farmer shrugged. 'Let's just say I like to take a belt-and-braces approach to my farming. I'm not ashamed to say that, just like the pagans did, I also believe in nature spirits. It's just a harmless little ritual of mine to leave them offerings around my land to ensure a good harvest.'

'And that works?' Joseph asked, unable to completely mask the sceptical tone in his voice.

'Who knows, but I like to think so.' She raised her hands. 'Look, I understand how that must sound to you, but me practising my pagan-based beliefs does no harm to anyone and never has.'

To Joseph, this woman certainly sounded sincere. Her beliefs aside, it was increasingly feeling to him like he was putting his own gran in the dock. Instinct was telling him this woman was exuding innocence from every pore of her skin. But he still had a job to do.

'I hear everything you're saying, but we will still need our forensic team to examine your farm, including the incinerator, and maybe even other fields across your land.'

The farmer nodded. 'Of course you do. But I can tell you now, I have nothing to hide. However, you're basically telling me I won't be sowing my winter wheat anytime soon, thanks to what I assume you'll be treating as a crime scene in my bottom field?'

'Aye, that's the measure of it.'

'Then do whatever you have to, but please get to the bottom of what happened as soon as you can. Of course, I will help in any way I can.'

'Thank you for your understanding, along with the tea and biscuits,' Joseph said, setting his cup down on the table.

'No problem at all, but you haven't tried any of my shortbread. If you're heading off again, please take some with you for the road.'

'That would be wonderful, thank you,' Megan replied before Joseph had a chance to get a word in. 'Oh, and if you could give us that tow, that would be a great help as well.'

'Of course.' Charlotte stood and gathered up some shortbread, wrapping it in paper napkins and handing a parcel to each of the detectives. 'Maybe you should borrow a set of wellies for the return leg, Detective Stone. I have some of Mike's old ones knocking around that should fit you.'

'That would be very much appreciated,' Joseph said, as he pocketed the shortbread. Megan, however, had wasted no time in taking a bite from one of her pieces.

Her face lit up. 'That's some of the best shortbread I've ever tasted in my life.'

'That probably has a lot to do with using my own milled organic wheat, and my grandmother's secret recipe. I used to sell it in my temporary old farm shop, along with my organic produce. But when I tried to get planning permission in an attempt to make it all above board and official, Maggie Trelawney went out of her way to make sure my application was blocked by the parish council. For good measure, she forced me to close down the shop as well. If she had her way, I'd literally be run out of town.'

'I see,' Joseph replied. It was becoming increasingly clear that, for all her fine upstanding credentials, the local shopkeeper might also have a very specific agenda here, based on a desire to settle an old score with a former love rival.

A short while later, the two detectives were standing outside the farmhouse as Charlotte went to fetch a vehicle.

'So, what do you think?' Joseph asked.

'I think Charlotte makes a very good point about letting an archaeological team dig on her land. Definitely not the act of someone trying to hide bodies.'

'Aye. As I thought before we even got here, that's not exactly the act of a guilty woman.'

At that moment, they heard an engine start up in one of the outbuildings. A few seconds later, an ancient green Land Rover emerged with Fergus in the back of its flatbed.

The farmer leaned out of the vehicle's window. 'Let's go and get your car pulled out of the slurry pool,' she called out.

As the detectives headed over, several crows flying figure eights into the howling wind gave up the uneven battle and were finally swept away towards the incinerator's chimney. Joseph cast his gaze towards it, questioning his instincts about the farmer. It would certainly offer someone a convenient way to burn their victims to ash. The question was, could the amiable woman they'd just shared a cup of tea with really be a murderer?

CHAPTER SIX

AFTER RETURNING FROM SHADOWBROOK FARM, Joseph and Megan sat in the incident room with all the other detectives and uniformed officers who were waiting for the briefing to begin. Chris, who'd already been designated the SIO to the case, stood in front of the large team that had been assembled for the investigation. For once, and thanks to the gravity of the case involving so many potential victims, the superintendent had loosened the budget strings.

Amy had joined them, ready to present the initial findings from the dig site. As always she'd gone out of her way to keep things professional with Joseph at work, making sure not to catch his eye. But it was something of a moot point, because by now there wasn't a person in St Aldates, and probably the Cowley station too, who didn't know the two of them were an item.

Derrick was also in attendance, standing at the back of the room. That underlined like nothing else could just how important this case was. Privately, the DSU had already agreed with Joseph to maintain the illusion of their ongoing less-than-warm working relationship. If Chris, or anyone else for that matter, was involved with the Night Watchmen, hopefully they would report back to their masters that the two men seemed just as hostile to each other as ever. The last thing they needed was for the crime syndicate to realise the two of them were working together.

Chris held up a tabloid newspaper to show the headline, *'Ritualistic Serial Killer Burned Victims for Decades!'*

'As you can see, the gutter press are already on the case,' the SIO said. 'That means we're going to be carrying out this investigation under the full glare of the public eye. So watch your Ps and Qs whenever you're around any journalists and avoid any off-the-record comments.' The SIO's gaze lingered on Joseph.

Although he hadn't mentioned Kate in person, the DI knew full well that's what that look meant. Not that he ever divulged anything he shouldn't during an investigation to his journalist ex-wife. Of course, it also wasn't lost on him that Chris hadn't even bothered glancing at Derrick. Not that the SIO would know that the superintendent and his wife were currently estranged. But even if he did, it would be putting his neck on the line to even dare suggest there might be any pillow talk between the two of them.

Ian took a sip of tea from his Batman mug. 'Yes, caution is the watchword with the press, because otherwise...' He paused for dramatic effect. '...they'll have a *field day* with this case.'

There was a series of collective groans from the detectives gathered together in the room.

Sue was already holding up a jam jar with *'Bad Pun Fines'* written on its side. The jar was already half full of pound coins.

Scowling, Ian dug into his pocket and slipped another coin through a slot in the lid to add to the growing collection.

Chris shook his head at the DS. 'Thank you for that contribution, Ian, but moving on.' He placed the paper back down on the table. 'DS Sue Evans will be the designated officer for the point of contact for the press, so direct any journalists who approach you to her.'

Sue shrugged. 'Yes, I don't know exactly what I've done to upset the boss, but here I am anyway.'

That raised some laughter, even from Derrick.

Chris turned to Amy. 'Okay, to kick things off, could you brief the team on what you've discovered?'

'Of course,' the SOCO replied, as she pulled her notes up on her tablet. 'First of all, we conducted a chemical analysis on the ash. While the high temperatures of whatever cremation process was used destroyed most of the organic material, there are trace elements present that suggest the ash originated from human remains. We also found higher levels of calcium and phosphorus. That's consistent with human burnt bone material.'

'So basically this confirms it wasn't animal bone fertiliser?' Joseph asked.

'Correct, although maybe whoever our murderer was, hoped that was what it would be mistaken for. But that's where they made a slip-up, thanks to the teeth fragments that were found among the ash layers. Talking of which, Professor Amanda Bailey, the forensic archaeologist who was running the dig, got back with her lab analysis of the fragments. Obviously, we couldn't use carbon dating as we normally would due to the cremation process and the age of the remains. However, teeth are composed primarily of enamel and dentine. Enamel, the hardest substance in the human body, has a dense, highly mineralised structure that is primarily made up of hydroxyapatite, similar to bone. I'm going to refer to Amanda's notes she sent over with the results.'

Amy started reading from her tablet. '"Because of the nature of the remains, we performed a thermoluminescence, TL, dating technique on the bone ash samples. This method measures the trapped electrons accumulated in the minerals over time, which are released when the sample is heated. Since teeth are generally more dense and robust than bones, they are potentially better at preserving their crystalline structure, even at high temperatures. This could mean that the TL signal from teeth might be less disrupted compared to bones, potentially leading to more accurate dating results. Additionally, teeth often undergo less post-mortem alteration than bones, which could help maintain a clearer luminescence signal. Thanks to that, we were able to roughly date the samples we were given to a specific number of years. The most recent samples date to about thirty years ago, and the oldest around 1966.'"

Amy looked up. 'This also confirms our initial theory for the dates based on the depth of the ash layer in the soil.'

'Okay, not that we really needed it, but this also obviously confirms we're dealing with a serial murderer here,' Chris said.

'But if it was the same person, wouldn't that mean they would have to be very old by now, if not passed away?' Megan suggested.

'Maybe not. We could be looking at more than one person working together,' Joseph said.

The SIO gave the DI a thoughtful look and nodded. 'Amy, I don't suppose you found any fragments of remaining DNA to identify the victims?'

'Sadly not, thanks to the high temperatures. However, there is one small detail that may lead us to a breakthrough. In one of the samples, there were larger fragments from what appear to be a single tooth, possibly a molar from the earliest victim. My team is painstakingly trying to put it back together. It appears to have been drilled at some point for a filling.'

Joseph's eyes widened. 'So you're saying you might be able to check it against a dental record?'

Amy smiled at him. 'Just so. We'll also cross-reference the dental records with missing people from the sixties through to nineties in the Fernbridge area to see if we can confirm the identity of the remains.'

'You little beauty,' Joseph said.

Amy gave him a small smile. 'Well, I'll take the compliment for all my colleagues, as it was very much a team effort.'

'Of course,' Joseph said, feeling the heat of embarrassment threatening his face. Several detectives in the room were giving him amused looks. If only they knew how complicated his personal life was becoming, not least because of Kate. He made a point of making sure he didn't look anywhere near Derrick.

'Anyway, to wrap things up from my side, we're going to extend the investigation to the surrounding fields to see if we can find any more human remains,' Amy continued. 'We're also going to examine an animal incinerator Joseph and Megan discovered on Charlotte Harris's farm. Okay, that's it from my side.' She nodded to Chris.

The SIO crossed to the incident board, where numerous photos of the dig site and the human remains had already been put up. Chris tapped his finger on a map centred on Shadowbrook Farm and the nearby village of Fernbridge.

'To kick things off, I want a complete list of missing people within a twenty-mile radius of the murder site. As you can see, that includes Oxford, so we're going to have our work cut out. Of particular interest right now is the earliest victim's remains that Amy's team is trying to identify. That will narrow our search window to 1966. We also need to build a picture of the murderer or murderers' MO. Did they kill random people, or was it premeditated? What was their motivation? Based on where the remains were found, could there be a ritualistic, occultist angle to the murders?'

'You're suggesting these were human sacrifices, boss?' Sue asked.

'It's just a theory at the moment, although we do have a local parish councillor who has accused Charlotte Harris of being a witch,' Chris replied. 'Joseph and Megan, how did you get on with your meeting with the farmer?'

'Well, she's certainly a unique character and admitted to believing in earth spirits and the like,' Megan replied.

Joseph nodded. 'But possibly more damning, and already mentioned, is an old animal incinerator. However, before we all get too excited, it's situated a reasonable distance away from the farmhouse, so in theory, someone else could have had access to it. I've already contacted Wallingford for Uniform to stand guard until Amy can get over there. But regarding Charlotte Harris being any sort of witch... I really don't think so. Quirky, most definitely. A member of the dark arts, no. Megan, what are your thoughts?'

'I agree,' the DC replied. 'Apart from anything else, anyone who can make shortbread as well as she can, can't be a witch.'

'You have read Hansel and Gretel, right?' Sue asked.

Several officers in the room, including John, chuckled.

'So based on your initial assessment, it sounds like we should look elsewhere for our murderer,' Chris said.

'Yes, but we can't rule Charlotte out either,' Joseph replied.

'Considering the range of dates we're looking at, could anyone else living at Shadowbrook Farm have been responsible?' a detective at the back asked.

'I already checked the electoral register and Charlotte is the only person living at that address today,' Megan replied. 'There were only two other people to live there. Charlotte's father, Jacob Harris, who died in 1972 and bequeathed her the farm. Then there was her ex-husband, Mike Clifford, who left her in 1978.'

Derrick spoke up. 'Which certainly puts them both in the frame for the earliest murders, at least.'

'Yes, but not the latest, which TL analysis places as late as the mid-nineties,' Amy added.

'That rules out Charlotte's father, at least for the later murders,' Chris said.

'That's what the evidence suggests,' Amy confirmed.

'I think we should make it a priority to track Mike Clifford down. Ian, can I task you with that?'

'Leave it to me, boss,' he replied.

Joseph turned the thought over in his mind. 'Maybe we should consider it's someone who's not been mentioned.'

Chris gazed at him. 'Such as?'

'What if somebody knew about this lost Celtic temple and decided to re-enact an ancient sacrifice ritual there? Maybe, as we've already speculated, they weren't acting alone.'

Derrick peered at him. 'Hang on, are you seriously suggesting there is some sort of satanic cult based around Fernbridge who is sneaking onto Charlotte's land to murder people?'

Joseph raised his shoulders. 'I wouldn't rule anything out at this point.'

The DSU rolled his eyes at Joseph, playing his *arse-wipe* role to a T. Although maybe, in this instance, it was actually what the big man thought of the DI's theory.

'Well, there's someone out there who doesn't believe that Charlotte Harris is as innocent as you may think she is,' Sue said. 'Ms Trelawney contacted the station. She said she has valuable information about the farmer that she needs to tell us. I did ask her what, but she said she needed to talk to an officer in person.'

Joseph sighed. 'No surprise there, then. There is one interesting fact that we learned from Charlotte about our local parish councillor. Ms Trelawney apparently was in love with Mike Clifford, who then chose Charlotte. Thanks to that, we may have a motive for our local parish councillor to want to frame the farmer.'

Chris looked sceptical. 'You're not suggesting Ms Trelawney may have carried out the murders?'

'I agree, she doesn't exactly seem the type, just as Charlotte doesn't, but there is the added motive of jealousy that we can't afford to overlook either, boss.'

'Well, then maybe in the name of balance, as you've already interviewed the farmer, you should interview Ms Trelawney as well,' Chris said. 'Besides, we need to follow through on this valuable information she has for us.'

Joseph sighed. 'How did I know you were going to say that?'

Even as Chris grinned, the DI could already guess what the meeting with the busybody was going to be like. All conspiracy theories and no proof. But he was also more than interested in seeing Ms Trelawney's reaction when they put her on the spot about her infatuation with a man who'd gone on to marry a woman who the parish councillor now seemed so determined to prove guilty of murder. This had the whiff of a secret agenda if he'd ever smelled it.

CHAPTER SEVEN

Joseph was driving the unmarked Volvo V90 through the village of Fernbridge as Megan looked out of the side window at all the honey-coloured stone cottages.

'This is all rather picturesque,' the DC said, as she took in the gentle, babbling brook running along the edge of the road.

'According to Dylan, this village also has a fair amount of history. But, of course, that's true for most villages around here. Did you notice the large ponds a little way back?'

'Yes, what about them?'

'According to the professor, that's one of the oldest watercress farms in the country and dates back to the nineteenth century.'

'The facts that man knows without ever using the internet never ceases to amaze me,' Megan said.

'Tell me about it. Anyway, talking of the professor, he was telling me he feels it's his personal duty to help solve this case.'

'That's hardly surprising since he was there when we discovered the remains.'

'Aye, and not that he was looking for my permission, but thanks to that, he's taken it upon himself to take on an unofficial investigative role, digging around in Fernbridge on our behalf to see what he can turn up. Apparently, he knows someone who might be able to help.'

'Hang on, with all due respect to Dylan, isn't that our job?'

'Don't I know it. But Dylan has a knack for teasing out the truth that the police might otherwise miss. We both know how often his insights have led directly to a breakthrough.'

'I'm certainly not going to argue with that.'

They passed a couple of police cars, one of which Joseph knew was driven by PC John Thorpe, who just happened to be dating his daughter. He, along with a number of Uniforms, had already descended on Fernbridge to carry out door-to-door inquiries. But if there really was a satanic cult being run out of this sleepy village, Joseph doubted they'd confess it to the officers anytime soon.

'Hang on, isn't that Dylan?' Megan said.

Joseph glanced over to where Megan was pointing. Dylan was walking along the pavement with a woman, her arm linked through his. The DI recognised Dylan's friend at once. It was retired Professor Iris Evans. He'd only met her once at the board game café during the Hidden Hand investigation, but she'd left an impression on him. Ahead of them, Dylan's dogs, Max and White Fang—a Beagle and a Terrier—were sniffing the base of a tree they had just passed. Then they took turns cocking a leg to mark it, before scraping the ground with their back paws and moving on.

'Who's that woman with Dylan?' Megan asked.

'That's Iris. According to him, she's an old friend from his college days, but between us, I think there might be more to it than that.'

Megan's eyebrow shot up. 'Really?'

'Aye. It seems the man is a bit of a dark horse,' he replied as they pulled up alongside the two professors.

As Megan lowered her window, and much to Joseph's amusement, Dylan quickly unhooked Iris's arm from his. Apparently, he wasn't ready to admit he might be romantically involved with anyone just yet.

'Ah, Joseph, good to see you again,' Iris said, spotting him in the driving seat.

'And you,' the DI replied, politely ignoring the blush spreading across Dylan's face. 'Let me introduce you to my colleague, DC Megan Anderson.'

'Pleased to meet you, Megan,' Iris said. 'Do you like board games, by any chance?'

The DC briefly looked confused, before a look of comprehension crossed her face. 'Of course, you're the woman who helped us during the Geoff Goldsmith murder investigation.'

'Yes, and I have to say it gave me a taste for it. When Dylan asked for my help digging up information about the murders at the dig site, I jumped at the chance.'

Dylan nodded. 'Among other things, we're planning to go through the local historical records to see if anyone had prior knowledge of the ancient Celtic temple.'

Iris nodded. 'The placement of the human remains indicates that someone here knew about it. We're heading to the parish council records to trace the oldest families in Fernbridge and the surrounding area. I've lived here my whole life, so we'll also talk to the locals to see if anyone knows anything.'

'As always, I'd certainly appreciate any insight you can give us,' Joseph replied. 'The investigation team will be up to its eyeballs researching missing persons within a thirty-mile radius of Fernbridge over the last sixty years.'

'Then we're glad to be of assistance,' Dylan said.

'Much appreciated. Speaking of local knowledge, Iris, do you happen to know Margaret Trelawney?' Megan asked.

Iris practically rolled her eyes. 'It would be hard not to know

Maggie, she makes it a point to stick her nose into everyone's business.' Her eyes narrowed. 'Let me guess—she's told you she has information about Charlotte?'

'Why would you say that?' Joseph asked.

'Well, talking of old families, the Trelawneys and Harrises go way back. Maggie has a vendetta against Charlotte due to a family feud. She's been trying to drive her out for years.'

'What sort of feud?' Megan asked, keeping her expression neutral.

'It goes back to their fathers, both farmers. Maggie's father, Nigel, was very ambitious. He tried to buy up neighbouring farms, but was ruthless in how he went about it. Those who wouldn't sell, he made life difficult for. He even deliberately spread salt on the Harrises' best arable land once, ruining it for years. But Jacob Harris stuck to his guns and refused to sell. But as they say, karma is a bitch. Nigel eventually lost his farm after a failed investment, but Jacob hung in there, eventually passing Shadowbrook Farm down to Charlotte when he died. Needless to say, Maggie inherited her father's grudge against the Harrises, something which, notably, Charlotte didn't. However, Maggie has made it her life's mission to turn the village against her perceived rival.'

Joseph nodded as Megan jotted down this gem. It seemed Ms Trelawney had taken on a new significance in their investigation.

'Thank you for that,' the DI said. 'It certainly helps explain why she's so hostile towards Charlotte. Context is everything.'

'Indeed,' Iris replied. 'I'd definitely take anything she says with a large pinch of salt.'

'We'll bear that in mind,' Megan replied.

With a wave, the detectives set off again. In the rear-view mirror, Joseph spotted Iris linking her arm through Dylan's again, and smiled to himself.

'So, are you thinking what I'm thinking?' Megan asked, as they headed towards the village shop near the small green, where a group of men stood talking together.

'Almost definitely. Our local gossip might be trying to frame Charlotte.'

'Okay, but you do know the problem with that theory, right?'

'That wanting to drive someone out isn't the same as murdering a number of people over several decades.'

'Exactly, but we also shouldn't rule anything out just yet.'

'You took the words right out of my mouth,' Joseph replied.

As they left their vehicle, Joseph noticed the way a group of men watched them with a certain wariness. Even in an unmarked car, it seemed every stranger stood out in Fernbridge.

Then, he spotted the lowest of the low, tabloid reporter Ricky Holt, heading towards the group with his cameraman. It seemed the vultures had already descended on the small village.

Shaking his head, Joseph followed Megan towards the shop, curious to hear what Ms Trelawney had to say when they turned the tables on her.

CHAPTER EIGHT

Joseph and Megan entered a shop stuffed with all the essentials one might need in a village like Fernbridge—loo paper, baked beans, artisan mustard spoons, luxury cat treats, and, of course, the ever-essential scented drawer liners.

Joseph cast a bemused look over the contents of the small shop-cum-post office, before fixing his gaze on Ms Trelawney, who had just put down her copy of *Miss Marple's The Murder at the Vicarage* on the counter in front of her.

Why am I not surprised? Joseph thought. Certainly based on the way she'd already been telling them how to do their job, he'd more than a hunch the woman probably saw herself as something of an amateur Miss Marple. That was, if she wasn't deliberately trying to frame Charlotte for something she had nothing to do with.

He traded a knowing look with Megan, who'd also spotted the shopkeeper's literary choice as they headed towards the counter. Unfortunately, Ms Trelawney's eagle-like gaze missed nothing. She took off her reading glasses and let them dangle from their chain, before giving them both a hard stare.

'What's so amusing, Detectives?' she asked.

'Sorry, I was just debating with my colleague...' Joseph gave Megan a slightly helpless look.

Megan made a valiant effort to come up with an excuse, pointing towards a packet of scones in the bakery section near the door. 'The proper way to cover a scone—jam or cream first.'

'Oh, good grief, no wonder the crime rate is as high as it is if two Oxford detectives are focused on such fripperies rather than concentrating on the job at hand.' The woman pursed her lips as though she'd been sucking on an extra-sour lemon. 'Anyway, I imagine you're here to follow through on my phone call to your police station?'

'We actually needed to talk to you anyway, Ms Trelawney,' Joseph replied. 'Is there somewhere we could talk in private?'

The woman peered at them as she got off her stool and opened a hatch in the counter. She went over to the door, turning the sign over to *Closed*, then, not bothering to lock it, she beckoned for the two detectives to follow her through a door at the back.

Joseph and Megan headed through a post office letter and parcel sorting area into a small rear office. Ms Trelawney gestured to two seats for them. But the DI wasn't exactly surprised when there wasn't an offer of tea, or, God forbid, a biscuit.

'To begin with,' Joseph began, 'I believe you called the station with what you referred to as crucial information regarding our investigation into the human remains found at the archaeological dig site?'

'Indeed, I do,' Ms Trelawney replied, placing her reading glasses back on her nose as she picked up her own flip notebook, which looked remarkably similar to the one Megan had open on her lap.

The shop owner licked the tip of her finger and thumbed

through her pages until she found what she was looking for, then fixed the detectives with a hard stare, making Joseph feel guilty, although he had no idea for what.

'Before I start, I assume you've now interviewed *that* woman?'

'I'm sure you can understand we can't go into specific details of an ongoing investigation,' Joseph replied.

Ms Trelawney scowled at him and wrote something down in her notebook, no doubt so she could report their supposed misdemeanour to his superior at the first opportunity. One thing Joseph was certain of, this woman was going to be trouble with a capital *T*.

The shopkeeper looked at both detectives as though they were on the wrong side of an interview table. 'No doubt you've spoken to Charlotte and have already been taken in by her lies. So it's just as well I'm here to set the record straight.'

You fine upstanding citizen, you, Joseph thought, keeping his expression neutral.

'To begin with, did you know there have been countless stories about what the Harrises have been up to on Shadowbrook Farm?' she continued.

'Such as?' Megan asked, her pen poised.

'To begin with, why Charlotte keeps herself to herself.' Her mouth turned down as though that lemon inside it had become even more bitter. 'That woman has a reputation for being difficult, and that's putting it mildly. She's got a temper on her, and she's not above making enemies. There's been talk about her grandfather being involved in some unsavoury activities as well.'

'What sort of *unsavoury* activities?' Joseph asked.

'Not to put too fine a point on it, devil worship,' Ms Trelawney replied without batting an eyelid. 'The rumours are they had orgies and did worse up on that farm of theirs.'

Megan's eyebrows shot up almost into her hairline. 'Such as?'

'Animal sacrifices. Apparently, that's why the Harris family used to keep goats.'

The DI only just managed to hold back the scoffing sound he was desperate to make. 'What proof do you have of this?'

'Over the years, plenty of people have seen strange things happening on their land at night. The rumours are that Charlotte's father, Jacob, ran a cult from his farm, founded by his father. And now, based on what you've discovered, it seems it wasn't only animals that awful man sacrificed.'

Although this was startling information, Joseph was mindful this was the second time he'd heard the word *rumour* in this conversation.

'Did anyone report this to the police at the time?' he asked.

'Of course they did—my father, Nigel Trelawney, God bless his soul. Not that it did any good, because the officers from Wallingford station refused to take him seriously.'

Joseph wasn't exactly surprised to hear that, because it certainly sounded like a tall tale—or someone deliberately trying to discredit a man he had a vested interest in seizing land from. But Joseph also knew there could be an element of truth they couldn't afford to overlook.

'So how does this involve Charlotte?' Megan asked.

'That woman is determined to keep her family's evil traditions alive. You see, some of these sightings happened long after her father died. And then there's the mysterious disappearance of Charlotte's husband, Mike Clifford. People say she drove him away, but others... Well, some think she did something much worse. No one's seen or heard from him since the eighties.'

'So, what exactly are you accusing Charlotte of here?' Joseph asked, not wanting to put words into the woman's mouth.

Ms Trelawney raised her palms. 'I'm just laying out the facts for you. The rest is up to you to figure out. Or do you expect me to do your jobs for you?'

Oh, wouldn't you just love that? Joseph thought, feeling his irritation grow.

He took a mental breath before responding. 'We'll certainly look into it, Ms Trelawney. So moving on, we've heard there was a feud between your father and Jacob. Mr Harris wouldn't sell his land to him, is that correct?'

Her voice dropped to an icy whisper. 'Yes, and picking up where he left off, Charlotte's always been fiercely protective of Shadowbrook Farm. She's had plenty of offers, but she won't sell. Now you've found those human remains, perhaps we finally know why. The question is, what are you going to do about it?'

The smug look on her face was enough to tip Joseph over the edge. Time to rattle the old woman and see how she responded when put in the hot seat.

'Can you tell us whether you ever had a relationship with Mike Clifford?'

The shopkeeper stared at him. 'Who told you about that?'

'Can you please just answer the question?' Joseph took a certain amount of satisfaction in seeing the blush creep up the woman's face.

'Yes, we were involved for a short while. But that witch ended up stealing him away from me. No wonder he ended up having all those affairs. He even had one at the very beginning of their marriage. She was never good enough for him.'

Megan wrote that juicy titbit of information down in her notebook.

Although Joseph already knew from Charlotte herself that her husband had a roving eye, he was still keen to hear Ms Trelawney's take on it. 'You're saying Mike strayed in his marriage?'

'That's what people said at the time, and who could blame him when he was married to that creature?'

'I see. And going back to your relationship with Mike, how exactly did Charlotte *steal* him away from you?'

The woman's eyes flashed with real anger. 'Because Charlotte threw herself at him using sex as a weapon.'

'That must have been difficult to deal with,' Megan added with her most sympathetic expression.

Ms Trelawney held up a hand. 'I'm going to stop you right there. I see where you're going and you're utterly wrong. I'm just doing my best to explain to you what a dangerous woman she is and why there is every reason to suspect her of those murders.'

Joseph fixed her with a steady gaze. 'So none of this is about settling an old score, then?'

Ms Trelawney straightened, her jaw tensing. 'Of course not! I wouldn't stoop so low. The fact of the matter is, that woman is a wicked witch. If you won't take this seriously, I'll take it to your senior officer.'

Megan jumped in. 'Rest assured, we'll certainly be following up on this. We're already trying to track down Mike Clifford.'

The shopkeeper sniffed. 'That's more like it.'

But Joseph wasn't letting the woman off the hook just yet. 'I still have to ask, do you think the family feud, not to mention your feelings towards Mike, might have coloured your view of Charlotte?'

Ms Trelawney's glare was fierce enough to make Joseph feel like she was trying to turn him to stone.

'Don't be so bloody ridiculous.'

Joseph knew his next comment would be like throwing petrol on a fire, but he had to say it anyway. 'You do realise how this looks for you, Ms Trelawney?'

She blinked. 'I don't follow.'

'Without proof, Charlotte could accuse you of slander. Or even something worse, like deliberately trying to frame her as a murderer. She might also ask why you would want to do something like that. So, Ms Trelawney, we must ask, are you the one responsible for the series of murders up at Shadowbrook Farm?'

Ms Trelawney was speechless for a moment. 'You can't be serious!' she finally said in a rush.

'You tell us?' Megan said.

The shopkeeper looked between them. 'How dare you suggest anything of the sort! I'll certainly be contacting your superiors about this harassment.'

Joseph sighed. 'Trust me, this isn't harassment. Just please answer the question.'

The shopkeeper glowered. 'I'm not trying to frame that witch. But I promise you this—my solicitor will be more than happy to take this up on my behalf. Now, you've wasted enough of my time. I need to get on.'

Joseph bit back the fact that it was the shopkeeper who'd summoned them. Instead, he managed a polite smile.

'Then I think we're done for now. Thank you for your cooperation.'

Ms Trelawney's glare was set to eleven as she crossed her arms.

Megan closed her notebook, and she and Joseph followed Ms Trelawney back into the shop.

The first thing the detectives saw was Charlotte Harris waiting outside the shop door, her trusty Land Rover parked up just behind her.

Ms Trelawney's expression turned to thunder the moment she spotted the woman. She marched up and practically threw open the door, getting right in Charlotte's face. 'What do you want?'

'I'm just here to drop off a parcel,' the farmer said, casting a wary look at the detectives behind the shopkeeper.

Ms Trelawney turned on her heel and stalked back to the counter. 'Name?' she asked, without making eye contact.

'For God's sake, you know who I am,' Charlotte replied.

'Name,' the shopkeeper repeated.

Joseph shook his head at Megan as they left the shop to leave the women to their escalating spat.

'Jesus H. Christ, if that woman were any more tightly wound, her knicker elastic would break,' Joseph said.

'Isn't that the truth?' a man's voice said from behind them.

They turned to see a dapper elderly grey-haired man in a smart jacket, a black felt fedora on his head, and a blue paisley cravat wrapped around his neck. He was smiling genially and gestured towards the shop.

'Unfortunately for Charlotte, Ms Trelawney has her squarely in her sights,' the man continued. 'She's been spreading tall tales about Charlotte for as long as I can remember.'

'Such as?' Joseph asked, keeping his expression neutral.

'Her favourite is that Charlotte's a witch. Listen to Ms Trelawney, and she would have you believe Charlotte sacrifices babies. All utter nonsense, of course. The only truth is that Charlotte has a slightly alternative worldview.'

'Well, there are plenty like that these days,' Joseph said, thinking of shops selling dream catchers, crystals, and all the rest.

'Exactly. But Ms Trelawney refuses to stock Charlotte's honey, even though it's far superior to the stuff she sells.'

At that moment the door flew open and the farmer charged out, tears streaming down her face. Ms Trelawney appeared behind her moments later.

'You and that farm are nothing but bad news for Fernbridge!' she shouted as Charlotte jumped into her Land Rover and sped away.

The shopkeeper shot the detectives an *I told you so* look before heading back inside with a small smirk curling her lips.

'As I said, no love lost between those two,' the man observed.

'So it would seem,' Megan replied.

The old man nodded. 'It's spats like that which make me thankful I live outside the village and far away as possible from Ms Trelawney. For someone who calls herself a Christian, you'd be hard-pressed to know it by how she treats people. Thankfully, my art studio is my sanctuary and well away from her and her poisonous village politics.'

'What sort of art is it that you do?' Joseph asked.

'Modern pieces, mostly in a variety of media. I've had some small success with London galleries. If you're ever in the area, pop by.' He handed them a gilt business card with Arthur Cleaves written on it.

Joseph nodded as he took it.

'Anyway, I'll leave you to your investigation. Good hunting, Detectives.' Arthur took a deep breath, squared his shoulders, and headed into the shop.

'We didn't tell him we were police officers, did we?' Megan said.

'In a village like this, the grapevine's probably already buzzing. Everyone knows who we are by now.' Joseph discreetly dipped his chin towards the men still watching from the nearby green. 'Especially, it seems, if Ms Trelawney has anything to do with it. Having said that, we still need to kick the tyres on what she told us. Once we're back at St Aldates, I'm certainly keen to see the original Wallingford police investigation into Nigel Trelawney's complaint about the strange goings-on up at Shadowbrook Farm. Not to mention, find out how Ian has been getting on with tracking down Mike Clifford.'

'You and me both,' Megan said as they headed towards the Volvo. 'So, are we any the wiser as to whether Ms Trelawney is still in the frame as our potential serial killer?'

'My instinct says no, but we shouldn't take her off the board until we've unearthed more information.'

'Even though she might throw her solicitor at us?'

'Even then,' the DI replied with a wry smile.

CHAPTER NINE

When Joseph got back to the incident room, with three cups of coffee from the *Steaming Cup* barista van, it was a hive of activity. A dozen detectives were trawling through what was rapidly turning into a mountain of research. To underline the scale of the task, Chris was currently looking at a list of at least a hundred names on the evidence board.

'Are those all the names of the people who went missing during our time frame, then?' he asked Megan as he deposited the cups on her desk.

'Apparently so, and the team is still ploughing through even more.'

Sue put her head above the partition and gestured towards the massive pile of folders on her desk. 'Some of these are so old that they haven't ever been scanned and archived on the database. I swear these case reports multiply when you're not looking. Give me fieldwork any day of the week over this.'

Joseph chuckled as he put his cup of coffee down on his desk.

Ian looked up from his screen. 'Hey, where's mine then?'

'You're forgetting you already owe me for at least three cups this month alone,' Joseph replied.

Sue nodded. 'With all due respect to my esteemed colleague, and based on bitter experience, he'll get round to settling up about a year later—and only when you threaten him with a court summons.'

Ian pulled a face at her. 'You're exaggerating.'

The DS just held his gaze until the DI broke eye contact and found the contents of his screen suddenly very interesting indeed. Some things in the universe were constant, and DI McDowell was definitely one of them.

Joseph raised his eyebrows at Megan as he took a sip of coffee. He sat in his chair, taking in the growing spiderweb of red string linking names to locations where people had last been seen on the map on the evidence board.

'Admiring my handiwork?' Chris asked, appearing beside the DI's desk.

'Aye, it looks like you've had a busy time of it while we were away.'

'Like you wouldn't believe. This is already looking like a long haul, trying to eliminate people from the list of possible victims—that is, if we ever can. So far, all we have is a single molar from the first victim, and we're hoping that name is somewhere on this list. I just hope we get a match in the dental records.'

'That could be the key to unlocking this whole case,' Megan said.

Joseph traded a frown with Chris.

'What's that look for?' the DC asked, glancing between the two officers.

'I used to have your wide-eyed enthusiasm, believing that a single clue could lead to a breakthrough,' Joseph replied. 'And of course, it can. But in a case like this, especially as so much time has passed, it's rarely that simple.'

Chris nodded. 'Even if we discover who the first victim is, that doesn't necessarily get us closer to who murdered them. That said, I'm expecting a call back from Amy any moment now. She's been at the old animal incinerator on Charlotte Harris's farm, taking samples. If bodies were burned there, we should know soon enough. But this is where good old-fashioned legwork comes in—Uniforms are still doing door-to-door inquiries in Fernbridge. Speaking of which, how did you get on with Ms Trelawney? Did she offer any evidence to support her claim that Charlotte Harris should be our chief suspect?'

Joseph rubbed the back of his neck. 'Well, there's certainly no love lost between the two women. We witnessed a full-blown argument between them in the village shop. That aside, Ms Trelawney had plenty to say about Charlotte being involved, and even claiming her father founded a devil-worshipping cult. She also said they sacrificed animals in the field where the old Celtic temple was found.'

'So, you're saying there may be some veracity to the sacrificial ritual angle?' Chris asked.

'If you listen to Ms Trelawney, that's certainly what she'd have you believe. Having said that, she also alerted us to an investigation into Charlotte's father, Jacob, back in the seventies, which might explain her attitude towards Charlotte.'

Megan nodded, gesturing to her screen. 'I've just found the summary of the Wallingford team's investigation. Apparently, after they looked into the rumours of occult practices at Shadowbrook Farm, it quickly turned out to be nothing more than hearsay. Jacob Harris even claimed it was all a smear campaign by Nigel Trelawney to discredit him.'

'I assume this Nigel Trelawney is related to our shopkeeper?' Chris asked.

'He's her father,' Joseph replied. 'And it seems she is doing her level best to keep the family feud alive.'

'And what was this feud about anyway?' the SIO asked.

'Jacob Harris wouldn't sell Nigel his land. My guess is that Nigel Trelawney was one of those large-scale farmers who always wanted more until he eventually fell on hard times himself.'

Chris gazed off into the middle distance. 'In light of the human remains we've discovered, this certainly casts this original investigation into Jacob Harris in a new light. The only problem is he died in the seventies from lung cancer, and we've got teeth fragments from the nineties.'

'So if it was him, maybe he had an accomplice,' Sue suggested.

Chris gave her a thoughtful look. 'I suppose it wouldn't be too big a stretch of the imagination. Could he have passed his occult beliefs down to his daughter who carried on his work? Maybe even her husband, Mike Clifford, was involved.' He looked over at Ian. 'How are you getting on tracking down his current whereabouts?'

'Not a sign. It's like the man literally disappeared off the face of the planet.'

Megan clicked her tongue against her teeth. 'Ms Trelawney had a theory about that as well. Without coming out and directly saying it, she suggested that he might have been murdered.'

'By Charlotte?' Chris asked.

'That was certainly what she implied. And if the farmer really is our serial killer, perhaps giving permission to the dig team was a double bluff intended to throw us off the scent. She could have thought refusing would be more suspicious if the bodies ever came to light.'

Joseph took another sip of his coffee. 'So you're suggesting it could be a bizarre form of insurance to keep her out of our spotlight?'

The DC shrugged. 'I'm just throwing ideas out there, seeing what sticks.'

Chris scratched his ear. 'It's as valid as anything else we've come up with so far. So, for now, we should definitely keep Charlotte in the frame as a suspect.'

'Even though my instinct says otherwise, I'm inclined to agree,' Joseph added. 'But there's one other thing we still need to consider—that someone is trying to frame Charlotte and maybe even her father. Someone who had a motive to do so.'

'You're suggesting we should be looking at Nigel Trelawney and his daughter, as well?' Chris asked.

'I think no one, however unlikely, should be above suspicion right now,' Joseph replied.

'That's a reasonable point. I'm also going to add Mike Clifford's name to the list of possible victims. Meanwhile, Ian, you need to keep digging, in case he decided to assume a new identity.'

'Will do, boss.'

At that moment, John walked into the room, looking decidedly exhausted.

'You look like you've had a long day of it,' Joseph observed.

'Like you wouldn't believe,' the PC replied. 'I tell you, doing door-to-doors in Fernbridge is a full-time job. Most people had nothing to say about the investigation but plenty of complaints about other things, including one elderly disabled guy contesting a speeding ticket.'

'Such as it ever was,' Joseph said.

'Aside from that, did you dig up anything useful?' Chris asked.

John nodded. 'Most were horrified by what's happened, but

a few weren't surprised that there were remains found at Shadowbrook Farm.'

'Why was that?'

'Some people believe Charlotte had something to do with it. They say—and I'm quoting here—"that woman is a wicked witch."'

'So it seems Ms Trelawney isn't alone in her opinion of Charlotte then,' Chris said.

John shrugged. 'Maybe, but the vast majority think she's a lovely woman.'

Joseph gazed at the young constable. 'It sounds to me like we're dealing with a split community.'

'That's putting it mildly, sir,' John replied.

Chris's phone warbled at that moment. He glanced at the screen and answered immediately. 'Any news, Amy? I'm going to put you on speakerphone. The rest of the team is here with me.'

'Hi, everyone,' Amy said. 'Just to let you know, the morphological analysis of the bone ash we found in the old incinerator at Shadowbrook Farm has just come back,' the SOCO said.

'Morphological analysis?' Megan asked.

'That's where we look at the shape of bone fragments,' Amy replied. 'Even in ash form, some fragments retain identifiable shapes, and along with microscopic examination, we can tell they're human, not cattle.'

'And you're certain of this?' Chris asked.

'One hundred percent.'

Chris looked at Joseph. 'Then it sounds like we've definitely reached the point where we need to pull Charlotte in for formal questioning.'

'You'll get no argument from me, boss,' the DI said, glancing at Megan, who nodded.

'Or me,' Amy said over the phone. 'Always follow the

evidence, I say. Anyway, Joseph, I'll see you later for our date night.'

'Yes, of course,' he replied, ignoring the amused looks from his colleagues as the call ended.

'If we're pulling Charlotte in for questioning, shouldn't we consider Ms Trelawney as well?' Megan asked.

'I don't think we're quite there yet,' Joseph said. 'Besides, can you imagine the earache she'll give us?'

Megan's forehead creased. 'All too easily.'

'We'll get to her in good time,' Chris said. 'But first, let's start with Charlotte and see where that takes us. Joseph, I'd like you to join me in the interview. Megan, I'd like you to watch from the observation booth.'

Joseph's gaze flicked to the clock, which had just ticked past four p.m.

Chris caught where he was looking. 'Don't worry, I'm sure we'll be done in time for your *date night* with Amy.'

Megan shot the boss an amused look as Joseph rolled his eyes at him. But part of him couldn't ignore the easy banter between himself and the SIO. It felt normal. In moments like this, it seemed impossible to believe Chris could be a bent copper. Joseph prayed that was the truth because the alternative —the ultimate betrayal—would leave a bitter taste in his mouth forever.

CHAPTER TEN

A COUPLE of detectives had been dispatched to collect Charlotte and bring her in for questioning. On Joseph's advice, they'd opted to take the Volvo V90, which, unlike Megan's Mini, had managed to navigate through the slurry spill on the way to the farm.

Thanks to that, Chris and Joseph now sat across the table from Charlotte. It would have been a serious understatement to say she was less than thrilled to have been dragged in—even though this was still technically just an informal chat. The farmer certainly hadn't wasted any time in asking an old family friend, who also happened to be a solicitor, to be there. Joseph wasn't exactly surprised. In Charlotte's situation, innocent or not, he'd have done the same, especially knowing Ms Trelawney had been spreading malicious gossip about her.

Joseph glanced at the one-way mirror behind which Megan was now seated, watching to see how things unfolded. In preparation for the interview, Megan had assisted Ian in his research into Charlotte's ex-husband. They had turned up something very interesting indeed that Joseph and Chris intended to fully explore once the conversation was underway.

Chris started the voice recorder and, after completing the usual formalities—stating who was present and the date of the interview—he looked at Charlotte. 'Now, as I mentioned earlier, I want to confirm this is just a conversation at this point regarding the human ashes found in your field at Shadowbrook Farm. We also need to follow up on your earlier conversations with DI Stone and DC Anderson, specifically about the animal incinerator on your land. Isn't it unusual to have one installed? I thought emissions were tightly controlled by the environmental agency.'

The solicitor nodded to Charlotte, giving her the go-ahead to answer.

The farmer met Chris's gaze. 'You'd be hard-pressed to get planning permission for one now. But back in the fifties, when my father built it, there was much less red tape in the post-war years. In those days, you could pretty much do as you pleased. Anyway, my father decided to build his own incinerator after a large TB outbreak in the county. He had to destroy a number of our cattle, which broke his heart and cost him a fortune. But being the canny businessman he was, Dad saw a business opportunity in it to expand the farm's operations. Obviously, not for TB-infected cows, as their ashes had to be carefully disposed of. Instead, he approached a local abattoir and undercut the prices they were being charged by one of the big companies. He didn't stop there and even produced bone fertiliser from the remains.'

Chris resisted the urge to dive straight into the big reveal about the human ashes in the incinerator. Instead, he dipped his chin slightly towards Joseph.

The DI leaned forward. 'So your father was quite the entrepreneur, then?'

'He was, and our farm, which has been in the family for generations, flourished,' Charlotte replied, a note of pride in her voice.

Joseph, having known a few farmers back in Ireland, had some insight into their struggles. 'It's impressive when anyone can make a farm thrive given the challenges.'

'You won't get any argument from me about that,' Charlotte replied.

Chris looked up from his notes. 'And how long was the incinerator in operation?'

'About fifteen years, until the early seventies, when it was shut down for not complying with the latest air quality standards.'

'And it hasn't been used since?' Chris asked.

Charlotte's lips thinned. 'I see where you're going with this, but to my knowledge, no, it's never been used again. Apart from anything else, that sort of thing is heavily regulated now—there's no demand for a small-scale incinerator like ours anyway.'

Chris sat back and took a sip of tea—their prearranged signal for Joseph to go for the big reveal.

Joseph fixed Charlotte with a steady gaze. 'In that case, can you explain why human remains were discovered among the cattle ashes in your incinerator? Using specialist lab techniques, our forensic team has found human ashes dating back to the eighties—long after you claim your father stopped using it.'

The farmer took an involuntary breath, her face paling, her eyes widening. 'No...'

The solicitor immediately placed a hand on Charlotte's arm. 'I advise we pause here for a moment, Charlotte. You shouldn't say anything until we've discussed this new information privately.'

She shook her head. 'As much as this is a shock, I've nothing to hide.' She scowled at the detectives. 'I can see what you're implying, but I promise you that you're barking up the wrong tree if you think I had anything to do with this.'

'So how do you explain the human remains?' Chris asked.

'Obviously, someone must have planted them there.'

'Who?'

Charlotte opened her mouth to reply, but this time, after a glance at her solicitor, she shook her head. 'No comment.'

Joseph narrowed his eyes. 'Could this have anything to do with someone your father was involved with?'

Her solicitor once again shook his head, but Charlotte ignored him. 'What do you mean by *involved with*?'

Chris sat forward. 'It's come to our attention that your father, Jacob Harris, might have been involved with a satanic cult that, among other things, sacrificed animals.'

Charlotte rolled her eyes. 'I don't even need to ask who put that ridiculous idea in your heads.'

'Why don't you tell us?' Joseph said.

'Margaret bloody Trelawney, of course. She's been spreading lies about my family for years, and this is just the sort of nonsense she'd come up with.'

'So you're saying it isn't true?'

'It's a downright lie—at least about my family.'

Joseph's ears pricked up at hearing that. 'Sorry, what do you mean exactly?'

'I *mean* there have been rumours about strange goings-on around Fernbridge for years. But I can assure you it has nothing to do with me or my father.'

Joseph knew they had to keep pressing. 'Okay, if it wasn't him, we obviously have to consider you a suspect. From talking to you before, I know you're aware that some in the village believe you're a witch.'

Charlotte shrugged. 'Yes, there are always people eager to slap labels on those who live an alternative lifestyle. But calling someone a witch isn't the same as accusing them of murder. Or are they doing that now too?'

Chris gave Joseph a pointed look. The time had come to drop the information Megan and Ian had uncovered.

Joseph dug into the file he had brought with him and pulled out a photograph, sliding it across the table.

Charlotte's expression pinched as she took in the image of a curly-haired man with a ruddy face, sitting on an old-fashioned tractor.

'For the benefit of the recording, I've just shown Charlotte Harris a photograph of her ex-husband, Mike Clifford,' Joseph said.

The farmer's eyebrows rose. 'And why are you showing me this?'

'Isn't it true that Mike disappeared from your farm without warning?'

Charlotte let out a sigh before giving them an amused look. 'Oh, don't tell me—you think I killed Mike and burned him in my own incinerator?'

'We're implying nothing of the sort,' Chris replied, even though that was exactly what he was thinking. 'But please answer the question so we can get to the truth.'

'Yes, we separated. He left me a note and took off. It's as simple as that. It was a long, long time ago.'

'I see, and what did he say in this note?'

'He admitted to having a string of affairs, saying I deserved better. He left in the middle of the night, but left a forwarding address for his things. And just like that, our marriage was at an end.'

'Do you still have this note so we can corroborate your story?' Joseph asked.

Charlotte crossed her arms. 'No. I burned it. I couldn't bear to look at his empty words of guilt and remorse. Anyway, I forwarded his things to a boarding house in Lancashire. He said he was going to start a new life up there.'

'Are you sure about that?' Chris asked.

Charlotte gave him a confused look. 'What do you mean?'

'Well, we ran a check on Mike Clifford to see where he is now, and there's no record of him. He's never paid taxes, and hasn't even registered to vote.'

For the first time, Charlotte looked rattled. 'That doesn't sound like Mike. He was a Labour man through and through. He'd never miss a chance to support them in an election.'

'And you've had no contact with him since?' Chris asked.

'No. He signed the divorce papers I sent to the boarding house, and that was the last I heard from him.'

'And you've absolutely no idea where he might be now?' Joseph asked.

'Not at all.' Charlotte looked between the two officers. 'Are you saying he's disappeared?'

'I'm afraid that's what it looks like. As a result, we're now treating your ex-husband as a missing person. Alternatively, of course, there is also a possibility that he might be implicated somehow with the bodies found on your land.'

Charlotte rapidly shook her head. 'Mike might have been a huge flirt, yes—but a murderer, absolutely not.'

'In that case, there is something else we need to consider,' Joseph said gently. 'I'm afraid we have to consider the idea that some of the human remains found belong to him. If so, that would suggest he never left the area.'

'You can't be serious?' The farmer's hands flew to her mouth, her eyes becoming saucers. 'But that doesn't make any sense. Someone signed the divorce papers,' Charlotte whispered, her eyes shining with tears.

'It does if someone murdered him and faked the note he left you,' Chris replied.

Charlotte nodded, spilling the tears building in her eyes.

If this hadn't been an official interview, Joseph would have reached across the table to comfort her.

Thankfully, the solicitor was already squeezing her hand. 'We can stop for a moment if this is too much,' he suggested.

'No, let's keep going,' Charlotte said, blinking away her tears. 'It won't lessen the heartbreak now that awful idea is in my head.'

The solicitor nodded and withdrew his hand.

'Obviously, we don't know if any of the remains belonged to your ex-husband,' Joseph explained gently. 'But we do need to explore the possibility. Can you think of anyone who might have had a grudge against Mike?'

'Mike didn't argue with anyone. He got along with everyone, and we were happy together at first. The only problem was his roving eye. In his note, he told me he'd even had an affair right at the start of our marriage.'

Chris leaned forward a fraction in his chair. 'That revelation must have hurt you badly.'

Charlotte met his eye and shook her head. 'I know where you're going with this. You think I killed him?'

Her solicitor piped up. 'Be careful here, Charlotte.'

She shook her head. 'Once again, I've nothing to hide.' She returned her attention to Chris. 'No, to answer your question, and for the record, I didn't kill him. Although...'

Joseph immediately spotted a troubled look behind her eyes. 'What is it?'

'I feel crazy even suggesting this, but could Maggie have had something to do with Mike's disappearance? I know she always had a bit of a thing for him. Although he never named names in his note, he did say he'd had affairs.'

Before the interview, the team had seriously considered the idea. But could Margaret Trelawney, even with such a significant chip on her shoulder, really be a murderer?

As if answering her own question, Charlotte shook her head. 'As much as I loathe her, I don't think she's capable of anything like murder.'

'I see. In that case, is there anything else you'd like to add before we wrap this up for the time being?' Chris asked.

'Only that you need to look harder at the people in Fernbridge. Even if Margaret has nothing to do with this, someone there must know the truth.'

'Don't worry, we're already investigating all possible angles,' Joseph replied.

Charlotte nodded as Chris leaned over towards the recorder.

'Terminating the interview with Charlotte Harris at five-thirty p.m.,' the SIO said. Then he dipped his chin towards Charlotte. 'Just give us a moment so we can consult between ourselves.'

A short while later, Joseph and Chris joined Megan in the observation room.

'What are your thoughts?' Joseph asked Megan, eyeing the copious notes she'd been taking.

'For what it's worth, I think Charlotte's reaction was genuine,' she replied. 'Whether Mike Clifford is involved in the murders somehow, or was a victim himself, remains to be seen.'

'Either way, we still can't eliminate Charlotte as a suspect,' Chris replied. 'For all we know, she was working with her husband to murder people before she killed him.'

'In that case, what's next, boss?' Joseph asked. 'I really don't think we have enough to formally charge her.'

'Don't I know it. I already know what the CPS would say if we tried to arrest her at this point. We just have a lot of theories, but no hard evidence to link her to the murders. So, we let her walk, and we keep digging as we have been, cross-referencing every missing person with the dates we have.' He became thoughtful. 'Maybe you were on the money, after all, Megan.'

'How so, boss?' she asked.

'If we identify the very first victim, everything else will become much clearer and things will start falling into place, like what set our murderer off and turned them into a serial killer. We also need to follow up on Ms Trelawney, namely sending Ian and Sue to talk to her about the possibility she had an affair with Mike Clifford.'

'Rather them than us,' Joseph said, making both his colleagues smile.

CHAPTER ELEVEN

Later that evening, Joseph was sitting with Dylan on board his boat, *Avalon*, finishing what could only be described as an exceptional chilli. In the DI's opinion, it was just the thing for a *freeze-your-nads-off* winter evening. The cosy warmth from the professor's stove was also helping to keep the icy grip of winter at bay.

'So, what's your secret ingredient?' Joseph asked, mopping up the last of the chilli with a hunk of malted bread the professor had also baked. 'There's a really rich velvety background taste I can't quite put my finger on.'

'Dark chocolate,' Dylan replied.

Joseph shot his friend a surprised look. 'Come again?'

'No, you heard me correctly the first time. Chocolate isn't just reserved for sweets and puddings, you know. Used in something like this, it adds a whole layer of subtle complexity to the flavour.'

'Well, colour me surprised. You're not wrong, but who'd have thought?' Joseph pushed his plate away, his eyes settling on his friend. 'So now you've fed my body and soul, we should get back to the case. You were saying you might have an idea about those wreaths that Charlotte Harris makes and leaves dotted around her farm?'

Dylan reached across and took down a book from among the hundreds cramming his shelves and thumbed his way through the hardback until he stopped at a page marked with a white feather. He held up the book with an illustration on the page that was similar to the twig wreaths Joseph had seen.

'Are these what you saw on Shadowbrook Farm?' Dylan asked.

'Yes. Charlotte said she believed in nature spirits and that they were offerings to ensure a good harvest.'

'That certainly corresponds with what I've been able to find out about them—they were often used by Pagans as offerings to deities, spirits, or the natural elements.'

'That all sounds harmless enough. Each to their own and all that.'

'Maybe, but there's also another use for these sorts of wreaths in nature-based magic. The act of weaving the twigs into a wreath could be a form of what is known as knot magic, by binding intentions or spells into the physical object of the wreath.'

'What sort of spells?' Joseph asked.

'There are quite a few associated with them, but perhaps the most interesting one is a protection spell.'

Joseph sat up straighter. 'Protection from what, exactly?'

'That's a good question, and if that's what Charlotte is using them for, only she will be able to tell you.'

'So you're basically confirming to me the woman really is a witch?'

Dylan pulled a face at his friend. 'I didn't actually say that. However, I think from what you've told me already about her, Charlotte is certainly acting like someone who has strong pagan beliefs. However, the really interesting thing for me, and maybe of relevance to your investigation, is that's exactly what the Celts did. Doesn't it strike you as something of a coincidence that, on a farm where a Celtic temple was discovered and allegedly long forgotten, the woman who now owns the farm just so happens to still share some of the beliefs of the people who once lived there?'

Joseph gave Dylan a thoughtful look. 'Aye, when you put it like that, I suppose it is quite the coincidence.'

'Coincidence, or something more? Just think about it. Human remains found buried above a forgotten temple?'

The DI contemplated the flames in the stove. 'We've been discussing exactly that theory at work. Someone, somewhere, obviously knew something about it before the dig. But regarding the idea of this being some sort of modern-day ritual, I thought Professor Bailey said animals were originally sacrificed in the temple there, not people?'

'That was certainly not unusual. However, human sacrifices weren't unknown among the Celts, either. Even Julius Caesar described the Druids as conducting human sacrifices. Large wicker effigies, known as Wicker Men, were filled with live humans and burned as offerings to the gods. Of course, that was made famous by the film of the same name.'

'Jesus H. Christ, you're not suggesting the ashes on the farm were from victims who were burned alive in a fecking giant straw man?'

Dylan quickly shook his head. 'No, as I'm sure we would have heard long ago if they were setting up Wicker Men around Fernbridge.'

'Aye, I suppose we would've. But that aside, are you saying that some psycho, or psychos, might be re-enacting some ancient Celtic sacrifice ceremony to the gods?'

'It's certainly not outside the realm of possibility. You see, human sacrifices were sometimes carried out—and this is where it gets interesting—to seek the favour of the gods for a successful harvest.'

Joseph peered at his friend. 'You're seriously suggesting that Charlotte might be murdering people, including her ex-husband, just to ensure that her wheat yield is up?'

Dylan shrugged. 'Some people take the fertility of their land very seriously.'

'Maybe in a horror movie they do, but in real life...' The DI shook his head. 'Having said that, I suppose we do need to consider this as a motive, even if it's absolutely out there.'

'Precisely. My advice is to try to keep an open mind and consider every angle, however unlikely it may seem at first glance.'

Joseph nodded. 'I'll do my best. So, was there anything else the two of you managed to dig up?'

'Actually, there is. I discovered an old newspaper article from the early twenties in the library. A journalist interviewed a gentleman in his nineties who used to live in Fernbridge. He spoke about how his grandfather had told him there were stories of strange goings-on around what's now known as Shadowbrook Farm that stretched back as far as anyone could remember.'

'So predating the sightings that Ms Trelawney told us about?'

'Yes, and by quite a margin—at least eighty years. The eyewitness recounted seeing a group of people in the middle of the night in what we now know was the site of the ancient temple. Apparently, these people were dressed in dark robes and looked like—and here I'm directly quoting—"*a bunch of Druids.*" Some people even thought that field was haunted by their ghosts.'

Joseph couldn't help but feel a mental shiver at hearing that gem of information, remembering the strange atmosphere he'd first felt at the dig site.

'Oh great, that's all I need. I can just see the look on the team's face when I tell them we're investigating a bunch of spectres...' A thought struck him. 'Hang on, you said a group of people—as in plural?'

'Correct. Apparently, going as far back as the nineteenth century, and possibly even earlier. It became something of a local legend until it eventually faded from memory. However, there is another interesting aspect to the story here. This old man also said that the numbers in those sightings dwindled as the years passed. Once they were ten strong, by the end it had dropped to just a couple of people.'

'So based on the assumption these weren't ghosts who got bored with haunting the place, are we talking about some sort of secret cult that faded away?'

Dylan steepled his fingers and nodded. 'There is also something very intriguing that Iris and I discovered at the local church in Fernbridge.'

'What flavour of intriguing?'

'You remember the triskelion symbol we discovered on that stone at the dig site?'

'Yes, those three interlocked spirals. What about it?'

'Well, imagine my surprise when we spotted that same symbol in the floor of the church, of all places. It had even been placed near the entrance, just like at the temple.'

Joseph whistled. 'That can't be a coincidence, can it?'

'Unlikely, and that certainly suggests to us once again that local people knew about the temple all the way back in the fifteenth century when the church was built. We asked the vicar about the origins of the stone, but unfortunately, he knew nothing about it.'

'So maybe this local cult had something to do with its placement. It is another religious building, after all.'

'That's certainly our best guess.'

'And now this cult has survived to the present day in one or more people, but has moved on from animals to people, sacrificing them to some Celtic god?'

'I suppose that's a possibility. But that isn't all. Iris dug up another newspaper article from 1966, where it was reported that a teenager heading home from a pub late at night claimed to have seen a lone person dressed in dark robes near Shadowbrook Farm.'

Joseph's eyes widened. 'Fecking hell. The same year our first victim was killed.'

'Yes, there does seem to be a link there to your investigation.'

'Aye. I don't suppose you have a copy of those articles, do you?'

Dylan reached over to a writing desk and took a manilla folder from the top of a pile. 'Iris printed them out for you,' he said, handing the folder over to Joseph.

'Thank you both so much for your sterling work.'

'Always a pleasure. I have to say it's rather nice to have a partner to help me with the research and share the thrill of the chase with.'

Joseph hitched his eyebrows up at his friend. 'Are you sure that's all Iris is to you?'

Dylan blinked. 'I don't know what you mean?'

The DI couldn't help but notice the red patches that had appeared on the professor's face. But before he could follow through, Max and White Fang let out short barks in unison, and Tux's ears pricked up. A moment later, someone knocked on *Avalon's* cabin door.

'Dylan, have you got my dad in there with you by any chance?' Ellie's voice called out. 'I've been trying to ring him, but he's not picking up.'

Joseph patted his pocket. 'Ah, I must have left my mobile on *Tús Nua*. You'd better come in.'

With claws clattering, White Fang and Max shot forward to meet and greet Ellie as the cabin door opened, letting in a brief snarl of biting wind before the door was closed again. She was wrapped up in a thick jacket, with John just behind her.

Joseph's daughter made a fuss over the two dogs. 'Yes, it's good to see you too.' Then she made her way over to Tux, who was sitting up in readiness to be stroked. 'Not forgetting you either, little man.'

Once the animal contingent had been dealt with, she finally turned her attention to the humans, giving both Joseph and Dylan a peck on the cheek. John gave both men a nod as he slipped off his coat.

'I take it by your presence here on this freezing night, it's something important?' Joseph said, as his daughter deposited her jacket on a bench seat and sat next to them.

Ellie's face became drawn. 'I think someone's been following me, Dad.'

Joseph felt his stomach slowly turn over. Dylan's brow furrowed.

'Why do you say that?' Joseph asked, already dreading the answer.

'There's this guy I keep seeing when I'm out and about in Oxford. I didn't think anything of it at first, but when I kept spotting him in completely different places, I realised it was too much of a coincidence. Once is fine, but a dozen times? I don't think so.'

Joseph had to fight hard to keep his growing sense of panic out of his voice. 'I don't suppose you managed to get a photo of this mystery man, did you?'

'No, although I tried to several times, he always ducked into a doorway or something similar, just at the wrong moment. But what I can tell you is he's a Caucasian male with a medium build, somewhere in his late thirties, or maybe early forties, with dark, cropped hair.'

'With a description like that, you're definitely a policeman's daughter,' Dylan said, smiling.

'Isn't that the truth?' John said, squeezing his girlfriend's shoulder.

'I'm just sorry I haven't got more info for you, Dad. I thought I was just being paranoid at first, until I spoke to John here.'

The PC nodded. 'I'm worried Ellie has picked up a stalker. I told her that she wasn't being paranoid, and that we needed to talk to you about it straight away.'

Joseph felt a surge of gratitude towards the young officer. 'Absolutely the right call. Okay, we're going to do whatever we can to track this guy down. Ellie, have you ever spotted him anywhere where there are security cameras so we could check the footage?'

'No. That's the first thing I thought of. But when I checked, there was never one around. It's almost like the guy knows where they all are and is deliberately avoiding being picked up by them.'

That sounded exactly like the sort of behaviour a professional criminal would exhibit. Joseph's mouth grew dry.

'Okay, first things first. From now on, I don't want you to go anywhere alone. Also, I'll sort you out another bottle of PAVA spray from work.'

John's eyebrows shot up. 'But members of the public are banned from carrying that.'

Ellie nodded. 'Oh, trust me, Dad knows. He nearly got into trouble at work with Derrick the last time he did that.'

'Don't worry about any of that now,' Joseph replied, knowing full well that he could rely on the DSU's support this time around. 'Anyway, I promise you, we'll sort this out one way or another. No eejit is going to intimidate my golden girl while I'm around.'

'Okay. How exactly?' she asked.

'Oh, I'd leave the details to your father to work out,' Dylan said. 'He can be quite resourceful when he needs to be.'

'So I'm starting to realise. Just no shallow graves like last time, Dad.'

John's eyes widened before a smile filled his face. 'That will be that famous Stone family sense of humour.'

'I certainly hope so,' Dylan said, shaking his head.

She grinned at them. 'Anyway, I'm going to have to love you and leave you. We're off to see a horror movie at the cinema.'

'Then have fun, you two,' Joseph said, before focusing his attention on John. 'I'm sure I can rely on you to keep an eye on my daughter as well?'

'Always,' John replied.

'Good man.'

As they slipped their jackets back on, Joseph stood, first shaking John's hand, before giving his daughter a hug. 'You just be careful and keep your wits about you. You hear me?'

'I hear you,' Ellie echoed, before bending over to kiss Dylan on top of the head, and making a fuss over all the animals again.

The moment the cabin door closed, Dylan's face fell. 'Joseph, I'm so sorry.'

'Aye, me too. This is literally my worst nightmare coming true. But as I've in no way done anything to piss the Night Watchmen off, I think this is probably another unsubtle message for me to play nice.'

'So you think they're just making a point by following her?'

'I have to believe that. If they wanted to rattle my cage, they've succeeded. But that also makes me suspect they're about to ask me to do something for them, and this is a reminder of who's pulling the strings.'

Dylan's brow furrowed. 'And I suppose the next question is, if so, will you play along?'

'Let's see what it is first. But make no mistake about it, Dylan. Right now, I'm wedged between a rock and a hard place, which is exactly where they want me.'

'Then you need to be ready for whatever they have coming your way.'

Another knock came from the cabin door, once again greeted with yips from the dogs and a modicum of interest from Tux.

'Did you forget something?' Dylan called out.

'Not that I know of,' Amy's voice said. 'You don't happen to have Joseph in there with you, do you, Professor? He's meant to be on a date night with me.'

Joseph grimaced as he glanced at his watch. 'Sorry, I completely forgot, but make yourself at home on *Tús Nua* and I'll be there in a moment.'

'Okay, but get yourself there quickly so we can make a start on this enormous amount of takeaway I got from that Turkish restaurant in Cowley that you like. See you in a moment.'

Joseph looked at his empty plate of chilli and then blew his cheeks out at Dylan.

His friend winked at him. 'Let's just hope you have the stomach capacity of a Hobbit.'

'Aye, because there's no way I want to hurt Amy's feelings,' Joseph replied as he stood. 'As far as the case, you and Iris have already struck gold, but keep digging.'

'Then, if you'll excuse the pun, we'll see what else we can dig up.'

Joseph raised his eyebrows at his friend as he patted both dogs. Tux jumped up onto the professor's lap, circling and trying to find the perfect place to sit.

'Why don't you make yourself at home?' the DI said to his feline companion.

'Oh, he always does,' the professor said, rubbing the cat behind the ear.

With a shake of his head, Joseph raised his hand in farewell and headed out of the narrowboat's door.

Amy was curled up next to Joseph in his bed, drawing lazy figure eights over his naked stomach. 'If I didn't know better, I'd say you were putting on a bit of weight.'

After eating a second meal that Amy really had overordered, it wasn't a surprise that Joseph felt fuller than a turkey stuffed in readiness for Christmas Day. Quite how he'd managed to cram the two meals into him, he'd absolutely no idea.

It was at that moment Amy made the fatal mistake of patting his stomach. That was all the encouragement it needed. A rattling, *shake-the-cupboards-and-cutlery* belch escaped the DI's mouth.

Amy's initial reaction of open-mouthed shock morphed into one of head-shaking laughter. She propped herself up on her elbow, looking down at him, making a show of flapping her hand in front of her mouth and nose.

'Better out than in, I suppose,' she said.

'Sorry, I don't know where that came from,' Joseph said, trying to keep the irony out of his voice. 'Anyway, isn't that a sign of appreciation for having enjoyed a good meal in some cultures?'

'Yes, but maybe try eating a bit less next time and spare us both your blushes.'

He chuckled. 'I'll do my best.'

Amy nodded. 'Anyway, now I've seduced you with food and had my wicked way with you, we need to talk shop. We've had a breakthrough with identifying that tooth from what appears to be the first victim.'

'You have?' Any remaining nausea was swept away as Joseph sat up.

Amy nodded. 'It was confirmed when one of the team managed to piece together a second tooth from the remains. Everything points towards it being a woman called Sally Blanchard, one of the people your team came up with during the search of missing people in the area.'

'Yes, that name rings a bell. Wasn't she a school teacher based in Bambleford?'

'Yes. She went missing in 1966, which also ties in with the thermoluminescence dating on the tooth as well.'

'So you're saying we now have confirmation of who our first victim was?'

'It seems that way. Chris was certainly over the moon when I told him. He wants to get the team together first thing in the morning to brief everyone.'

'Oh, you sweet talker, you.'

Amy nuzzled into the crook of his arm, this time leaving his stomach alone like an unexploded bomb, and traced the line of his jaw with her finger.

But as Joseph breathed in the scent of Amy, rather than feeling at peace, the DI felt more conflicted than ever. He cared deeply about Amy, and she definitely brightened up his life. But even though it was ridiculous—because he and Kate had been divorced for years—every time he was with Amy like this, it felt like a betrayal of his ex-wife. And then there was that kiss he and Kate had shared on board this very boat, where the planet had seemed to stop spinning for a moment. The only thing

Joseph knew for certain was that he felt confused to the core of his being.

Amy's hands started to spiral downwards, wisely bypassing his stomach, but still sending small sparks through Joseph's nervous system.

'Hey, what are you up to?' Joseph asked.

'Seconds,' Amy said, as she slid her right leg over his and manoeuvred herself into a straddling position.

'God, you're beautiful,' Joseph said, gazing up at the naked woman on top of him. He reached up and felt the rapid thrum of her heartbeat beneath his fingertips.

'You better believe it,' Amy replied, as she leaned down, kissed him, and the world melted away around them once again.

CHAPTER TWELVE

Having just briefed the team about the possible link to the ancient cult that Dylan had discovered, Joseph sat back down while the SIO took over.

Chris pointed at the photo of a blonde woman in her mid-twenties, wearing a tie-dye multicoloured dress and an embroidered white cotton blouse. Plastic flowers had been woven into the woman's long hair, in what, the entire team had agreed, was the overall hippy look of the sixties.

'This is Sally Blanchard, a primary school teacher in a neighbouring village to Fernbridge,' he said. 'We've now got a confirmed dental match for her from Amy's team. Sally was last seen at a school performance on the evening of the 26th of June in 1966 at Bambleford Village School. She was last seen riding home on her bicycle.

'Law enforcement couldn't find any evidence of foul play, especially as Sally sent a letter to the school a week later saying she had met someone and was resigning so she could travel the world with him. This also corroborated what a number of her colleagues had said, believing she was carrying on a secret affair, although they didn't know with whom.

'With no other evidence coming to light, investigators eventually concluded she had eloped with this mystery man, and the investigation was wound up due to a lack of evidence. But now, thanks to Amy and her team's efforts, we know exactly what happened to our school teacher. Sally was abducted and then her body was burned, her ashes scattered over the field where a Celtic temple once stood. Based on lab analysis, she was the first victim. Those are the facts we know so far. So what do we think?'

Ian blew out his cheeks. 'Doesn't this, *"I'm off to see the world"* letter, sound a lot like the note Mike allegedly left for Charlotte, saying he was going to start a new life? Could we be looking at our murderer's MO here, boss?'

Sue was already nodding as well. 'They could have forced their victims to write the letters to cover their tracks, before murdering them.'

'That certainly isn't beyond the realm of possibility,' Chris replied. 'So let's see if there are any other similarities between the missing people we have listed on the board. If nothing else, it could be a way of thinning down the number of potential victims.'

Everyone else was nodding now, a sense of energy palpable that they were finally on the right track.

'Hang on, what about this man she was allegedly going to run off round the world with?' Joseph asked.

'He was never identified in the original investigation,' Chris said. 'However, I did find something very interesting in the case notes. Mike Clifford was one of those interviewed. It turns out his mother was the headteacher and often roped him into helping with school performances.'

That got everyone's attention, including Joseph's, who sat up straighter.

Chris held up his hands. 'But before any of us jump to

conclusions, I've already checked the case notes and Mike wasn't under suspicion. He had a solid alibi during the time of Sally's disappearance.'

'So why didn't Charlotte mention Mike had been spoken to by the police during her interview with us?' Sue asked. 'That's surely suspicious in itself. It certainly seems one hell of a coincidence that a teacher who is murdered is also a person Charlotte's husband must have known.'

Joseph sucked in the air between his teeth. 'Charlotte did say that Mike had a roving eye. Ms Trelawney also independently confirmed that Mike had an affair at the start of his and Charlotte's marriage. I suppose it's not beyond the realm of possibility that the woman in question was actually Sally Blanchard.'

Ian jumped in with considerable enthusiasm as the idea started to gather momentum. 'So, Charlotte finds out about the affair, abducts Sally, gets her to write the fake letter, murders her, then scatters her ashes in the temple field as an offering to her pagan god. Bish bash bosh.' He sat back in his seat with something of a smug look, obviously believing he'd solved the case.

'Okay, this is certainly something we need to follow up with Charlotte,' Chris replied. 'But once again, there's a lot of theorising here rather than any hard evidence. However, what we do now know from Joseph's initial briefing is there's a strong possibility of an occult connection between this case and the practices of an ancient cult. That obviously puts Charlotte squarely in the frame, especially in light of the possible connection between her husband and Sally Blanchard. But I'm not ready to rule out Mike as a suspect, either. So let's brainstorm this further.'

Sue chewed her pen. 'Maybe Mike is just a regular psychopath who's changed his identity to drop off the map.'

The SIO wrote *Psychopath* under Michael's name, along with *Trying to silence Sally?*

'And put *Crazed witch* under the farmer's name,' Ian added.

Chris raised an eyebrow and instead wrote *Confirmed pagan beliefs* and *Acted out of jealousy?* beneath Charlotte on the board.

'I don't think we should rule out Jacob Harris, either,' Joseph said.

'Even though the murders continued after his death?' Megan asked.

'We can't afford to ignore the fact that he might have restarted the rituals and maybe even pulled his daughter into it. Maybe Charlotte even got Mike involved in it, too.'

'Right, we'll add all this to the board,' Chris said. 'Any other suspects?'

'Ms Trelawney,' Sue said. 'We know she had a motive to make Charlotte's life difficult after Mike broke off their relationship, not to mention their family feud.'

Chris added her name and motives to the board.

'Anyone else?' When no one spoke up, he continued, 'The next step is to determine whether the victims were just in the wrong place at the wrong time or if there's something more to their disappearances. Were they targeted, or was this opportunistic? If we can crack that, we might narrow down the list of potential victims even further.'

Everyone nodded, realising the importance of this analysis.

'Okay, we'll wrap it up for now. There's still a lot to dig through, so let's get to it, people.'

As Joseph returned to his desk, his phone vibrated and Dylan's name appeared on the screen. The DI picked up immediately.

'Do you have another juicy breakthrough for us?' he asked.

'Not yet, but you need to get to Fernbridge immediately,' the professor replied.

'Why the rush?'

'Because there's serious trouble brewing, stirred up by none other than Ms Trelawney. She's organised an emergency church council meeting. I can tell you, the mood here isn't pretty.'

'You're actually at this meeting now?'

'Yes, along with Iris, who alerted me. You need to get here, Joseph.'

'On my way.' He hung up and turned to Megan. 'Fancy a blue-light run?'

Megan grabbed her coat. 'Always, but why?'

'I'll tell you on the way,' the DI replied, grabbing his coat and went over to Chris to let the SIO know where they were heading.

The village hall was crammed with people, so many, in fact, that quite a few had spilled out onto the pavement. Because of that, despite the freezing temperature, the double doors had been flung wide open so the crowd outside could listen in on the debate currently going on inside the building.

Joseph and Megan had to make good use of their police warrants to persuade people to move aside so they could squeeze past. Dylan was standing near the back, next to a display cabinet with pottery in it. He spotted the detectives and waved them over.

A fierce debate was in full swing. It was between a man near the front of the audience and Ms Trelawney, sitting on a stage surrounded by a handful of other people behind a table, all of whom looked bemused.

Joseph recognised some of the reporters in the room, many

of whom had their recorders out, including Kate, who gave him a small wave. He spotted Ricky Holt among the pack, who, like a fly homing in on a turd, had a knack for sniffing out a story where he could spin other people's misery into clickbait. Unlike anything written by his ex-wife, Ricky's toxic coverage would be sensational, and would blame the police no matter what they did.

'So what's going on here exactly?' Joseph asked as they finally reached Dylan and Iris.

'Nothing good,' Dylan said. 'It seems Ms Trelawney is a woman on a mission.'

'That mission being?' Megan asked.

'To drive Charlotte Harris out by whatever means necessary,' Iris replied. She handed the detectives a flyer. *'Emergency Meeting in the Village Hall at 12 PM to discuss concerns about recent events at Shadowbrook Farm.'*

As the DI turned to take in the gathered crowd, his elbow knocked into the display case and the vase inside wobbled dangerously. Thankfully, Megan had lightning-fast reflexes and managed to steady the cabinet before the vessel toppled.

'Good grief, that was close,' Iris said. 'That would have been a disaster for the auction if that had shattered.'

'Don't worry, I'd have paid for it out of my own pocket if I'd broken it,' Joseph said.

'Are you sure about that? Arthur's vases are real collectors' pieces. The last one went for thirty thousand at auction.'

Joseph gawped at her. 'How much? What are his pots made from, solid gold or something?' The DI glanced at the vase, but there seemed to be nothing extraordinary about its design apart from its pretty green glaze.

Iris shrugged. 'That's the art market for you. Some art critic somewhere decided Arthur's work was a big deal and the next thing you know, the well-heeled were fighting each other to buy his pots. Not that Arthur makes them anymore. Anyway, no one begrudges him the success he enjoys because he gives most of the proceeds away to charity. That's why this pot is on public display here for an auction that's being held tomorrow, to help raise money for roof repairs for the local church. All the great and the good of Fernbridge are going to be there.'

'If this pot is worth that much, you'd think it would have an armed guard,' Megan said.

'Not when it's in what was meant to be a sleepy village—at least it was until these murders came to light,' Iris replied.

Ms Trelawney raised her voice at the man she'd been on the edge of having a blazing row with. 'We all know there's something not right about Charlotte Harris, and there never has been.'

'But she's done absolutely nothing wrong,' the grey-haired man at the front of the audience replied.

It was only as he shook his head and cast a beseeching look at those around him, that Joseph recognised who it was—Arthur Cleaves, the artist who'd given him his business card outside the village shop and who had made the pot he'd nearly knocked over.

'I know you mean well, Arthur, but we all know you've got too kind a heart for your own good,' Ms Trelawney replied. 'That woman and her family have been nothing but bad news for the reputation of Fernbridge. Now that human remains have been found on Charlotte's farm, we all need to be honest with ourselves. This basically confirms what we've all been thinking all these years. It's certainly not hard to draw a very obvious conclusion from all of this.'

'Just because those remains have been discovered on Charlotte's land, doesn't mean she had anything to do with it,' Arthur said.

'I'm liking that man more by the moment,' Joseph whispered.

'Arthur is certainly a good egg and not afraid to stand up for others,' Iris replied.

Ms Trelawney's gaze dropped somewhere below sub-zero as she glared down at the artist. 'Do you know your problem, Arthur? You try to see the best in everyone, even when the person in question is a witch.'

That got the shutters on the cameras clicking.

Ms Trelawney raised her eyebrows at the collective audience. 'Oh, come on, you're all thinking it. We've all heard the rumours about strange goings-on up at Shadowbrook Farm over the years. And now, at last, we know what was actually happening.'

'What's that exactly?' Ricky Holt asked with his usual snarky, nasal tone.

'Isn't it obvious? Satanic worship, that's what. Someone has obviously been abducting those poor people to murder them and then burn their bodies. Let's not beat around the bush any longer. We all know who that person is. Charlotte Harris.'

Ricky Holt grinned at the photographer next to him, who was busy taking photos of Ms Trelawney in full harpy mode.

Joseph didn't need to be psychic to know just how the gobshite of a reporter would turn all of this into an attention-grabbing headline for the following day.

'I've heard enough of this,' Arthur said. 'Charlotte is nothing but a kind woman, and you're making her out to be some sort of pariah.' He turned to look at the other people gathered. 'If you've got any sense, you'll not listen to any more of this rubbish and will get out of here now.'

When no one responded, Arthur shook his head at the other villagers and made his way out with a look on his face like a disappointed parent.

Joseph couldn't help but notice the triumphant look that filled Ms Trelawney's face as Arthur departed, having banished her nemesis from the room.

But people's heads were now bent together, and slowly, in ones and twos, some of the audience followed Arthur out, thinning the numbers attending the meeting considerably.

'You're all making a mistake,' Ms Trelawney said to their departing backs.

'Shouldn't we follow their example?' Dylan said.

'Not if we want to see what this rabble-rouser's agenda is, we don't,' Iris replied.

Joseph nodded. 'Aye, half of me wants to break this meeting up, but the other half wants to see what her agenda is here.'

'Apart from being downright unpleasant, we don't have any real grounds to intervene,' Megan said.

'True. Even if we did, I doubt it would take long for Ms Trelawney to go over our heads to complain.'

It was at that precise moment that the shop owner spotted them standing at the back of the hall. She frowned at the detectives before returning her attention to the rest of her potential flock.

'Well, I'm pleased that so many of you are prepared to listen, because mark my words, we have a real problem on our hands. Did you know that the police have already interviewed Charlotte about the murders and let her go? What do you have to say to that, Detective Stone?' She shot him a challenging look, and everyone in the room turned towards the two detectives standing at the back.

'Here we go,' Joseph muttered under his breath. Then he raised his voice so everyone in the hall, and hopefully the people outside, could hear what he was about to say. 'As I'm sure you're aware, we can't discuss any details of an ongoing investigation.'

'Yes, but why did you let her go after interviewing her?' a

man built like a bull and with a hard face asked from across the room.

Iris leaned in a fraction and kept her voice low so only Joseph could hear her. 'That's Charlie Pankhurst, a retired builder who loves nothing more than to create trouble. He and Margaret Trelawney are cut from the same cloth.'

'Noted,' Joseph replied under his breath, before giving the man his most winning smile. Raising his voice again, he said, 'I'm sure you can appreciate that we can't discuss a sensitive subject like that.'

Charlie glowered back at him. 'So, in other words, it's just like Ms Trelawney said. You're doing shit-all about Harris.'

Joseph scowled, and his expression was caught by Ricky Holt's photographer, who took a snap.

Ms Trelawney raised her hands. 'We are not here to criticise the police but to assist them where we can.'

'Even though you were the one who kicked things off,' Dylan muttered under his breath.

Ms Trelawney cast her gaze out over the audience. 'Does anyone here know anything, anything at all, that maybe you felt you couldn't discuss with the officers who did the door-to-door inquiries? Perhaps you felt you didn't want to say anything due to some sort of misguided loyalty towards Charlotte. But we all know just how serious this situation is, and I would implore you to say something if you've been holding your tongue.'

A ripple of conversation passed through the audience. Then, with a lot of encouragement from the woman sitting next to him, a man, roughly in his forties, stood up. He looked distinctly uncomfortable, particularly as the photographers in the room all now had their cameras trained on him.

The man cleared his throat, looking like he wanted to be anywhere but there. 'Twenty years ago, when I was a teenager, I was out walking the dog very late one night on the public footpath that crosses close to Charlotte's land when I saw something very strange...'

The woman reached up and patted his arm, giving him an encouraging look.

'First of all, I know how this is going to sound, but I swear I saw a hooded figure that looked just like a druid walking through that field where they found those human remains. They seemed to be scattering something as they went, and I could hear them chanting something, although I couldn't make out the words.'

Joseph traded a surprised look with Megan.

'Could that person have been Charlotte?' Ms Trelawney asked, as though she were a barrister interrogating a witness on the stand.

The man met her gaze. 'I couldn't say. Their body was hidden by the robe. But there was another thing. I did see Charlotte's old Land Rover parked up near that field. That was unusual because it was close to midnight.'

Ms Trelawney shot Joseph and Megan a triumphant look. 'There you go, Detectives. You have your woman. You should go and arrest her at once.'

Joseph had never taken kindly to being told how to do his job, especially by a jumped-up Miss Marple wannabe.

He held up his hands. 'In light of this new information, we will, of course, look into it, and my colleague here, DC Anderson, will take a statement from...?' He looked at the man.

'Mr Wickes,' the man replied.

Joseph nodded. 'If there is anyone else here who's been reluctant to say anything until now, I would urge you all to talk to us individually rather than in a public forum like this.' He couldn't help but glance across at Ricky, who smirked. 'Whatever you know, however small or inconsequential you think it is, you need to step forward. We'll be very grateful for any information you can give us.'

Several people nodded.

'Yes, don't be shy about this,' Ms Trelawney said. 'The sooner the truth comes out about what that woman has been up to and she is finally locked up, the sooner we can all put this unfortunate event behind us and be able to sleep soundly in our beds again. Trust me when I say that myself and the other parish councillors will also be looking at what steps we can take to deal with her.'

The other people on the stage with her traded frowns. To Joseph, at least, they didn't look like they were on board with that idea.

'I cannot believe you would stoop to something so low as this,' a woman's voice called out.

Everyone turned to see who'd joined them. Charlotte Harris was standing in the doorway, one of the flyers for the meeting crumpled in her hand. 'I knew you were capable of many things, Maggie Trelawney, but I didn't think you had it in you to pull a stunt like this.'

The shopkeeper stood up and glowered at the farmer. 'If this is what it takes to expose you for what you really are, then so be it.'

'And what am I, exactly?' Charlotte asked, her tone threatening.

'A witch and a murderer!' Ms Trelawney said, crossing her arms and jutting out her chin.

The camera shutters whirred as Ricky Holt, in particular, lapped it all up, his pen frantically scribbling in his notebook. Nearby, Kate met Joseph's eye and shook her head.

'Go to hell!' Charlotte shouted, turning on her heel and pushing past those in her way, and marched out.

Margaret Trelawney looked positively triumphant. 'There

you go. Notice Charlotte didn't even try to deny it.' Then the shopkeeper shot Joseph a *go on then* look, as though challenging him to arrest the farmer there and then.

The DI ignored her and turned to Megan and the others with him. 'Okay, I've seen enough. I'm going to head after Charlotte. Megan, you stay here and get whatever statements you can from anyone else who has any more information.'

'Got it,' the DC replied.

'This is bad business, Joseph,' Dylan said.

'Prosecution in the court of public opinion is never a good look for anywhere or anyone. But maybe something useful might still come out of this.'

Dylan nodded. 'Iris and I are heading back to Oxford. A librarian I tasked with digging through the archives has unearthed some old bound journals held in the Bodleian, which she thinks might be relevant.'

'Thank you both for your continued support. It's already making a huge difference to the investigation,' Joseph replied.

'More than happy to help, and it makes a welcome change from the crossword,' Iris replied.

'A woman after your own heart, hey, Dylan?' Joseph said.

The professor blinked. 'So it would seem.'

Joseph did his best to suppress a smile as his eyes met Kate's again across the village hall, where a line of people was keen to talk to her. With some satisfaction, he also saw that, in contrast, no one was eager to speak to Ricky Holt, who was waving his dictaphone under the nose of an old lady gathering her things to leave.

As the DI got outside, he spotted Charlotte's Land Rover already heading away down the street.

One thing was for certain, he needed to talk to the farmer as soon as possible and certainly before the likes of Ricky Holt got to her. Keys in hand, he walked towards the Volvo.

CHAPTER THIRTEEN

Joseph drove the all-wheel-drive Volvo V90 with much more confidence than he'd felt as a passenger in Megan's Mini Cooper. Sure, a police Land Rover might have been better suited to the track leading to Shadowbrook Farm, but the V90 didn't embarrass itself either. It even managed to make it through the temporary slurry pond without requiring the DI to wade through it again.

Ahead, the farm looked bleaker than ever under the heavy blanket of storm-black clouds. The constant moan of the wind only enhanced the desolate atmosphere as Joseph parked the car and stepped out. A flock of crows spiralling above the nearby wood drew his gaze towards the unmistakable figure of Charlotte, striding purposefully in that direction, with her Border Collie, Fergus, following behind. Maybe she was just going for a walk to clear her head after being so publicly vilified.

Joseph headed to the back of the Volvo and, after his last experience, grabbed his wellies from the boot. As he pulled them on, he noticed the nests in the bare branches of the trees, where crows and jackdaws were gathering to roost as the light began to fade. Glancing at his watch, he saw it had just passed four. Nightfall wasn't far off. Grabbing a torch from the glove compartment, he set off after Charlotte.

Before long, Joseph was striding along a well-trodden footpath across a ploughed field towards the wood where the farmer had disappeared. The wind howled, tugging at his jacket with a biting chill. He zipped it up as high as it would go, grateful he was wearing one of his better winter coats. On the ridge behind the farm, the lone chimney of the incinerator loomed, a dark silhouette in the dying light.

It was easy for Joseph to imagine the murderer bringing their victims to that isolated spot to dispose of their bodies. Even with all the circumstantial evidence stacked against her, the question in his mind remained—was Charlotte really the one responsible? Ms Trelawney certainly seemed to have already convicted the farmer in her own mind, and was doing a good job of convincing a fair portion of the village as well.

In some ways, it was hard to argue with her logic. All the victims had been found on Shadowbrook farmland, and Charlotte had easy access to an incinerator. Add in the mysterious robed figure, and it was a compelling case. But apart from a potential motive linked to her husband, and maybe Sally, Joseph couldn't figure out why she'd have killed all the other victims. Could it really be about offerings to some Pagan god? Even with Charlotte admitting she was superstitious, even as the avenues of their investigation all began to point to her, that still seemed unlikely to Joseph. Unless she really was the psychopath Ms Trelawney portrayed her as.

The sky darkened further, but the clouds were thinning in places. Through one of the gaps, Joseph caught a fleeting glimpse of a full moon before it disappeared behind the clouds again.

The wood was shrouded in darkness by the time Joseph reached it. A quick check of his phone confirmed it wasn't on any official footpath, but the ground looked well trampled, suggesting Charlotte had used this route often.

Cupping his hands around his mouth, he called out, 'Charlotte, if you're in here, I need to talk to you.' Other than the cawing of crows and the creaking of branches, there was no reply.

He checked the map again. Beyond the wood, there was nothing but open fields. If Charlotte had passed through the wood, he'd likely spot her on the other side. If not, he could wait for her in the comfort of his car until she returned to the farm.

Pressing on into the deepening darkness, the cries of the crows faded as they settled down to roost. Joseph was about to turn on his torch when he spotted a glimmer of light ahead on the path. He was about to call Charlotte's name again, but hesitated, his curiosity raised.

What's going on there? he wondered.

Intrigued, the DI moved closer and gradually the flickering lights resolved themselves into a dozen small flames, forming a circle. Sensing something significant, Joseph approached silently, not wanting to disturb whatever was happening in the heart of this isolated wood.

As he got closer, he realised the candles had been placed around a small circular structure made from young saplings. They had been bent over and their branches woven together to form a domed roof.

In the centre, he finally spotted Charlotte, her pale figure illuminated by the candlelight. To his shock, she was naked, her toned limbs reflecting the flickering light. She knelt before a rudimentary altar made from a roughly hewn log. On it had been placed an apple, a slice of cheese, several bread rolls, and a wooden cup.

Joseph froze, not sure how to react to the startling scene.

Bloody hell, what is this, a naturist's ploughman's lunch?

Then Charlotte's whispered words reached him.

'With this light, I cast this circle,' she said. 'Let it be a sacred space, protected and free from harm, a place between the worlds where magic happens. By the power of the moon and the elements, this circle is cast.'

Joseph knew he was intruding on something deeply private, but could this be proof linking Charlotte's occult beliefs to the murders? The one thing he knew for sure was that he had to see how this played out.

'Great Goddess, Lady of the Moon, Queen of the Night, I call upon you,' Charlotte continued. 'Shine your silver light upon me, guide me with your wisdom, and bless my circle with your presence. Hail and welcome.'

At that moment, the clouds parted, revealing the full moon, a brilliant orb in the sky. Its light illuminated the clearing, making Charlotte's skin glow silver. The scene might have been bizarre, but even Joseph had to admit there was a strange beauty to it. Could this be how the Celts once connected to the natural world at their temple?

'With the power of the full moon, I seek to manifest understanding and kindness in the hearts of those who wish me harm. So I raise this chalice, filled with moon water...' Charlotte's voice took on a sing-song quality. 'By the light of the moon, let my wish take flight. As I will it, so might it be.' She took a sip from the cup and placed it among her other offerings.

Joseph's phone vibrated in his pocket. Though muffled, it was loud enough to make Fergus, who Joseph hadn't noticed near the farmer, sit up and bark. Charlotte turned and locked eyes with the DI, her expression darkening at once.

'I thought you were a detective, not a peeping Tom, Detective Stone,' she said, standing to face him in all her nakedness. 'Or are you some sort of pervert who gets their kicks from this sort of thing?'

Heat rushed to Joseph's face as he quickly turned away. 'I'm sorry. I saw you enter the wood and followed because I need to talk to you about what happened in the village hall.'

'So, you're not here to get your kicks by seeing me naked, then?'

'No, of course not!' Joseph snapped.

'No need to be so adamant, Detective. A lady might take offence,' Charlotte said. 'You can turn around now.'

Joseph cautiously turned to see that Charlotte had dressed in her denim again, her expression amused.

'I doubt you'll forget this in a hurry,' she said.

Joseph raked a hand through his hair. 'You could say that again.' He gestured to the items on the log. 'Are those offerings to your goddess?'

Charlotte nodded. 'Exactly. To the moon goddess Arianrhod, to be precise. And, as you can see, no human sacrifices in sight. No orgies either, unless...' She gave Joseph a pointed look.

Before he could respond, she grinned. 'Just pulling your chain, Detective. Though I have to admit, Arianrhod might approve.'

Joseph held up his palms. 'Okay, okay, message received. But I do have questions, especially after what I just witnessed. Is this some kind of homemade temple?'

Charlotte ran her hands over the woven walls. 'Indeed she is, and made from living hazel saplings. It's my sacred space—not as grand as the Celtic temple in my lower field might have once been, but it has its charms.'

'I suppose it does. Now, about the village meeting...'

Charlotte sighed. 'Yes, it wasn't great, was it? But at least I had a chance to defend myself.'

'Actually, you weren't the only one who did that. Arthur Cleaves made an impassioned speech on your behalf. It convinced quite a few people to leave.'

A small smile touched Charlotte's lips. 'Arthur's always been kind to me. It's good to have a few people who don't turn their backs on you when you live life a little differently.'

'Arthur certainly didn't. But there's something else that came up before you arrived. Back in the eighties, a villager claimed to have seen a robed figure around midnight in the field where the temple was found.'

Charlotte pulled a face. 'And how much had they had to drink, or were they high on something?'

'So, you're saying it wasn't you?'

'No. I'd have been tucked up in bed. Besides, as you just saw, I don't wear clothes when I'm communing with my gods.'

Joseph gave her a sheepish look. 'Aye, I suppose you don't. But the witness also saw your Land Rover parked nearby. How do you explain that?'

Charlotte shrugged. 'I can't. If anyone had tried to borrow it, Fergus's great, great, great grandmother would have raised the alarm. Maybe it was just a similar vehicle.'

'And what about an alibi for that night?'

'Give me a date, and I'll ask Fergus to check his grandmother's diary,' Charlotte replied with a smirk.

Joseph rubbed his neck. 'So, in other words, you've no idea, then?'

'Could you remember what you were doing on any given night in the eighties?'

The DI sighed. 'Probably not.'

'Exactly. So, what now, Detective? Do you arrest me for indecent exposure, or as your prime suspect?' Charlotte held out her wrists.

Joseph raised an eyebrow. 'No need for that. What you do on your own land is up to you, as long as you're not hurting anyone. Do it on the village high street though, and we might have words.'

A sharp smile crossed Charlotte's face. 'That might be worth it, just to see Maggie's expression. As for the robed figure, unless you have hard evidence, it's just hearsay.'

'I agree. We need solid evidence, although I must admit the circumstantial case against you is building.'

Joseph considered asking her there and then about Mike's involvement with Sally Blanchard. But he was also painfully aware that particular discussion was best had in an interview room with a recorder running. Now wasn't that moment. Yet, at least.

The amused expression faded from Charlotte's face. 'A crazed old woman with Pagan beliefs and a secret temple, with human remains on her land—I know how it looks, Detective.'

'Even so, it doesn't make you a murderer.'

'You might not think so, but others seem more than happy to jump to that conclusion. In older times, I probably would have been burned at the stake already.'

'Thankfully, we live in a different era now,' Joseph said.

'I hope you're right,' Charlotte replied, packing the wooden cup into an old rucksack but leaving the food behind. 'So, how about a cup of tea and a chance to warm up by the fire?'

'That sounds like a grand idea,' Joseph said, switching on his torch to light the way back, as Fergus trotted ahead, leading the way.

CHAPTER FOURTEEN

Just as Joseph knew he would be, the DI was the focus of a lot of light-hearted banter in the incident room. After he'd updated the team about the rather startling revelation of what Charlotte Harris got up to in her woods, the reaction of his colleagues had been nothing if not predictable.

'So let me get this right, you're basically someone who gets their kicks by watching women of a certain age get their kit off?' Ian said with a wide grin.

'You right eejit, I'm not even going to bother honouring that with a reply.'

'Look, if Joseph has a secret thing for this sort of stuff, who are we to judge?' Sue said, the corners of her mouth twitching.

'Well, there is one benefit, I suppose,' Megan added.

'Which is?' Chris asked distractedly, as he concentrated on updating the incident board with the latest information about just how far Charlotte Harris's beliefs went.

The DI peered at her, waiting for the punchline to land.

'At least we all get to share this excellent shortbread thanks to Joseph's *sugar mummy*.' She took another bite of the biscuit in her hand.

Joseph scowled. 'Thank you for that contribution, really.'

'Look, I'm not complaining. Charlotte gave you enough shortbread to keep us going for a week.'

'Maybe, but I'm not touching a single one of those,' Ian said.

Sue gave him a surprised look as she dunked her shortbread in her cup of tea. 'Have you actually tasted these yet? Because if you haven't, you don't know what you're missing.'

Ian crossed his arms. 'I'm not going to take the risk. Who knows what ingredients she might have slipped into them?'

Joseph gave him a straight look. 'What, you're worried she added a love potion to them or something?'

Ian raised his eyebrows at him. 'Well, it's obviously worked on you, *toy boy*.'

The DI gave him his most powerful version of *the look*, which only made the eejit grin even more broadly.

When Chris turned around to face the room, even he was trying to suppress a smile. 'Okay, time to save Joseph's blushes—we need to move on.' He nodded towards Megan. 'Could you update everyone about the eyewitnesses who stepped forward at the village hall meeting?'

Megan finished off the last of her shortbread and nodded. 'It turns out the sightings of a lone mysterious figure stretched over at least three decades, starting in the sixties and ending in the nineties. They all claim to have seen a figure on or near Shadowbrook Farm, wearing a long, dark, druid-like robe with the hood drawn up over their head.

'Two of them also reported seeing a parked Land Rover in a nearby lane. Although no one could remember the number plate, they both said they thought at the time it belonged to Charlotte's father, Jacob Harris. It's the vehicle that he drove back then, and that Charlotte still drives to this day. Although they couldn't give me specific dates, their rough estimates about when they think it was correlated to at least three of the missing people on our list.'

Chris nodded. 'So the question we need to ask ourselves is whether these sightings coincide with any of our victims.' He turned towards the list of three names that had been added beside Sally Blanchard's on the board. Only Sally's name had been marked with a green tick, thanks to the dental records confirming her identity, and a line had been drawn from her to *The Cloaked Reaper* written at the top of the board.

That was the name Ricky Holt had come up with for the serial killer in his newspaper piece. True to form, his article had been an over-sensationalised account, naming Charlotte Harris as the prime suspect.

Joseph knew the little cockroach's work would only help fuel the paranoia already running rampant in the village. In contrast, was the far more measured piece that Kate had written for the Oxford Chronicle. Being the professional journalist she was, Kate had stuck to the known facts, making it a point of not trampling over anyone's life.

'Right now, we can't be sure that these other three people are victims, but for the time being, we'll assume they are,' Chris continued. 'Megan has already looked at the circumstances of their disappearances to see if any sort of pattern emerged. Megan, please tell everyone what you found.'

The DC joined Chris at the board. 'It could just be a coincidence, but in all three cases, the victims were on the road at the time. In Sally Blanchard's case, she was cycling home but never arrived. Another was walking home along a path next to a main road after experiencing car trouble. The third was a hitchhiker. All of these incidents happened within a ten-mile radius of Fernbridge. In each case, they left a letter saying they were leaving their old lives behind.'

Chris gestured to the list of names. 'Apart from possibly

confirming part of the serial killer's MO here, it also suggests they might have been in their own vehicle when they came across these victims.'

Several detectives in the room exchanged knowing looks.

Joseph nodded. 'They might have been an opportunist who, seeing someone alone on the road, seized their chance.'

'Like a certain individual who, for the sake of argument, drives a Land Rover,' Sue said, voicing what everyone else was thinking.

'Not to mention the fact that we now know that same individual has more than a passing interest in Pagan rituals,' Ian added. 'Someone whose husband was having an affair with Sally Blanchard. Maybe it's time to call a spade a spade and all agree that Charlotte Harris is our woman and formally arrest her.'

Joseph wasn't sure why, but part of him still wasn't ready to go there. Not just yet, at least. 'I realise everything is pointing towards Charlotte, but my gut is telling me that someone is framing her for this,' he said. 'I keep coming back to this: why risk burying the remains of your victims on your own land? Especially when you then give the go-ahead for an archaeological dig at that very location. Yes, I know we've discussed the double-bluff theory, but I'm still not convinced. After all, it's one hell of a risk to take.'

Chris gave the DI a thoughtful look. 'Well, if someone is trying to frame her, then who is it?'

'Margaret Trelawney certainly springs to mind,' Megan said.

Joseph frowned. 'I still don't see that woman as a murderer either. A right royal pain in the arse, maybe, but not necessarily someone capable of killing anyone. But that's not to say she isn't involved somehow. The problem is we have plenty of circumstantial evidence, but no definitive proof to tie anyone directly to the murders. Even the human ashes found in Charlotte's incinerator could have been planted there, just like the remains found in her field.'

'Are you sure it's not that you've got a soft spot for her, Joseph?' Megan asked.

Ian grinned. 'I'm not so sure about *soft* spot.'

Joseph was grateful that Sue, who was nearest to Ian, picked up a folder and reached over to clip her colleague over the head with it.

'Thank you for saving me the effort of having to do that,' Joseph said, giving Ian *the look* again.

Sue winked at him. 'Anytime.'

But even as Joseph chuckled, he couldn't help but wonder if Megan had a point. Maybe his opinion of the farmer was clouding his view.

'Well, we're certainly not there yet in terms of being able to arrest Charlotte Harris for anything the CPS would be happy with, but maybe we're closing in on the evidence that will,' Chris said. 'Meanwhile, I'll be talking to Sally Blanchard's only remaining relative, her brother, to let him know the news about the discovery of her remains. Needless to say, that's going to be a very difficult conversation. Sue, as the press liaison officer, you can let the media know about our discovery once I give you the nod.'

'No problem, boss. I'll get a press release written up for you to sign off on,' the DS replied.

'I'd say today has been productive,' Chris said, 'and we're slowly but surely closing in on our murderer. Keep up the good work, and we'll crack this case sooner than later and help bring closure to a lot of people who have lost loved ones over the years. Now, let's call it a night, shall we?'

As the meeting broke up, Joseph pulled open his desk drawer to grab his things and spotted an envelope with his name printed on it. He took it out and opened it to see a photo inside, along with a note.

A tight feeling was already filling his chest as he took the photo of Ellie out. She was walking through the High Street in Oxford with a woman he recognised as a friend from college. Joseph felt physically sick as he read the short message written in decidedly shaky handwriting.

'It's time to prove yourself, Stone. We need the investigation file on the Shotgun Raider gang, and we need it now. Text us on this number when you have it.'

For a moment, the room seemed to spin around the DI and he slumped back into his chair.

'Are you okay?' Chris asked, passing by on his way to his desk.

Joseph stared at his boss. He already had a good idea who had likely placed the envelope in his desk for him to find.

'All good,' he replied, unable to keep the edge out of his tone.

'Okay...' Chris frowned slightly. 'I was wondering if you fancied joining me to work on restoring the Aston Martin DB5 tonight. The big moment has come of putting her engine back in.'

Even though Joseph knew the best strategy was to play along without tipping the DCI off, he couldn't quite bring himself to play nice at the moment.

'Sorry, I'm busy,' the DI replied, stopping himself from adding, *because I'm doing my hair.*

'Right,' Chris said, his lips thinning.

So much for our supposed friendship, Joseph thought as he watched his boss walk away. How could the gobshite do something like this to him and his family? Threaten his daughter's life—that was the implicit message here—backed up by the fact Ellie herself had told Joseph that someone had been following her. No doubt one of Chris's lackeys, making sure he got the message that the Night Watchmen meant business.

The only thing for sure was that he needed to talk to someone about what he was going to do next, and that conversation needed to happen sooner rather than later.

As he stood up, his mind a wall of noise, Megan held out the box of shortbread to him. 'Please eat some of these before I finish the lot.'

'Sorry, I need to see someone about something, but keep a few back for me.'

'No promises,' Megan replied through a mouthful of biscuit.

'Right,' the DI said, managing to force a smile for the benefit of his colleague.

With a lead weight in his stomach, Joseph grabbed his things, stood, and headed out to have an urgent meeting with DSU Derrick Walker. He needed to discuss this with someone who really understood the situation and who could help him decide what the hell he was going to do next.

CHAPTER FIFTEEN

Joseph knocked and headed into Derrick's glass office, closing the door behind him.

The big man looked up from the spreadsheet he'd been working on. 'I'd appreciate it if you'd wait for me to invite you in.'

'No time for niceties,' Joseph said. 'Look what I just found in my desk.' He dropped the envelope onto the DSU's desk.

'What's this?' Derrick asked.

'A message from the Night Watchmen. It seems the time for that favour you warned me about is finally here.'

Derrick closed his eyes for a moment before opening them again. 'Joseph, I'm so sorry. Part of me hoped they wouldn't do this.'

'Well, that doesn't seem to be the case. And just to make sure I really get the message...' The DI gestured to the envelope on Derrick's desk.

The DSU shook out the photo of Ellie and sighed. 'When was this taken?'

'Recently. Ellie spotted their man following her, although he never got close enough for her to get a photo. But it's very clear that they mean business.'

The superintendent's face became drawn. 'You can be certain of that. Exactly what is it they want you to do?'

'Read the note.'

Derrick did exactly that, the lines on his forehead growing deeper. 'Why do they want the investigation file on the Shotgun Raiders? As far as I know, the Night Watchmen have nothing to do with them.'

'They've already told you that?' Joseph asked.

'No, just an educated guess on my part. If they had been, they would have instructed me to turn a blind eye to what was going on.'

'Aye, that's what I guessed during the Geoff Goldsmith case. At the time, you made catching those bank robbers a priority, which told me it couldn't have anything to do with the Watchmen.'

'I like to think, even if they had been involved, I would have had the balls to say no to them. Like I did when I turned down the bribe money they sent via Chief Kennan.'

'Talking of which, surely there will be consequences for you doing that?'

Derrick gave the DI a thin-lipped smile and tapped the photo of Ellie. 'What do you think this is, Joseph? It's a way of pulling me back in, making sure I stay in line. I might have rejected their offer outright, but as we both know, they have ways of exerting pressure that gives you no choice but to bend to their will. Seizing Kate was a timely reminder for both of us of just how far they're prepared to go.'

'You're saying they will get their way one way or another?'

'You tell me. Are you going to download the investigation file for them?'

Joseph squinted at the big man. 'So, I've got no choice in this?'

'Based on personal experience, no. Although...' Derrick's gaze strayed to the photo of Ellie again. 'Maybe there's another play here.'

'I'm all ears. The thought of doing anything to help them makes me sick to my core.'

'What? You don't want to end up a bent copper like me?'

A wave of guilt crashed over Joseph and he held up his palms. 'Jesus, I didn't mean to imply that. Look, I realise now they backed you into a corner by threatening Kate. Anyone would have broken under that sort of pressure. And I know you had no way of knowing when you slipped them the information about the prisoner transfer, that they would end up shooting people when they ambushed us.'

Derrick pinched the bridge of his nose. 'Yes, but I still buckled, and because of that, I have blood on my hands.'

Not for the first time, Joseph felt real sympathy for Derrick. It wasn't that long ago that he'd loathed the man's guts, but that was all history now. Such was the new reality Joseph found himself living in.

'So tell me, how can I avoid being compromised and tempted to sell my mam's soul in exchange?' he asked.

Derrick held up his hands. 'No need for that. Although, it will involve me selling a little bit more of mine.'

Joseph's eyebrows pinched together. 'Sorry, I don't follow.'

'I mean, I'm going to do my best to make sure you don't get your hands dirty doing this. I'm going to download the files for you so your conscience can remain clear. That way, at least one of us will be able to sleep at night.'

'You'd seriously do that for me, Derrick?'

'Yes, because when there's a price to be paid eventually, I

don't want to drag you down with me. Besides, don't I owe you that for all the shit I've put you through over the years?'

A smile crept across the DI's face. 'Aye, I suppose there's been a fair bit of that.'

The DSU's face softened. 'Then let me do this. Please.'

'But I can't let you take the fall for me.'

Derrick made a show of holding up his hands. 'You might not be able to see it, but my hands are already covered with dirt thanks to them. So what difference will a little bit more make? Besides, this is a way to redeem myself in a small way.'

Joseph sighed. 'Are you absolutely sure?'

'I am. In fact...' The big man pulled out a USB memory stick from his desk drawer and plugged it into his computer, navigating through dozens of folders. Then, finding what he was looking for, Derrick dragged it over, copying it onto the USB.

When the green light stopped flashing on the memory stick, the DSU pulled it out and slid it over the desk. 'There you go, all the records we have about the Shotgun Raiders. Message the Night Watchmen on the burner phone number they gave you. They'll tell you where to drop off the files.'

Joseph took the memory stick. 'I don't quite know what to say. You do know if any sort of IT audit is conducted, they'll be able to trace the files being copied back to your machine.'

'That's the general idea,' Derrick said.

Joseph pocketed the USB stick. 'I don't know how to thank you.'

'Don't worry, I'll think of a way. Maybe a rare single malt.'

'You name it, as long as I don't have to sell a kidney to pay for it.'

Derrick actually chuckled, which was the first time Joseph had heard him do that in a long time.

Then the DSU's expression grew serious again. 'One question—where did you get that envelope anyway?'

Joseph gave his colleague a drawn expression. 'I found it in my desk.'

'So you think Chris put it there?'

'That's my guess. Although, I suppose it could have been another detective assigned to the Cloaked Reaper case. The thing is, I still don't want to believe Chris is involved in any of this, but no one else quite fits the bill like he does. Fast-tracked under mysterious circumstances, right place, right time, and all that.'

Derrick frowned. 'You're not the only one finding it hard to believe. I swear that man is as straight as they come.'

'I know, but we can't bury our heads in the sand. As we both know, the Night Watchmen have a knack for knowing exactly which buttons to press to break a person. But talking of bent coppers, how are you getting on putting that list together of any officers who've been fast-tracked by Chief Kennan?'

'It's been slow going, but I'm getting there. So far, I have a list of ten possible officers across the Thames Valley force.'

'That's a start.'

There was a knock on the door, and Derrick's expression momentarily froze. When Joseph glanced around, he spotted none other than Chris standing there.

Derrick raised his eyebrows at Joseph a bare fraction. 'Talk of the devil.' Then he gestured to the DCI to come in.

It was then that Joseph realised the photo and note were still in plain sight on Derrick's desk. He quickly leaned forward, putting his bag on top of them as Chris entered. Joseph could have sworn he spotted the slightest frown on the DCI's face as he glanced towards the desk, but then it was gone.

'What's Joseph done now?' Chris asked, glancing between them.

'Oh, the usual,' Derrick replied without missing a beat. 'God knows how you cope with him on your team.'

'As I keep telling you, the DI is a major asset and always has been,' Chris replied.

'Well, we'll have to agree to disagree about that,' Derrick said, keeping true to his classic arsehole attitude towards Joseph.

'You'll see it my way one day. Anyway, I thought I should get you up to speed with the Fernbridge investigation.'

Derrick nodded and fixed Joseph with his best steely gaze. 'Okay, you can get out of my sight, Stone.' He jutted his chin towards the door.

'It would be my absolute pleasure,' the DI replied, scooping up his bag and what lay beneath it and heading for the door. As he passed Chris, they shared a look, as if to say, *the bastard never changes, does he?*

But as Joseph headed down the corridor, he was full of admiration for the superintendent. The man had just taken the fall for him. Maybe he should have tried harder to talk him out of it. But the truth was he felt a tremendous sense of relief, and of all people, he had Derrick to thank for that.

Joseph looked at the text on his mobile phone's screen. '*St Barnabas Church. Leave the memory stick stuck beneath the lectern in the pulpit,*' the message said. He'd received it exactly five minutes after texting the mystery number that he had the files.

The DI had just parked his mountain bike outside the church, situated in the quiet back streets of Jericho. Dylan had once told him, as they'd sailed past on the nearby canal, that the architect had been someone called Sir Arthur Blomfield. He was a man who had obviously wanted to make a statement with the design of this church. The austere Gothic-style building, with its domed bell tower, loomed over the surrounding houses with an almost brooding presence.

Joseph looked around him, but in contrast to the bustling heart of the city less than a mile away, there was not a sign of anyone around. It was little wonder the Night Watchmen had chosen the church for the drop-off. There would be no one to witness whoever collected the memory stick.

He headed towards the church's door and pushed it open. Out of pure habit from his Irish Catholic upbringing, Joseph made the sign of the cross as he entered.

The DI stepped into the large, vaulted interior. Faint lightbulbs cast a dim orange glow, barely illuminating the interior but creating plenty of shadows where someone might be lurking.

Joseph crossed the rear row of benches towards the lefthand aisle, slowly walking the length of it, checking behind each and every column that flanked the side passages. He didn't want anyone witnessing what he was about to do.

His footsteps sounded impossibly loud in the quiet church. If anyone else was there, they would certainly know they had company.

After checking the rest of the church and ensuring the vestry door was locked, Joseph was finally reassured that he was alone.

Not wanting to waste any more time, the DI took a trail cam out of his pocket and climbed the stairs up into the pulpit.

For the first time in his life, he found himself with a priest's eye view of the church, looking out over the rows of benches. He could easily imagine one of the old-school fire-and-brimstone priests berating his congregation for being such sinners.

The DI looked up for a hiding place for the trail cam, examining the supporting struts of the ornate roof over the pulpit until he found a suitable recessed corner. Carefully climbing onto the stone edge of the pulpit—and feeling glad that Father Michael from St. Mary's back in Ireland couldn't see this act of wanton desecration—Joseph turned the trail cam on, reached up, and placed it in its shadowy hiding place. Hopefully, it wouldn't fall mid-sermon and hit an unsuspecting vicar on the head before he had a chance to retrieve it.

Joseph jumped back down into the pulpit. Even though he knew it was there, the camera was almost invisible to the naked eye. Job done.

He completed his final act with a far heavier heart, reaching down and sticking the memory stick to the bottom of the lectern with some tape. Derrick might have been the one who retrieved the files, but here Joseph was, handing them over to the crime syndicate. He could dress this moment up as much as he liked, but this single act still felt like a betrayal of everything he believed in as a police officer—even if it was supposedly for the greater good. He just prayed that would end up being the case here, otherwise, he wasn't sure he'd be able to live with himself.

As he headed back towards the exit, Joseph imagined Father Michael shaking his head and saying, *What have you done, Joseph?* If this had been a Roman Catholic church, he would have seriously considered stopping off at the confessional right then.

Outside, the night was growing icy, cold rain threatening to turn to hail, stinging his face. The DI drew his jacket tighter around him and was heading back to his mountain bike when he spotted a slight movement at the end of the road. His gaze snapped to a man who'd been standing on a street corner. The figure quickly turned and headed away. Even though Joseph had only seen him for a split second, he was a hundred percent certain it had been Chris Faulkner.

So he hadn't needed his trail cam, after all. It looked like his worst fears had been confirmed. The man he had considered a friend really was a traitor to everything the DI believed in.

Instead of fury, Joseph felt a wave of grief rush through him. The itch of tears scratched the back of his eyes as he fumbled with his lock. From this moment on, Chris was dead to him. The DI wouldn't rest now until he brought the little fecker to justice.

CHAPTER SIXTEEN

THE DARKNESS PRESSED in around Margaret Trelawney as she clutched her stomach, rushing away from the charity auction in the village hall.

On tonight of all nights, she thought.

The shopkeeper had learned long ago to recognise the telltale signs of gluten entering her system—the bloated stomach, the headache threatening to take hold, and the sharp pain in her gut. Thankfully, she already had a course of steroids from her GP at home for just these sorts of gastric emergencies.

But Margaret was seething inside.

This was meant to be her night, basking in its reflective glory as she ran the auction. She'd always craved the spotlight, so it was little wonder she'd looked forward to the annual charity auction. But tonight she'd been denied that experience.

All because some stupid waiter mixed up my order and gave me a chocolate sponge pudding, she thought.

Well, she would sue the caterers and demand financial compensation. Then, more importantly, because it was a point of principle after all, she would do everything she could to make sure that blonde waitress with her vacant smile was fired.

Maybe she'd demand a written apology from the woman too, for good measure. Yes, she'd make that woman sorry.

Margaret hurried along the pavement, praying she'd reach her toilet in time to ride out the stomach gripes strengthening by the second. She passed the church onto the small, dead-end cobbled lane where her pretty stone cottage stood by itself.

The shopkeeper was opening the gate to her home when she heard a soft footfall behind her.

With the hairs on her neck prickling, Margaret turned and gasped. An apparition was walking up the lane towards her, dressed in a long, dark, monk-like robe, tied at the waist with a length of cord. Rather than a crucifix, a strange silver pendant with three interwoven spirals hung from a long chain around the figure's neck.

'Charlotte?' Margaret asked, still unable to see the figure's face in the shadow of their hood.

In answer, the figure increased their pace.

Margaret let out a small cry as she turned on her heel and moved as fast as she could towards her front door. Her hand shook so violently that it took three attempts to get her key into the lock. Finally managing it, the door swung open and she almost fell through it. Catching herself, she turned to slam it behind her. Mid-swing, the door stopped dead as a gloved hand appeared at the edge.

Heart hammering, the shopkeeper threw herself against the wood, trying to stop the intruder from forcing their way inside. With the impossible strength of the devil on their side, her nemesis kept pushing. Then, a single massive shove sent Margaret toppling backwards.

She caught herself on a side table, a sharp pain in her back from the impact. She'd just managed to right herself and saw the silhouetted figure framed in the doorway. The blood roared in her ears as her stalker stepped inside.

Margaret raised her hands. 'Please, Charlotte, don't do this. I'm sorry for everything.'

Again, there was no response as the figure closed the distance and grabbed Margaret by the wrist. Adrenaline surged through her system, and with a scream, she pulled free with a strength she didn't know she had. Half running, half throwing herself up the staircase, she tried to get away.

Margaret managed to reach the landing just as a hand locked onto her right shoulder, ripping her wool coat open at the seam as she tried to pull away. Then, like she weighed nothing at all, she was hurled around. Pops of light briefly swam in her vision as her skull slammed into the wall and slid along it. But her assailant wasn't done.

Still hanging onto her shoulder, they swung her around again until Margaret was facing down the stairs. Just for a moment, the toes of her sensible wellies teetered on the edge, her wide eyes fixed on the darkness at the bottom. Before she could grab the banister to steady herself, she felt her assailant's other hand seize her by the back of the neck and push.

Time slowed.

She toppled forward, registering flecks of mud on her immaculate stair carpet.

She'll pay for that, she thought.

Then, like a bubble popping, time caught up, and the steps rushed up to meet her.

Margaret's head struck with the full weight of her body, snapping her neck with a sickening crack. Her lifeless body kept going, tumbling down the stairs until finally coming to a rest in a heap at the bottom.

The robed figure headed down the staircase after her, breathing hard. They stepped over Ms Trelawney's dead body, their eyes gleaming in the darkness as they took long, steadying breaths and let the buzz of adrenaline fade. It had been a messy kill, but at least now the bitch was dead. They leaned down to scoop up their victim...

'What the fuck do you think you're doing?' the hulking shape of Charlie Pankhurst bellowed from the doorway.

Before the giant of a man had a chance to take in the whole scene, the robed figure rushed at him, a cosh in their raised hand. Bringing their arm down, they slammed it into the builder's head.

Caught off guard, Charlie sagged to the floor, his eyes fluttering shut as he collapsed, unconscious.

That was all the chance the assailant needed. They jumped over the prone man and ran into the night.

CHAPTER SEVENTEEN

THE FOLLOWING MORNING, Joseph woke from a dreamless sleep feeling wrung out. After arriving back from St Barnabas the previous night, he'd made a point of briefing Dylan about spotting Chris lurking outside the church. Grim-faced, the professor had listened and after hearing everything, he finally agreed that Chris must be in the Night Watchmen's pocket.

After that conversation, Joseph had been awake for hours, still trying to come up with an excuse, however implausible, for how his boss might be innocent. But unable to come up with anything plausible, he'd finally had to accept that Chris really was working for the crime syndicate.

That had broken something deep inside him. If a good copper like the DCI could be turned, was there any hope for the rest of them?

Tux, sensing the wakefulness of his member of staff, immediately jumped up on his chest and started kneading, the cat's purr like an engine. It was as though Joseph was his favourite person in the world—at least if there was even the faintest chance of getting fed.

'You're so transparent, my furry friend,' Joseph said, rubbing the side of the cat's head.

Tux leaned into the attention, but as soon as the DI even hinted he was about to get up, Tux jumped down and began herding him, as effectively as any sheepdog, towards his food bowl.

Joseph was opening a food pouch, with Tux winding around his legs, when his phone pinged. His mouth went bone-dry. Was this going to be a message from the Night Watchmen saying they'd discovered his trail cam? Had Ellie already paid the price for his recklessness?

What the hell was I thinking? His mind spiralled towards the darkest possible outcome. Joseph squeezed his eyes shut for a moment, mentally bracing himself for whatever the message contained.

His shoulders dropped from around his ears when he saw it was from Kate.

'I've dug up some interesting info about Kennan. I'll pop over to discuss it before you head to work. x'

Joseph's gaze lingered on the single kiss far longer than he should have, like a drowning man in a stormy sea spotting a life raft. It was several long seconds before he eventually tore his gaze away to finish feeding Tux, get showered, and grab some breakfast before his ex-wife turned up.

He was just eating a bowl of porridge when his phone pinged again. Expecting to see another message from Kate, unease filled him when he saw it was from an unknown number.

As the DI started to read, he could feel the tension spreading across his shoulders.

'Well done, DI Stone. You've proved yourself. We've received the memory stick, and we'll leave Ellie alone.'

Joseph let out a long breath as he sank into a chair. So Chris hadn't realised he'd been spotted and, perhaps more importantly, hadn't discovered the trail cam in the pulpit.

A knock came on the door.

'Joseph, are you decent?' Kate's voice asked.

'I'm not sure I'll ever be decent, although I do have clothes on, if that's what you mean.'

The door opened, and Kate walked into the cabin, a laptop bag slung over her shoulder.

Joseph turned his phone around so she could read the message.

Kate's eyes widened. 'That sounds like good news, but what's this about a memory stick?'

'I'm afraid it's the price we had to pay to secure Ellie's safety. They demanded all our files on the Shotgun Raiders investigation.'

'The gang believed to be involved in a spate of bank robberies across Oxfordshire?'

'That's the one. For some reason, the Night Watchmen wanted to know more about the gang, suggesting it's a rival group.'

She peered at him. 'And what exactly are they going to do with that information?'

'Nothing good, that's for sure,' Joseph said.

'Hang on, doesn't that implicate you in all this mess just as much as Derrick?'

'Tell me about it, but what choice did I have, Kate?'

She chewed her lip as her gaze searched his face. 'Yes, I'd have done exactly the same in your position.'

Joseph felt a surge of relief that she understood. 'Derrick insisted on taking the bulk of the responsibility for this by downloading the Shotgun Raiders investigation files. He said that way it couldn't be traced back to me when this all eventually comes to light.'

Kate's eyebrows shot up. 'You mean he's trying to protect you from any fallout down the line?'

'That's the measure of it. Derrick insisted on throwing himself under the bus on my account. Admittedly, he's a right royal pain in my arse sometimes, but it turns out that deep down, your husband really is one of the good guys. So maybe cut him a bit more slack than you have been.'

Kate narrowed her eyes at him. 'You mean by letting him move back in with me?'

Joseph quickly raised his palms. 'Hey, I'm not going to stick my nose into your marriage. That's between the two of you and nobody else.'

With an unreadable look, she gazed out of the window. 'If Derrick hadn't lied to me in the first place, I would find it easier to forgive him.'

'Oh, come on, Kate. Everyone deserves a second chance.'

She shrugged. 'Maybe. Anyway, down to business, and about that coffee.'

Joseph recognised someone shutting down a conversation when he heard it. He also knew from bitter experience when it was best to back right the hell away from a sensitive subject with Kate. This was definitely one of those occasions.

He flashed her his best winning smile. 'Coffee is coming right up.'

A short while later, Papua New Guinea coffee bean brew in hand, the two of them were sitting side by side on the small sofa, looking at Kate's laptop screen.

'So, as I said in my text, I've been able to dig up some very interesting information about Chief Kennan.' She clicked on a folder and opened up a list of files, the first of which was a spreadsheet. Another click, and Joseph was looking at a long list of very large numbers.

'What am I looking at here?' he asked.

'A lot of evidence that Kennan is making a lot more money than a chief superintendent on salary should be. I've been doing a lot of old-fashioned investigative journalism, trawling through Companies House and even the land registry records. It turns out Kennan has her finger in a lot of pies. She's listed as a director for three different companies. From those, she draws a collective annual salary in excess of five hundred thousand, not to mention owning a portfolio of property worth well over five million. And that's just what I've been able to discover so far. Who knows what investments and offshore bank accounts she has in her name.'

'I don't suppose there's an easy explanation for that, like coming from a wealthy family or marrying into money?'

Kate shook her head. 'Her dad worked in the Cowley Mini factory and her mum was a cleaner. She's married to a teacher, and as far as I'm aware, she's never won the National Lottery. But if the quite eye-watering numbers on that spreadsheet aren't enough to convince you, it turns out at least one of those new start-up companies she's a director of can be linked directly to the Night Watchmen. Also, all three companies sprang into existence fully funded only three months ago. I'm sure you can see the significance of that.'

'You mean they were founded after the NCA shut down all the ones owned by the Night Watchmen last summer?'

'Exactly. And these are only the new companies I've been able to find out about. It seems the crime syndicate just brushed themselves down and funnelled their drug money and the rest of their ill-gotten gains into these new companies, handing out some tasty jobs in the process to their most loyal subjects.'

'And you have definitive proof that Kennan is one of them?'

'I still need to do some more digging, but let's just say I'm putting together a very incriminating file for when we're ready to go public with this. But that's not all, and this is perhaps the most worrying aspect because it points to what the Night Watchmen's mission statement really is. Talking to people who know Kennan well, it turns out she has serious ambitions.'

'Such as?' Joseph said, before taking a sip of, if he said so himself, a rather excellent Papua New Guinea coffee.

'The rumour is she has her sights set on becoming Chief Constable.'

Joseph let out a soft whistle. 'Shite, with that role, she would have complete oversight of the Thames Valley Police.'

Kate nodded. 'Can you imagine the benefit to the Night Watchmen if Kennan gets anywhere near that position?'

'Jesus H. Christ. The consequences would be off the charts.'

'And this is only part of the Night Watchmen's playbook. I'm fairly sure they have several politicians, not to mention a couple of judges, in their back pocket already. Whatever the Night Watchmen are, this isn't just another run-of-the-mill crime syndicate.'

'You think they have a long-term goal in all of this?' he asked.

'I do, and I dread to imagine what that might be. That's why we need to stop them.'

'Well, let's begin with taking down the person who has been making our lives difficult—namely, DCI Chris Faulkner. I saw him watching St Barnabas Church, where I did the drop last night. He must have picked it up and sent me that message.'

'You think or you know?' Kate asked.

'Don't worry, I thought of that and left a trail cam hidden in the pulpit to record whoever they sent to pick it up.'

'You mean you may have video evidence?'

'I'll know for sure when I swing by later today to pick it up.

Then we should have definitive proof.' He looked down at his hands encircling his mug, then added, 'I have to admit, I feel very conflicted about this.'

'Because it will confirm that Chris is compromised?'

'Aye, that's certainly how it's looking to me. There I was, having him pegged as a good guy, my friend, and now this...' He shook his head.

Kate reached out, massaging the back of his hand with her thumb. The moment stretched on, an unspoken conversation between them.

It confirmed to Joseph just how deeply his ex-wife still cared for him, and God knew, it was certainly true for him.

She glanced down at his lips. That old magnetic force was drawing them together, and they leaned towards each other, just as a knock sounded on the door.

They leapt apart as the door opened to reveal Amy standing there. The smile she'd had on her face faded as she looked between them, lines spidering out from the corners of her eyes.

'I bought you some almond croissants from that patisserie you like...' She shook her head and placed the pastry box on the step. 'Sorry to interrupt.' Without another word, the SOCO turned away and closed the door behind her.

Kate turned to Joseph. 'You can't let her go like that.'

Joseph jumped to his feet. He raced outside, only just managing to avoid crushing the croissants underfoot in the process. The unfortunate metaphor that would have created, wasn't lost on him.

It had only taken him moments to get to the towpath, but Amy was already a receding figure, marching away with a determined stride.

'Amy, please,' he called after her.

But if she heard him, she chose to ignore him. Rather than slow her stride, if anything, she increased it.

Even though he and Kate hadn't actually done anything, an enormous weight threatened to crush his soul. If Amy had entered even a few seconds later, who knew what she might have witnessed. He turned back to *Tús Nua* to see Kate emerging from the cabin, coat on, her laptop bag slung over her shoulder.

'Oh, Joseph,' she whispered.

'Aye, I know.' He looked into the dark pools of her eyes, feeling the familiar pull as always.

Kate shook her head slightly, as though trying to rouse herself from a waking dream. Then she leaned in and kissed him on the cheek. The next moment, she was hurrying away down the towpath in the opposite direction to the one that Amy had taken.

Joseph watched her go and felt something rubbing his legs. He looked down to see Tux, looking up at him and giving him a questioning look.

'Well, at least I can head off a lecture from you by feeding you your second breakfast of dry food.' With a heart heavy with guilt and the feeling of being pulled in two different directions, he walked back into the sanctuary of his boat.

Joseph had barely had time to open the cat food when his phone rang, and he saw Chris's name on the screen. His jaw tightened. Had his boss rumbled him after all? With more than a small amount of trepidation, he pressed accept.

'Joseph, there's been a major development on the Hooded Reaper case.'

The DI felt a surge of relief wash over him and his jaw relaxed. 'Why, what's happened?'

'Ms Trelawney has been found dead in her home. A local man, Charlie Pankhurst, disturbed the murderer. Someone dressed like a druid, hit him round the head with a cosh and escaped whilst Charlie was unconscious. As soon as he came round, he called the police.'

'Shite, I'm on my way,' Joseph said. But as he ended the call, he already knew what the implications were. Apart from suspicion falling once again on Charlotte Harris, he was bound to run into Amy at the crime scene as well.

This day just gets better and better, he thought to himself. He quickly dished dried cat food into Tux's bowl as he dialled Megan to let her know the news.

CHAPTER EIGHTEEN

Joseph was at the wheel of the unmarked Peugeot, with Megan riding in the passenger seat. The vehicle wasn't by choice. They'd lost the police pool car lottery to Ian and Sue, who'd already grabbed the Volvo V90.

Having arrived in Fernbridge, they parked behind a line of police cars, along with Amy's SOC van. She must have been driving at light speed to beat them to the crime scene.

At the foot of a cobbled lane where a lone, picturesque cottage stood, Ian and Sue were talking to an old woman, and trying to ignore the pack of journalists shouting questions at them beyond the outer perimeter on the main road.

Joseph and Megan exited their vehicle and, with a nod to their colleagues, headed towards an inner cordon of police tape stretched across the gateway, where PC John Thorpe was standing guard.

The DI gestured with his chin towards the house. 'How's it going in there?'

'Chris is already inside with Amy.' John gestured to the SOCO van. 'You'll need to do the usual if you want to go inside. Amy is running a tight ship with this one.'

'No problem,' Joseph replied, looking forward to this encounter with about as much enthusiasm as he had for karaoke night at the Scholar's Retreat.

As he and Megan pulled on their white forensic suits, it was hard to ignore the telephoto lenses of the tabloid press trained on them. Among them, Joseph spotted Ricky Holt badgering a passerby for a comment.

'It seems the grapevine is working hard as usual,' he observed to his colleague.

'Sue was telling me that they've pretty much set up camp in the local pub,' Megan replied.

'Why doesn't that surprise me,' Joseph said, now suited and booted, heading towards the crime scene.

The first thing they saw as they entered the cottage was a female SOCO with shoulder-length blonde hair tied back at her nape, dusting the polished wooden floor for prints. Beyond her, Amy and Chris were standing over Margaret Trelawney's crumpled body at the foot of the stairs. Joseph felt a spin of nausea at seeing the victim's head snapped back at an unnatural angle to her body. Amy leaned closer to the body with a camera and took a close-up of a gash on the right temple.

Joseph took in the trail of dried blood that had run down from the wound over the shopkeeper's face. After taking a snap of that, Amy took another shot of Ms Trelawney's brown wool coat where the right shoulder had been torn.

Chris's gaze narrowed slightly as he spotted the DI before the look vanished. After the run-in with Amy on the boat earlier that morning, Joseph had been bracing himself for her reaction. With that wall of noise swamping his thoughts, it had temporarily drowned out his encounter with the SIO outside St Barnabas Church the previous night. But based on his neutral expression, it seemed the boss was going to keep the charade going, at least for now. This was neither the time nor the place, but at some point, Joseph knew it would be.

When Amy finished taking photos, it was her turn to register his presence. Rather than the hardness he'd been expecting, there was actually a look of sadness in her eyes. That twisted Joseph's heart like nothing else could. But the SOCO remained professional, giving Joseph the smallest of nods, as if to say, *We both have a job to do, the rest can wait.*

He dipped his chin in response, understanding far too well. Then her usual professional mask was back in place, their colleagues totally unaware of the weighted non-verbal conversation the two officers had just had.

'Good, you're here,' Chris said, heading over. 'Amy, can you repeat what you were just telling me and why you think this is murder?'

Megan was already casting her gaze up the staircase. 'I'd certainly like to know that. At first glance, it just looks like Ms Trelawney fell down the stairs, hit her head on the way, and broke her neck during the fall.'

'And this is where you'll discover why Amy is so good at her job,' Joseph said.

Normally, that would have elicited at least a small smile from the SOCO, but her mouth didn't so much as faintly curl at the corners. The DI knew then that he was well and truly in the doghouse and no amount of Irish charm was going to get him out of there anytime soon.

Instead, Amy focused her attention on Megan. 'There are all the signs that Ms Trelawney didn't just trip. That's corroborated by the eyewitness account.'

Chris nodded. 'Charlie Pankhurst, a local builder, disturbed the intruder. He claims to have seen a robed figure standing over Ms Trelawney, getting ready to lift her.'

'Shite, so Ms Trelawney was meant to be another sacrifice?' Joseph asked.

'That's certainly what it looks like.'

'I don't suppose there's anyone else to corroborate his version of events?' Megan asked.

'Another passerby saw the same robed figure running off into the night, ruling Charlie Pankhurst out as a suspect, unless forensic evidence says otherwise.'

'Even so, how can you be certain Ms Trelawney was murdered by this intruder?'

'If she'd simply fallen down the stairs, we'd expect to see the corpse far closer to the bottom step,' Amy replied. 'So what does that tell you?'

Joseph already knew the answer, having seen this sort of thing before, especially in domestic disputes that had spiralled out of control. Chris also kept quiet, no doubt as intrigued as the DI to see how the DC answered the question.

But Megan was razor-sharp as ever. 'She was pushed or thrown and the extra momentum carried her further from the stairs than if she'd just fallen naturally?'

Amy gave Megan a wide smile. 'Correct. But that's not the only clue here. What else can you see?'

Joseph's gaze travelled up the stairs to see a splatter trail down the right-hand wall. Chris gave him a knowing look as Megan zeroed in on the detail as well, and frowned.

'Is there something about the gash on her head where she hit it on the wall, that indicates it wasn't just a simple fall?' the DC asked.

'Now you're on the right track,' Amy replied. 'Come up the stairs for a closer look and it'll become clear what really happened here.'

Joseph followed Chris and Megan as they stepped around the body and headed up to join the SOCO on the landing.

The first thing the DI noticed was that the blood-splatter pattern started abruptly and then smeared away in a line to the right.

'What can you tell from that, Megan?' Amy asked, pointing it out.

'That's obviously where the victim first hit her head.'

'I agree. So what's wrong with this picture?'

The DC gave her a blank look. 'I've honestly no idea.'

But Joseph could already see what didn't stack up if this had been just a fall.

Megan turned to Joseph. 'What am I missing here?'

'I'll give you a hint. The victim's injury should be on her left temple if she tripped and fell forward down the stairs,' he said.

Megan's eyes widened. 'In other words, she was heading up the stairs, turned around, and then fell?'

'Almost, but if you look closely, you can see a slight indentation in the wall,' Amy added.

Joseph had spotted the groove in the plasterwork and had a fair idea of what had actually happened.

Megan leaned in for a closer look at the damage, then nodded. 'Her head must have hit the wall with considerable force before she toppled forward.'

A smile lit up Amy's face. 'Exactly. We also found paint and plaster fragments on the right side of the victim's head, indicating she struck it very hard indeed.'

Joseph pictured the scene as Amy had described it. In his mind's eye, he watched Ms Trelawney walking up the stairs, reaching the landing, and...

Then the sequence of events slotted together in his head. 'So, Ms Trelawney was being chased up the stairs,' he said. 'She reached the top, but whoever was chasing her caught up and grabbed her right shoulder—hence the tear on her coat's seam. They spun her around so that her head initially slammed into the wall on the right-hand side, but she was swung around until she was facing down the stairs. That's when her assailant gave her a final shove. That's why the head injury is on her right temple and not her left.'

Amy hitched up her eyebrows at him. 'I'm sure that's the answer Megan was about to give me if you'd given her a chance.'

Joseph grimaced at his colleague. 'Sorry, me and my big mouth.'

Megan smiled at him. 'No problem. Although I had missed the connection with the ripped coat.'

Chris gave Joseph an impressed look. 'It seems hanging around with Amy has had its benefits.'

Normally, that would have resulted in a bit of banter between Joseph and Amy, but not on this occasion. Both officers avoided each other's eyes and simply nodded.

It struck Joseph how surreal the situation was. On the one hand, he was in serious shite with Amy, trying to pretend nothing had happened until they had a chance to talk in private. On the other, Chris was carrying on as if nothing had happened. If Joseph hadn't spotted him outside the drop the night before, he'd be questioning whether he'd dreamed the whole thing. It was almost like they'd all become actors in some play Joseph didn't have the script for, but he could already guess how it worked out—not well for any of them.

Megan, thankfully, was oblivious, looking lit up as she studied the blood splatter. She was lapping up the details of forensic work, learning as all good officers did from moments like this.

'It'll be interesting to see if Doctor Jacobs discovers anything during the autopsy,' she said.

'Hopefully, to start with, he'll be able to confirm the time of death,' Amy said. 'The algor mortis suggests it was around nine last night.' At the confused look Megan gave her, she clarified, 'The body's temperature.'

Megan nodded her thanks.

'That would coincide with Charlie Pankhurst's account of when he arrived and what he saw,' Chris said.

'Right, and I think we're pretty clear on the cause of death,' Amy said, 'but you never know what Rob and Claire might be able to discover.'

At that moment, the female SOCO, who'd been dusting for prints, called up the stairs. 'You're going to want to take a look at this, Amy.'

'You found something interesting, Alison?' Amy replied.

'Partial boot print,' the blonde woman replied.

The detectives followed Amy back down the stairs to join her colleague, who was pointing at the black forensic dust, revealing an imprint near the door.

'It looks like a Hunter Welly based on the tread pattern,' Alison said. 'I'd estimate somewhere around size eight or nine by the look of it.'

Chris gave Joseph a knowing look. 'Not exactly standard footwear for a druid, but for a farmer...'

The DI held up his hands. 'I still say we shouldn't jump to conclusions yet. It isn't just farmers who wear wellies.'

'But it's hard not to, especially when Ms Trelawney, a very vocal critic of Charlotte Harris, is found murdered in her own home. Not forgetting that there's been a long-running family feud between the Trelawney and Harris families. At the very least, there's plenty here to suggest a motive.'

Joseph raked a hand through his hair. 'But surely, if Charlotte is our killer, she wouldn't want to draw attention to herself in this way. Okay, maybe allowing the dig was a double bluff, but this would always point straight back to her as the most likely suspect.'

Megan tapped her fingertip on her lips. 'But what if this was a crime of passion? After all, we all know there was no love lost between her and Ms Trelawney. Maybe Charlotte came here to have things out with Margaret, and their argument got out of hand?'

'I'm not sure that line of thinking stands if the farmer turned up here wearing ritualistic robes,' Chris replied. 'That doesn't seem like the sort of thing you'd wear for a cosy little chat over tea and biscuits.'

Joseph turned back to examine the corpse, turning the thought over in his mind when he noticed something glittering on the back of the victim's neck, where a bruise had bloomed.

He pointed it out to the others. 'What's that?'

'One of the bruises she sustained during the fall, or a possible grab mark by whoever murdered her when they shoved her down the stairs,' Amy replied.

'No, not that. If you turn your head slightly, you can see something sparkling on the skin. Here, let me show you.' He switched on his phone's torch, and immediately a small area glimmered as it caught the light.

'Now I see it,' Amy said, squatting behind him, all distance forgotten as her professional curiosity kicked in. 'That also looks like a left-hand thumb indent. We know the assailant's right hand seized her by the shoulder to hurl her against the wall from the direction in which the fabric was torn, but they must have grabbed her by the neck with the left, before shoving her down the stairs.'

'And what? They had some chemical residue on their hands that left that behind?' Megan suggested.

'Possibly, although we haven't been able to lift any prints, so they were likely wearing gloves. Maybe the chemical, whatever it is, came from those.'

Chris gave Joseph a pointed look before addressing his question to the SOCO. 'Like some kind of fertiliser?'

'We'll need to wait for the lab to confirm that one way or another, but I suppose that's certainly a possibility,' Amy replied.

The SIO nodded, his expression taking on the look of someone who'd already made up his mind. 'Okay, then I look forward to seeing the results,' he said to Amy. 'In the meantime,' he said to Joseph and Megan, 'I think we have no choice but to arrest Charlotte.'

'Aren't we getting ahead of ourselves here?' Joseph said.

'Oh, come on, this is all stacking up too heavily against her for us to ignore it anymore.'

'Aye, but until we have hard evidence to link her, I'm still not convinced.'

'You do know you're sounding like you may have a bit of a blind spot towards her?'

Like I did with you until recently, Joseph couldn't help thinking to himself.

John appeared in the open front door. 'There's a woman here who claims to be a friend of yours and who urgently needs to talk to you, DI Stone. She said something about a group of local people taking matters into their own hands.'

Joseph exchanged a concerned look with Chris and headed outside, followed by Megan.

Iris was standing there, face etched with worry lines. 'Joseph, you need to get up to Shadowbrook Farm as quickly as possible.'

'Why's that?'

'The village grapevine has been humming. A hard-core group of people are convinced Charlotte's responsible for Ms Trelawney's murder. They've decided the police aren't doing enough, and that it's time to take matters into their own hands.'

Megan glanced at Joseph. 'At that village hall meeting, the mood was already pretty ugly. It wouldn't take much to send some of those people over the edge.'

'Then we'd better get up there fast and arrest Harris, if only for her own protection,' Chris said.

Iris looked between the detectives. 'You'd better hurry. The rumour is, a group set off for her farm a good half-hour ago.'

'Okay, I'll call in the cavalry,' Chris replied. 'Joseph, you and Megan better get up there pronto. Grab Ian and Sue as well. Hold the fort until backup gets there.'

'You've got it, boss,' Ian said.

Joseph glanced at their parked Peugeot and then at the Volvo Ian and Sue had brought. 'We'd better take that if we don't want to get stuck in the mud again.'

Megan nodded as they raced towards their colleagues.

CHAPTER NINETEEN

Ian wasn't taking any prisoners as he drove up the rutted track towards Shadowbrook Farm in the dying light of another storm rolling over the countryside. Sue sat in the front passenger seat, while Joseph and Megan were in the rear, bouncing around like coins in a washing machine on its spin cycle.

'This isn't a bloody rally car, Ian,' Joseph muttered, hitting his head on the ceiling for the third time.

'And I thought you were a speed demon these days,' Ian said, grinning at him in the rear-view mirror.

The DI scowled back at his colleague.

Ahead of them, Joseph could see a group of vehicles parked on either side of the track. A Nissan Qashqai stuck in the slurry running across it, creating a temporary blockade.

'That's one piece of good news,' Megan said. 'Looks like Charlotte's temporary moat has slowed down the lynch mob a little bit.'

'Aye, but that includes us with that vehicle in our way,' Sue replied. 'We're going to have to walk from here.'

Ian grinned. 'Don't be so sure about that.' He gunned the

engine. The Volvo roared forward straight towards the slurry pool, aiming for a gap that was barely there.

They all lurched forward in their seats as the Volvo ploughed into the lake of effluent like a boat being launched off a ramp. A huge bow wave of liquid cow muck exploded from the nose of the vehicle, throwing a curtain of it up either side of the Volvo and over the stranded Qashqai. One moment, the Nissan resembled a vehicle, the next it looked like a giant floating turd.

The Volvo fared little better as Ian flicked the wipers to their highest speed to clear two triangular windows on the slurry-covered windscreen. More by luck than judgement, Ian squeezed their vehicle past the Nissan. Despite the wheels spinning, despite the traction control's efforts, somehow he managed to get them out the other side and back on the solid surface of the track.

'See, told you. Piece of cake,' Ian said, with what could only be described as a smug look.

'Don't think the guy in charge of the police fleet will say that when he sees this,' Megan said.

Joseph chuckled. 'He's almost certainly going to make you clean it as punishment.'

Ian grinned. 'Those are the breaks.'

Just then, the open gate of the farmhouse came into view, as did a group of at least sixty people standing in front of the building, all wearing raised hoods or face coverings.

Ian flicked on the blue lights and siren as he brought the Volvo to a slithering stop, thanks to all the muck still jammed into its tyre treads.

All four officers were out of the vehicle within seconds. Joseph led the way towards the group of people, who were shouting and baying at the farmhouse like a pack of wild animals. One big man, wearing a plastic pig mask, was thumping on the front door hard enough to make it shake in its frame.

'Feck, this isn't looking good,' the DI muttered to the other officers.

'So how are we going to deal with them?' Megan asked.

'Make them see sense long enough to stop them from doing anything stupid,' Sue replied.

Together, the detectives pushed their way through the crowd towards the big man banging on the door.

With the officers now between the house and the crowd, they turned to face the mob, which had fallen silent at the sight of them.

Joseph raised his hands. 'Whatever you think your business here is tonight, I suggest you turn round and go home before we arrest the lot of you for...' He cast a look at the others for inspiration.

'Trespass,' Megan immediately said.

The giant of a man, with broad shoulders and fists like shovels, slowly turned around.

'I don't think so,' he said in a low, dangerous tone. 'If you hadn't noticed, there's a lot more of us than you.'

Joseph recognised the voice from the village hall—the same man who'd apparently been knocked out by Ms Trelawney's murderer. Yes, of all people there, he would definitely have a grudge to bear.

The DI's eyes narrowed as he squared up to the man towering over him. 'Not for much longer. I suggest you and your chums head off home now, because backup will be here any moment.'

'Well, they're not here now, are they?' a woman's voice called out from the back of the crowd.

'Maybe not, but do you all really want a criminal record?' Ian said.

The giant crossed his arms. 'You'll need to be able to identify us all first.'

'Like that's going to be difficult, Charlie Pankhurst,' Joseph said, with just the right amount of sarcasm in his voice.

The man didn't reply, but his hands flew to his mask, no doubt to check if it was still in place.

'As for the rest of you, we took down all your number plates as we passed your vehicles on the track just now,' Megan said, not batting an eyelid at the blatant lie. But of course, the mob didn't know that.

Another man spoke up. 'Well, if you were doing your jobs in the first place, none of us would be here. More importantly, Ms Trelawney would still be alive.'

There was a lot of nodding as people muttered among themselves.

'Trust us, we're going to do everything in our power to bring whoever killed Ms Trelawney to justice,' Sue said.

The response was hollow laughter and slow handclaps from the crowd.

Charlie found his voice again. 'Like you have for all these other missing people that Harris—and no doubt her father before her—murdered?'

Joseph had plenty of experience dealing with mobs and recognising the moment when things would kick off. Charlie's words were exactly that spark and were answered with angry shouts and cries from the people gathered.

The DI ducked instinctively as he saw a stone lobbed from the middle of the crowd. The projectile sailed overhead and smashed a window on the upper floor. It was like someone had fired a starting gun. A fusillade of improvised missiles was thrown—bottles and rocks smashing into the house and breaking more windows as the mob whooped.

'Shit, this is worse than when things kicked off with the

Millwall fans at the Kassam Stadium after Oxford United unexpectedly beat them,' Ian said.

'You're telling me,' Joseph replied, sidestepping a bottle spinning past him towards a lower window.

'Well, stuff this for a game of soldiers,' Sue said, flicking out her telescopic baton.

Megan followed her lead and did the same.

Ian shot Joseph a look. 'Did you bring yours?'

'Nope. You?' the DI replied.

Ian shook his head. 'Not even pepper spray on me.'

Charlie, emboldened by the moves of his comrades, ignored the officers and returned his attention to the door. He started raining blows and kicks so hard it actually began to splinter. 'We're coming to get you, witch!' he bellowed.

If Charlotte was inside, Joseph realised, she had to be terrified thanks to this group baying for her blood right outside her home.

'You need to stop what you're doing,' Megan said calmly, as though she were discussing the weather.

Charlie ignored her and continued to rain blows into the door.

'Last warning,' Sue said, already holding her PAVA spray.

Rather than strike the builder as Joseph had expected, Sue simply reached forward and tapped the man on the shoulder with the tip of her baton. The moment he turned to see what was going on, Sue sprayed him straight in the face with the artificial pepper spray. Coughing and desperately rubbing his eyes, the giant sank to his knees. In a lightning move, Megan followed through and cuffed his hands behind his back.

Joseph exchanged an impressed look with Ian.

'Ten seconds, start to finish—the guy didn't stand a chance,' his colleague said.

'Which is grand and all that, but...' Joseph gestured to the group, still hurling projectiles at the house. That was when he spotted exactly what he'd been worried about—someone had come prepared with a fuel can and was busily filling bottles, a group huddled around him.

'Okay, this is about to get even uglier,' Ian said, having seen it too.

'Then what are we waiting for?' Joseph said.

The detectives headed towards the group, who were already stuffing lengths of rag into their Molotov cocktails.

Before the detectives had a chance to shout out a challenge, one of the men had lit a bottle and thrown it with a shot that would have impressed a professional basketball player. It sailed through a broken upstairs window. With a whoosh, flames almost instantly began to lick the curtains.

'Shite, we'd better get the fire brigade up here pronto,' Joseph said, just as one of the men got ready to light another bottle.

'As God is my witness, if you throw that fecking thing, I'm going to shove the next one right up your arse and then light it,' Joseph bellowed at them.

The group traded looks among themselves. But when the DI growled like a pissed-off bear, all the men quickly dropped their bottles, which smashed onto the ground, spreading into puddles. The DI was so worked up at that point, he almost ordered them to find a brush and clean up their fecking mess. Instead, he grabbed the bastard who'd thrown the first projectile, and within moments, Ian had him cuffed.

Sue ended the call she'd been on. 'Fire brigade is on the way.'

'Good, but we need to disperse this mob before someone does something even more stupid,' Joseph replied.

At that moment, they heard a siren getting louder. They

turned to see a police Land Rover with Chris at the wheel, screaming into the yard.

'About time the cavalry got here,' Sue said, shaking her head.

The SIO leapt out with a megaphone already in hand, as a group of uniformed officers, including John, bundled from the back of the vehicle.

Chris's voice boomed out. 'This is a police order: disperse at once. If you don't comply, you will be arrested and charged.'

Even though the crowd still heavily outnumbered the officers, the sight of actual uniformed police seemed to make the mob think again. In ones and twos, they began to drop their projectiles and gradually the whole group, heads down, started to skulk off in the direction of their abandoned vehicles.

Ian nodded towards the SIO as he reached them. 'Never underestimate the power of the shouty voice, eh, boss?'

Chris hitched his eyebrows up at the DI before his gaze swept over the farmhouse and the flames licking from the smashed upstairs windows.

'Looks like things turned ugly here.'

'Let's just say we appreciate the timely intervention,' Joseph replied.

The SIO gestured towards the handcuffed giant, as tears streamed down his face thanks to the PAVA spray.

'And what exactly did he do?' the SIO asked.

Megan exchanged a look with Sue. 'That's the ringleader, Charlie Pankhurst. He resisted arrest.'

Ian raised his eyebrows at Joseph, who did his best not to smile. The female detectives hadn't exactly given the thug much time to comply. Megan, in particular, was learning the best of his bad ways and he utterly approved.

The flames upstairs were really taking hold, filling the room with flickering orange light as smoke billowed out.

'Have you got eyes on our farmer yet?' Chris asked.

'Not yet—we were rather busy dealing with that mob, boss,' Ian replied.

'Okay. We need to get her out of here as quickly as possible and back to St Aldates,' Chris said, heading towards the house, followed by the others.

'Charlotte Harris, it's DCI Faulkner—it's safe to come out now,' Chris said through the megaphone.

There was no response from inside.

Joseph clicked his tongue against his teeth. 'What if one of that fecking lynch mob already got inside?'

'Only one way to find out,' Chris said, grim-faced. 'Joseph, Ian—do a sweep of the inside, while the rest of us check the outbuildings in case she's hidden herself.'

The two DIs nodded and headed to the front door that Charlie had nearly kicked off its hinges. With a combined shoulder charge, the two detectives finished the job, and the door toppled inward with a bang that reverberated through the house.

'You take the ground floor; I'll cover upstairs,' Joseph said as they both rushed inside.

Ian nodded and headed off down the corridor, calling Charlotte's name as he went.

From somewhere upstairs a smoke alarm began blaring.

Joseph didn't hesitate, running up the stairs two at a time. When he reached the landing, he saw smoke billowing from under a door to his left. Then, an almighty whoosh came from inside and the door shook as something struck it from the other side.

Confused, Joseph spotted water flowing out from beneath the door. He opened it a crack to see the bedroom floor swimming with water. The curtains and bedding, which had been on fire, were now all soaked through. Thankfully, the thing he'd feared most—finding Charlotte's body—was nowhere to be seen.

Had the fire brigade already got here? But how had they navigated the slurry pit to reach the farm?

The DI crossed to the broken window, and looked down into the yard.

John, lowering a large hose to the ground and spotting the DI, waved. 'I noticed this in the yard and thought it was worth trying to dampen the fire until the professionals get here,' the PC called out.

'Grand job. You've completely extinguished it,' Joseph called back.

The PC gave him a thumbs up as the DI turned and headed back to the landing.

He began searching the other rooms without success. He opened the final door into a small guest room at the back of the house, and with a view of the hill behind it. On the summit stood the silhouette of the old furnace chimney, like a sentinel against the skyline. But that wasn't what drew the DI's attention now.

Flames were rising from the middle of the small wood where he'd followed Charlotte to her makeshift pagan temple. A sense of deep foreboding filled Joseph as he rushed downstairs, nearly colliding with Ian.

'Any sign of Charlotte?' he asked in a rush.

Ian shook his head. 'I've checked everywhere, there's no sign of her.'

'Her dog?'

Ian shook his head again.

'She wouldn't have left Fergus behind with that mob baying for her blood. I've a good idea where she's gone, though I'm praying I've got it wrong.' He rushed outside, followed by his colleague.

'Any sign of her?' Chris asked, seeing them emerge from the house.

Joseph shook his head. 'No, but I think she may be at her temple in the wood behind the house, which looks like it's on fire.'

Charlie, who John had been escorting to the police Land Rover, glanced over at them and smirked. 'Then you're already too late.'

The SIO glowered at him. 'What the hell do you know about this?'

'A couple of guys thought they saw someone running from the back of the house and went after them.'

'You fecking gobshite, you could have told us that before!' Joseph broke into a run, heading for the side of the farmhouse.

Although the DI had a head start on the others, he heard someone gaining on him fast. When he glanced around, he wasn't surprised to see Megan—like a human gazelle—closing the gap. She was well ahead of Chris, Sue, and John, with Ian bringing up the rear in a lumbering half-walk, half-run.

The DI heard frantic barking coming from the wood where smoke and flames were rising into the sky.

As they neared the edge of the shadow-filled copse, they saw two men rush from the woods, with Fergus barking in pursuit. Despite his age, the old Border Collie had a real turn of speed on him and was rapidly gaining. The two men, spotting the officers charging towards them, scattered in different directions. But Fergus was having none of it. The collie launched itself at the nearest man, knocking him to the ground.

Chris was already shouting orders to the others. 'Don't let them get away!' He led the charge with Sue, John, and Ian in tow.

Meanwhile, Joseph and Megan raced into the woods, following the narrow path through it. There was no need for a torch. Their way was lit by a beacon fire, blazing in the middle of the wood, casting dancing shadows past them.

'Bloody hell, this is starting to remind me way too much of the Burning Man case,' Megan said.

'Aye, no need to tell me,' Joseph replied. His imagination was already there, recalling when he'd pulled the blistered body of Mathew Forbes, a professional criminal, from the remains of his burning garage. Was that what he'd find now—a farmer set alight by two thugs?

As the detectives approached the clearing where Joseph had last seen Charlotte worshipping in her temple, they slowed to a stop. The trunks and woven-branch roof of the living structure had flames licking over them in a surging fury of conflagration, consuming everything in its path.

Through the swirling flames, Joseph stared into the middle of the clearing. A shape lay motionless on the ground. Despite the intense heat radiating from the fire, his blood iced.

Megan stared at him. 'Don't even think about it—it's already too late.'

'But I have to, Megan.'

With no thought for his own safety, Joseph moved forward when he felt a strong hand seize his shoulder.

He turned to see Chris just behind him, shaking his head. 'Don't be a fool.'

Joseph opened his mouth to argue, but a loud crash stopped him dead. He spun around to see one of the trees had toppled straight onto the top of the temple, crushing it completely. The shape he'd seen was now lost among the roaring flames.

Chris patted his shoulder gently. 'I'm sorry, Joseph, but if Charlotte was in there, she was already dead.'

Joseph nodded slowly, staring at the man he'd been so determined to expose for the hypocrite he was. The same man who'd almost certainly just saved his life.

CHAPTER TWENTY

THE FOLLOWING MORNING, after some much-needed rest, Joseph and Megan headed back towards the wood, having already passed several weary-looking fire officers with soot-covered faces. They'd spoken to one of the officers who'd told them the ploughed field had made it impossible to get their fire engines anywhere close to the wood. Instead, they'd had to rely on hooking up their hoses to a mobile water bowser they'd towed close to the wood with their four-wheel-drive truck. But thanks to their efforts through the night, the fire had finally been extinguished just as dawn was rising, saving the rest of the wood.

The two detectives arrived back at the charred remains of Charlotte's once-living temple, now little more than a sooty circle in the middle of the wood. Amy was already hard at work with her team. All of the SOCO's white suits were covered with ash as they worked together in the clearing.

Joseph's gaze fell onto the dark shape he'd seen lying in the middle of the temple and almost laughed when he saw what it was. 'For Christ's sake, what I thought was Charlotte was actually her log altar.'

Hearing him, Amy turned and nodded. 'Unless she

managed to cast some sort of spell that turned her into a tree.' A smile tugged the corner of her mouth.

Joseph felt a weight coming off his shoulders in more ways than one at this chink of light between them. 'That's good news then.'

Amy nodded, and for a moment, the two of them just stood gazing at each other. Before either of them could say anything else, Chris materialised in their midst.

'I take it you've heard the good news about our missing farmer?'

'That she wasn't barbecued by those yobs last night, you mean?' Joseph replied.

'Indeed. It also confirms what the two men we captured fleeing from here said in their interviews with Ian and Sue. It turns out they stole the fuel from one of her outbuildings and followed Charlotte into the wood where they came across her temple and set fire to it. The idiots even filmed it for their social media channels with the highly original *Burn the Witch* caption. But then Charlotte's dog erupted from the woods and chased them into our waiting arms.'

'Fergus deserves a medal,' Joseph said. 'Talking of which, where is the fella?'

'Staying at my house and being looked after by my neighbour,' Chris replied. 'It seems I'm taking a leaf out of your book like you did with Tux.'

'Good man, but hopefully it won't be too long before he's reunited with his owner.'

'Any sign of our missing prime suspect?' Megan asked.

'None at all, but after having that mob of people baying for her blood, who can blame the woman?' Chris said. 'Anyway, that's why I've called in the dog teams to look for her. After what happened last night, the sooner we find Harris, the better. Apart from anything else, Fernbridge appears to have far too many people who are prepared to take the law into their own hands.'

Megan frowned. 'I'm still finding it hard to believe that a group of villagers in a peaceful place like this could behave like they did last night.'

'That's just how it is when people's blood is up,' Joseph replied. 'I'm sure everyone in that mob considered themselves decent folk. It shows just how dangerous a mob mentality can be, turning those people into savages.'

'Don't forget that before she died, Ms Trelawney did a fantastic job of stirring up a lot of animosity towards Charlotte. But of course, she had no idea that it would be her own death that sent a lynch mob after Harris. It seems that if the farmer really did murder our shopkeeper, she nearly ended up sealing her own fate.'

Joseph looked at the blackened circle in the clearing. 'And what if somebody else did it?'

'You're still not giving up on her being innocent, then?' Chris asked.

'What if we're being played here, boss?' Megan said, before Joseph could. 'Just think about it. Charlotte would have known full well that if Maggie Trelawney was killed, the spotlight would immediately fall upon her. What if the real murderer realised that too, knowing it would put some people in the village on the warpath? Perhaps they were even among that mob last night, egging them on.'

'But equally, Harris may just be a killer who overplayed her hand,' Chris said. 'Either way, we'll squeeze the names of the rest of that rabble from the people we already have in custody. Once we have that information, we'll take a long hard look at everyone involved.'

The radio clipped to his belt, chirped.

'DCI Faulkner, one of the dogs seems to have picked up a scent. Over,' a woman's voice said.

Chris unclipped his radio and pressed a button on the side. 'Okay, send us their position and tell them we'll join them. Out.'

He looked at the others. 'Okay, let's leave Amy's team to get on with things here, while we see whether we can have Charlotte Harris tucked up in a nice, cosy interview room before the day's out.'

Joseph hung back a moment to meet Amy's gaze. 'See you later, maybe?'

'We'll see,' the SOCO replied with a small shrug.

The DI wanted to say more, but stayed mute. Amy obviously wasn't in any mood to forgive him just yet. He gazed at her for a moment, considering. Did he actually want her to?

Maybe the time had come for Joseph to be honest with himself. The spark between him and Kate was not only still there, but actually getting stronger. Whether that moment together on *Tús Nua* had just been a moment of madness or the start of something more, Joseph couldn't be sure. The one thing for sure was, the moment he came up for air from this case, he needed to have a heart-to-heart with Kate. That was the only way he was going to work out what to do next, and hopefully not break anyone's heart in the process—at least more than he had to.

Amy frowned at him, and just for an awful moment, he thought she might have developed the ability to read thoughts. But then she made a shooing motion.

'You better shift yourself.' She pointed past him.

Joseph turned to see Chris and Megan disappearing away down the path.

'Aye, I'd better,' he replied, dipping his chin towards her, before turning and making his way after his colleagues.

Joseph, Megan, and Chris were following the dog handler, PC Andy Jacobs, and his Alsatian dog, Kaiser, along a path running along a hedgerow.

The dog's nose was down, his tail up, as he guided the group.

'Kaiser has definitely picked up her scent again now,' PC Jacobs said over his shoulder to the detectives.

'You had me a bit worried when we crossed over that field covered with slurry,' Chris replied.

'That was a bit of a challenge for his nose, but he's trained to ignore it,' the dog handler replied.

'I wish my nose could,' Megan replied. 'I feel like the smell of the manure has soaked into my skin.'

Joseph made a show of taking a deep breath in. 'The smell of the country—there's nothing quite like it. Having said that, I think I'll stick to the smell of a fresh cup of coffee from the Covered Market back in Oxford.'

Chris chuckled. 'I think I'm with you on that one.'

The path the group was on started to dip towards a wooded valley that Kaiser was dutifully leading them towards.

Joseph could picture Charlotte heading down this route, constantly glancing back to see if she was being pursued by members of the mob. He could easily imagine the fear the farmer must have felt. The question he was increasingly unsure about was whether she was a fugitive or, as instinct was still telling him, someone who had simply been persecuted for having alternative beliefs and was entirely innocent.

Kaiser raised his head and started to pull harder on his lead. He let out a short bark and his tail began to wag.

'That looks promising,' Chris observed.

'Oh, it is. That means the farmer's scent is really strong here,' Andy replied, as the dog almost pulled his arm off, yanking him down the path.

Megan scanned the wooded valley ahead of them. 'There certainly looks like plenty of places Charlotte could hide out down there.'

'Yes, but in the middle of winter?' Chris replied. 'I doubt she had much time to prepare. If she is down there somewhere, and if she hasn't been able to light a fire, she will probably be half frozen to death by now.'

'I wouldn't be so sure,' Joseph said. 'Charlotte strikes me as a very resourceful and determined person. You have to be if you're going to make a go of farming when so many are struggling.'

They entered the wooded valley. The trees were spaced apart, leaving a view of brown reedbeds on either side of a stream cutting through the bottom of the valley. The officers followed the dog, whose tail was waving even more frantically.

They had almost reached the bottom of the slope when Joseph spotted a squat structure resting against a tree bough. It seemed to be made from a frame of woven branches covered with a layer of turf. If he was in any doubt of what they were looking at, that was swept away when he spotted a small burned-out campfire next to it that Kaiser was heading towards.

'That firmly answers the question about Charlotte's resourcefulness then,' Chris said.

The dog barked excitedly at Andy, who rubbed his neck and gave him a doggy treat from his pocket.

Joseph bent down and slipped his gloves off, carefully pressing his fingers into the ashes of the campfire. 'Still some warmth left. Charlotte can't have left here that long ago.'

The SIO gave him an impressed look. 'Where did you learn

that trick from? Have you been on a tracking course or something?'

'Actually, watching the Coen Brothers' No Country for Old Men. There was a scene in it where one of the characters was tracking someone and did the same thing.'

Megan looked past him and her eyes narrowed. She crossed to the makeshift shelter and pulled out a piece of paper from under a rock, examined it, and frowned.

'It seems Charlotte has left us a little message,' she said, showing it to them.

Written in neat handwriting, the note read, *'I'm going to track down the person who is actually responsible for the murders. Don't bother trying to find me because I promise that you won't. Not until I'm good and ready to be found.'*

Megan looked at Chris and Joseph. 'So, according to this, she isn't fleeing for her life after all, but is a woman on a mission to clear her name.'

'Why am I not surprised,' Joseph replied.

'If you believe this note,' Chris said. 'Don't forget she could have simply left this to throw us off the scent. Talking of which, if Kaiser keeps on like he is, her wish or not, I wouldn't be surprised if we caught up with her before much longer.'

Almost as though the dog was answering him, Kaiser barked and headed towards the edge of boggy ground among the dying reedbeds bordering the closest side of the stream. He started to pace up and down it.

'What's wrong with Kaiser?' Megan asked.

'By the look of things he's lost the scent, but that's hardly surprising,' Andy said. 'This farmer we're trying to track down knows exactly what she's doing. She's probably headed along the stream, meaning Kaiser won't be able to detect her scent over water. So now we'll have to walk all the way up and down the embankment, hoping he picks up her scent again, but I wouldn't hold out much hope.'

'Bloody hell, Derrick isn't going to be happy if we have to send a police helicopter out to search for her,' Chris said.

Joseph nodded, but he suspected that Charlotte, who'd already proven herself highly capable, would be able to evade even a set of eyes in the sky.

It turned out to be a very long, fruitless day of searching. Charlotte had been true to her word and had appeared to completely disappear off the face of the planet. Despite extra dog teams being brought in, and an extensive search of the area by the police helicopter using thermal imaging, there hadn't been a single sighting of her anywhere. That hadn't been helped by the sightings that had been rung in by the public to the hotline that had been set up and proved useless.

Joseph, who'd helped with the search, felt tired to the core of his being. Although desperate for his bed, he had one last thing to do before he was prepared to call it a day. He'd been so busy with everything that had happened, he hadn't been able to pick up his trail cam. Soon, he'd have the evidence to confirm that Chris was working for the Night Watchmen. To say he felt conflicted, especially after the same man had saved his life, would have been the understatement of the century. But he had to know.

That was why the DI was once again outside St Barnabas Church, casting a wary look around him as he headed inside. Thankfully, it appeared empty again. Even so, he did a quick lap of the church just to make sure.

Then, a sense of anticipation rising inside him, Joseph

headed up onto the pulpit. But when he looked up into the canopy, he couldn't see his trail cam anywhere. He'd obviously hidden it better than he'd realised.

He glanced around to make sure there really wasn't anyone to witness the minor bit of sacrilege he was about to commit again, then he pulled himself up onto the edge of the stone pulpit and reached into the shadows beneath the wooden canopy.

That's strange, he thought when, despite probing everywhere with his fingertips, he still couldn't find it. Then his hand brushed something and a piece of paper fluttered down.

Joseph had a bad feeling as he jumped back down onto the pulpit and scooped up the note.

'Don't be so bloody stupid in future,' the note said in shaky handwriting.

Joseph's stomach clenched into a ball and he breathed through his nose, reaching out to the balustrade to steady himself.

So he hadn't been anywhere as clever as he thought he had. The Night Watchmen, specifically Chris, must have done a thorough sweep when he'd come to pick up the memory stick. Just as, if he'd paused to think about it even a moment, he would have done if their roles had been reversed. But now, thanks to his own pigheadedness the crime syndicate knew he wasn't playing along and had given him this final warning. One slip up now, and Ellie would pay the price.

The DI scrunched the note into a ball and shoved it into his jacket pocket. He'd gambled and lost. The Night Watchmen well and truly had him in their pocket and there was nothing he could do about it.

He would have to tell the others just how badly he'd lost. Dylan would understand, Derrick would probably call him a fool, but it was Kate he was most worried about. She'd probably never forgive him for this feck up. Joseph wasn't sure he would be able to either.

Then Ellie's face filled his mind and tears beaded in his eyes. He smudged them away before he headed out of the church, lost in the darkness of his own thoughts.

CHAPTER TWENTY-ONE

A BAD NIGHT's sleep hadn't helped Joseph at all. By trying to be clever he'd royally screwed everything up. Also, despite his best efforts, he still didn't have the proof to take Chris down. What had he been thinking putting his daughter's life on the line like that?

The DI sat in the incident room lost in the spin cycle of his own thoughts, an island to himself. He was barely able to bring himself to look at the SIO, who was currently briefing the team about the extensive search for Charlotte. The one thing the DI would give the man—he was the best actor on the fecking planet.

Since the DI had arrived at work earlier that morning, not once had his boss implied that he had Joseph in the palm of his hand. If Chris told Joseph to jump for the Night Watchmen, the DI's job was to ask him, *how high?*

As predicted Dylan had been understanding when he'd told him, saying it had been worth a shot even though it hadn't worked out. But as predicted, Derrick had called him an *absolute idiot* and told him there was nothing more he could do to protect him.

What would twist the knife of his failure even further, was when he had to tell Kate. He was already mentally preparing himself to suggest the time had come to send Ellie off on a trip somewhere far enough away that the crime syndicate couldn't get to her. Australia, or maybe even New Zealand. But that wasn't his only reason for not contacting Kate.

There was also the whole landmine of a subject of what had *almost* happened between them on his boat, the spark that yearned to turn into a bonfire. There was also the matter of Joseph feeling like he was betraying Amy. Right now, the DI couldn't help but feel that life had served him a steaming shite sandwich, admittedly mostly of his own making, and was laughing at him as it watched him eat it.

He mentally sighed at himself as he tuned back into the briefing.

'So I'm afraid there is still no sign of Charlotte, despite the extensive use of search parties, dog teams, helicopters, and even drones,' Chris was saying to everyone.

Joseph looked up from the doodle of something that resembled a devil he'd been absentmindedly working on in his notebook. He noticed the SIO had ringed Charlotte's name several times as *chief suspect* on the evidence board. From the snippets the DI had heard during the briefing, that seemed to be the consensus of those present. Perhaps it was finally time for him to join the others in that. As much as he liked Charlotte, someone he saw as a mild-mannered rebel, even he had to admit, despite her note, that she was most likely their murderer.

Chris held up the rag of a newspaper that Ricky Holt worked for. The headline screamed, *'Mad Witch Murderer Seeks Revenge on Local Village.'*

'Classy piece of journalism as usual from that rag,' Ian said.

'You can rely on certain things in life, and attention-grabbing articles that help fan the fires of hate and fear, in this—and I use the word loosely here—*newspaper*, is of the worst sort of reporting,' Chris replied. 'And of course this reporter also blames the police for letting the prime suspect in a murder investigation get away.'

Megan's eyebrows drew together. 'Only because a mob tried to burn down her house, forcing her to flee.'

'Yes, but like always, why let a fact get in the way of creating clickbait. Anyway, be under no illusion that the pressure is on for us to make an arrest as soon as possible. That aside, after a thorough sweep of the Shadowbrook Farm, it turns out an old Land Rover registered to Harris is missing.'

'In other words, she could be anywhere in the country by now,' Ian said.

'Possibly, and which is why I've sent a national alert out across the country. But so far we've heard nothing, and no recorded sightings with any ANPR cameras, either. Of course, she could have just changed the plates.'

Amy walked in. Joseph noticed she was holding an evidence bag with a piece of paper in it.

'You have something for us?' Chris asked, also spotting it.

'Nothing major, but I thought you'd like to know we managed to lift a DNA sample from the note Charlotte left in her shelter in the woods. It matched a sample taken from her hairbrush, and a fingerprint on it matched one taken at her home.'

'It never hurts to be thorough, just in case someone else was planting a false trail,' the SIO replied.

Inspired by what Amy had said, Joseph's thoughts wandered. He'd been in such a state when he'd discovered the note at the church, it hadn't occurred to him that it might have any evidence on it. He suspected whoever had left it, had written it with their non-dominant hand because handwriting was so shaky, but what about the ink used? Joseph had seen the

DCI use a rollerball pen on many occasions. Could the ink used to write the note be a match?

'Okay, I think that's it for now. Carry on with your work, everyone,' the SIO said.

Megan was chatting to Amy, who was doing her best to look anywhere but in Joseph's direction.

As Chris headed past the DI, Joseph seized his chance and made a show of shaking his biro. 'Bloody thing is always drying up on me. I don't suppose I could borrow your pen for a moment, boss?'

Chris didn't even pause and handed the DI his expensive-looking pen from his inside pocket, no doubt paid for with crime syndicate backhanders. 'Give it back to me when you've finished. Then, for goodness' sake, go get yourself a decent fibre tip pen from the stationery cupboard. I don't know why you persist in using biros anyway.'

'Old habits and all that,' Joseph replied.

Chris shook his head and headed towards his desk.

The DI turned the page over in his notebook and then, discreetly fishing the crumpled note from his pocket, and tore off a small section with writing on it. Then he signed his own name with Chris's pen in his notebook before tearing the page out as well. He grabbed an evidence bag from his desk drawer and slipped the two pieces of paper into it. Finally, with a look to check his boss's attention was now firmly on his computer screen, he headed over to Amy and Megan, still deep in conversation.

'We're hoping to get that chemical sample analysis of the glittering substance we found on Maggie Trelawney's neck, back within twenty-four hours,' he heard Amy say as he neared them.

'Good, because if it's fertiliser, it will be the first piece of evidence that could link Harris to Trelawney's murder,' Megan replied, as the DI joined them.

'Only if she happens to use the same fertiliser on her land,' Joseph said, joining them. 'Don't forget she's meant to be an organic farmer, which will restrict the use of many, if not all, modern farming chemicals she can use. Even then, unless you can find it on her farm or some DNA evidence directly linking her, it's still circumstantial.'

Amy narrowed her eyes at him. 'You're still holding onto the idea the woman is innocent?'

'Maybe just a thin thread of hope. But even I have to admit the weight of circumstantial evidence is getting hard to ignore. Anyway, I just need a quiet word with you, Amy.' He raised his eyebrows at Megan.

'Oh, right.' The DC looked between them, obviously assuming this was personal, and headed away.

Amy frowned at him. 'This really isn't the time or place to get into it, Joseph.'

He held up his palms. 'It's nothing like that. I just need to ask a favour.'

The SOCO gave him a perplexed look. 'Such as?'

He glanced over to check Chris's eyes were still on his screen, before slipping the evidence bag to Amy.

'Put that into your pocket before anyone in here sees it,' he said under his breath.

'Why?'

Joseph saw Chris's head come up. 'Please just do it, then I'll explain.'

Amy gave him a confused look, but did as instructed a second before the boss glanced over in their direction. However, when the boss saw the two officers together, he smiled to himself, obviously thinking they were having a private moment.

If only you knew, Joseph thought to himself, before returning his attention to the SOCO.

'So what's this about?' Amy asked him, crossing her arms.

'In that evidence bag are two pieces of paper. One has my signature on it. The other is from a note I found yesterday. I need you to sample the ink on it and see if it's a match for the ink I used to sign my name. Also, have you got DNA samples from all of the detectives involved in the murder investigation team?'

Her brow furrowed. 'Of course I have. As you know, it makes it so much easier in case someone slips up at a crime scene and leaves any of their DNA behind. That helps save everyone involved a lot of time and wasted effort.'

'In that case, I'd like you to check to see, mine notwithstanding, if there's the DNA of any serving officer you have on file that matches anything on that torn note fragment.'

'What's this about, Joseph?'

'I really can't say at this point. But please, I need you to do this for me and keep it to yourself. Then get back to me with the results as soon as you have them.'

The SOCO gave him a perplexed look. 'Joseph?'

He sighed. 'I know how this all sounds, but I have my reasons. I'll tell you everything when the time comes, but this isn't that moment. You have to trust me on this.'

'I always trust you.' Amy gently reached out and briefly touched his arm before withdrawing her fingers again.

For a moment, Joseph wasn't sure if they were talking about work or their personal life, or maybe a bit of both. But before he could reply, Derrick came rushing in.

'I need every available officer in here to assist at a major incident over in Abingdon.'

Chris jumped to his feet, grabbing his jacket. 'Something to do with Harris?'

Derrick gave a sharp shake of his head. 'No, the Shotgun Raiders gang.'

'They've hit another bank?' Ian asked, taking a last slurp of tea from his Batman mug.

'Yes, but this time, they were ambushed. They've all been shot dead, even the getaway driver. And not by our tactical unit either. It appears to have been a ruthless strike by a rival gang. Now shift your bloody arses!'

The room seemed to swirl around Joseph for a moment as he took a deep breath in through his nose. He knew exactly what this meant. This was why the Night Watchmen had been so keen to have everything the police had on the bank robbery gang—to take their competition out.

His eyes briefly met Derrick's as he rushed out of the room with Megan and the others. The big man looked as pale as he felt inside. The DSU might have tried to protect Joseph, but right now, they both had blood on their hands.

There were police cars everywhere by the time Joseph and Megan arrived with Sue and Ian in the Volvo. John and another officer were finishing tying off the inner perimeter, cutting off both ends of the high street where the bank was situated.

Along the street, four ambulances had been parked, their crews waiting as a team of forensic officers, visible through the shattered windows of the bank, worked inside. Another two were taking photos of a black Audi S6 parked outside, its windscreen punched through with dozens of bullet holes.

Amy pulled up behind the detectives in her SOC van and she quickly headed over to join her colleagues, one of whom was placing yellow numbered markers on the ground next to the spent bullet casings that seemed to be all over the pavement.

Joseph took in the chaos along the street. There were abandoned vehicles, including a double-decker bus. There were also dropped bags everywhere and even a lone shoe on the pavement. The DI could easily imagine the chaos when the shooting started. Already, a sizeable group of onlookers had gathered beyond the outer perimeter at the end of the high street, many with their phones out to capture the moment.

Megan shook her head as she took in the scene. 'Bloody hell, this looks like a war zone.'

'That's exactly what it is,' Ian said. 'Normally, rival gangs keep it between themselves, but to do this when members of the public are caught in the firing line...' He shook his head, as a squad car and police van pulled up behind them.

Underlining just how serious this situation was, Derrick got out of the first vehicle, taking a rare excursion from behind his desk. Uniform officers emptied out of the van and within moments, the DSU had a dozen of them gathered around him.

'I need you to get as many witness statements from that lot.' He jerked his thumb over his shoulder towards the crowd of onlookers. 'We need to piece together a picture of what exactly unfolded here.'

The officers, including John, nodded and headed away.

At that moment, a woman wearing dark blue trousers and the jacket of a bank employee was led out of the bank by an ambulance worker. The medic was holding a wad of bandage to the woman's cheek to halt the blood flowing from a wound.

Derrick turned to Ian and Sue. 'Okay, you two start with her and find out what you can.' Then he gestured to Joseph and Megan. 'You're with me. Let's head inside and see exactly how bad this shitshow is.' He traded a look with Joseph. They didn't need to say anything. They both knew they'd had a part to play in what had happened here.

Joseph fought a swirl of nausea as they all headed inside the bank and took in the carnage. Two men wearing balaclavas lay dead in pools of their own blood, their bodies riddled with bullets. Two shotguns were next to them, no match for the firepower the Night Watchman had brought to bear, probably submachine guns based on the number of bullet casings scattered over the polished floor.

'Bloody hell,' Megan muttered, summarising what they were all thinking.

SOC officers in their white suits seemed to be everywhere, the floor a sea of yellow markers next to casings and bullet damage that riddled the interior of the bank. The lingering smell of cordite scratched at the back of Joseph's nose and throat.

True to form, Chris had driven like a Formula One driver to beat the rest of them there and was already examining the other side of the counters. Joseph couldn't help but notice how haunted the man looked.

As well he should, Joseph thought, *the little fecker and the crime syndicate are the ones responsible for this slaughter.*

When the SIO spotted them, he gestured for his fellow officers to join him.

When they reached the far side of the counter, nausea roiled in Joseph's gut as he spotted another bank robber lying dead there. The man's head was little more than a bloody pulp, having been hit by so many rounds. A shotgun was still clutched in his hand. Next to him was a bag stuffed full of banknotes.

'It looks like he didn't go down without a fight,' Derrick said, gesturing to the two spent cartridges lying next to the dead man.

Joseph found himself staring down at the corpse. He'd seen plenty of awful murder scenes in his time and was hardened to it. But this one brought the tang of bile to the back of his throat. He quickly popped a Silvermint into his mouth, breathing in its scent to try and fight the growing nausea. Megan, who was standing next to him, gave him a questioning look that he chose to ignore.

'Were any members of the public killed?' Derrick asked, his face drawn.

'Thankfully not, although we have reports from the people in the bank that one of the attackers was winged in the shoulder,' Chris replied. He gestured to Alison, who was carefully scraping some blood samples from a pillar and putting them into a sample bottle. 'Hopefully, we'll get some DNA from that.'

Joseph might feel like he had a hand in what had happened here, but he couldn't believe how Chris could stand there and carry on doing his job like he wasn't the bastard ringleader of this feck up. If Ellie's life wasn't on the line, the DI would have punched him in the face there and then—to hell with the consequences.

'But I don't understand. Why didn't whoever ambushed them take the money?' Megan asked.

'Perhaps they were trying to send a message to other rival gangs in the area that this isn't about the cash,' Chris said.

Derrick tucked his chin in. 'What sort of message?'

'A power play, pure and simple,' Joseph said. 'They're warning off any rivals. Operate on our patch and you'll pay the price.'

Derrick nodded. 'I agree. That's exactly what this is.' The two officers met each other's gazes for a moment, expressions tight. Neither of them was able to look at Chris, who had betrayed all his colleagues for this bloodbath.

CHAPTER TWENTY-TWO

Joseph hadn't served as long as he had without having some bad days, but this was one of the worst. Helping interview the traumatised bank staff, along with members of the public who'd been caught up in it, weighed heavily on him. Even though the DI hadn't actually been there, in his mind he was as guilty as any of the criminals who'd been in the shootout. He'd as good as pulled the trigger to end the lives of those men.

Joseph pulled his mountain bike up next to *Tús Nua*, weighed down to the bottom of his soul. He, Megan, Ian, and Sue had been sent home early for a short break.

The DI noticed Tux on the roof, watching something intently. When he followed the cat's gaze, he spotted the squirrel hanging upside down on Dylan's latest bird feeder, filling its face with sunflower seeds.

'*You see these metal rods the birds perch on, see what happens when you put your finger on one,*' Dylan had told him when the parcel had first arrived, courtesy of an Amazon courier a week earlier.

Joseph had done as instructed and immediately the flap had

slid closed over a hatch, shutting away the seeds within the feeder.

The professor had grinned at him. *'The weight of a bird won't trigger that, but a flipping squirrel will!'*

Joseph had nicknamed the tree-climbing rodent Raffles, thanks to his ability to get past all the previous squirrel-proof feeders. Until recently, this marvel of modern engineering had fended off the tree rodent's best efforts. Until now.

Raffles was currently hanging from the underside of the feeder. The creature had braced its two rear legs at the base of the tube and, with some considerable ingenuity—even Joseph had to admire—it extended the front half of its body up to the fading hatch, bypassing the spring-operated perching rods. The DI could swear he could see a grin on the squirrel's face as it stuck its head into the feeding chamber and filled its chops.

A bellow came from his neighbour's boat, followed by a squirt of water hitting the squirrel squarely in the body. The creature immediately dropped off the feeder, landed on its feet, and zipped away along the path, with Tux giving chase. Not that the cat had any chance of catching the thing. Joseph had seen Raffles, despite his much shorter legs, put his cat to shame during many chases. It could switch directions and hurtle straight up trees far faster than his cat could even dream of. If *Tom and Jerry* ever needed inspiration for a reboot, they could do worse than look at those two.

The DI turned to see the professor standing in the cabin of his boat, *Avalon*, with a huge Super Soaker water pistol in his hand.

'And good riddance to you,' Dylan called out. He turned to see Joseph, who was heading in his direction with an amused expression.

'I see your new'—Joseph made air quotes—'"*squirrel-proof*" feeder is doing well then.'

Dylan glowered at him. 'No need to flipping tell me. I've a good mind to complain to the manufacturer. That thing isn't fit for purpose.'

'Well, you're up against the natural cunning of a squirrel who knows a thing or two about getting what it wants when it comes to food.'

The professor narrowed his eyes as Joseph drew closer. 'And what brings you home in the middle of the day? Not a problem at work, is there?'

'Chris sent some of us home so we could catch our breaths before heading in to cover the evening shift in the hunt for Charlotte Harris.'

'And why would you need to take a breather?'

'We've had one hell of a morning, Dylan. We all got pulled in for a bank robbery that went south over in Abingdon.'

'Oh, I heard about that on Radio Oxford. Something about a shootout between two rival gangs...' Dylan closed his eyes for a moment. 'Hang on,' he said, dropping his voice, 'this isn't anything to do with that file, is it?'

'In one. Four dead, one of the bank tellers injured, and one of the Night Watchmen winged—and who still got away.' Joseph patted his chest. 'And this is on me, Dylan.'

The professor shook his head. 'I can understand why you think that, but it really isn't. You were forced into a corner. They threatened Ellie if you failed to comply. And before you beat yourself up, here's the thing. I've actually been giving the whole situation a lot of thought, and I can't see why Chief Kennan couldn't have done it herself. After all, she would have had access to those files, too. That leads me to the conclusion that it was all about testing you, Joseph.'

'Aye, I can see the sense in what you're saying, but I still did their bidding, and a lot of people died. There is at least one piece of good news.'

Dylan's raised an eyebrow. 'Which is?'

'I managed to get a sample of Chris's pen's ink. I've given it to Amy to run some lab tests, comparing the pen he uses at work to the ink in the note that was left in St Barnabas to see if they're a match.'

'So Amy knows about this now, as well?'

Joseph shook his head. 'Not the details, and no doubt she'll want some answers in due course. But for now, she's doing me a favour and running the tests without any questions.' He looked at his friend, briefly considering asking Dylan for his advice about the situation he'd found himself in with Kate and Amy, but decided against it. For now, he'd fall back on his well-tested strategy for when anything to do with his personal life was getting too complicated. Ignore it and hope it either goes away, or simply sorts itself out.

The professor studied his face. 'What is it, Joseph?'

'Sorry, I got lost in my thoughts for a moment there. But as I was saying, even if I don't have video proof of Chris picking up that memory stick, if the ink is a match, it will still confirm it. Then, God help him after today's events, he'll deserve everything that's coming to him and then some.'

'And if it proves Chris isn't involved?'

'That's so unlikely that I'm not even going to bother giving it headspace.'

'I see...' Dylan gave him a small nod. But whatever he was thinking, he was keeping it to himself. Then his expression brightened. 'What do you say to a spot of date and ginger spiced cake? I'm on something of a baking run at the moment. I tried out a recipe I found online. It's fresh out of the oven and should have cooled enough by now to eat. What do you say? Also, it will give me an excuse to tell you about the latest gossip Iris has about the good people of Fernbridge. She's also on her way over to give me an update about some historical research she's been doing.'

'Then count me in,' Joseph said, relieved to have something else to talk about other than the Night Watchmen.

With the flames in Dylan's stove flickering and the fragrance of spiced cake filling *Avalon's* cabin, the atmosphere was exactly what Joseph needed to distract him from the brutality of the morning's events. Time out from his own complicated work and personal life.

Max and White Fang were curled up in their doggy beds. However, Tux, who'd turned up shortly after Joseph had entered the boat having abandoned the squirrel chase, had taken up residence on Joseph's lap. Even his cat, it seemed, realised he needed some TLC right now.

'Go on then, give me your verdict,' Dylan said, gesturing to the slice of cake on Joseph's plate.

The DI didn't need to be asked twice and took a bite. The sweetness of dates and carrots had a rich, almost caramel-like taste, perfectly balanced with warming spices.

'Is that a hint of cinnamon I'm tasting here?' Joseph asked.

'Indeed it is, along with nutmeg, ginger, and also a sprinkle of cloves.'

'Well, fair play to you, because this is an absolute masterpiece of baking.'

Dylan smiled at him. 'It's not bad, is it? And the smoky taste of the Lapsang Souchong tea goes really well.'

The DI took a sip of the brew Dylan had made to accompany the cake, and the smell of campfires filled his nose. His first taste confirmed everything that the professor had just said.

'Now that really hits the spot.'

'It certainly does. Anyway, let's get down to the latest update. Iris, who's obviously been keeping her ear to the ground in case anything interesting came up regarding Charlotte, briefed me before she headed over.' He glanced at the clock. 'She should be here in about ten minutes, but I'm going to tell you anyway.'

'And?' Joseph asked, before taking another bite of the delicious cake.

'Well, as you can probably already guess, paranoia has been well and truly stoked by what happened to Ms Trelawney. Basically, anyone who has anything even vaguely to do with that mob who went for Charlotte is convinced she's going to return the favour. Some have become so paranoid they've temporarily moved out of the village and are staying with friends, family, or at nearby hotels until things blow over.'

'What, they think she's going to murder them in their beds or something?' Joseph asked.

Dylan gazed into the flames of the stove. 'Basically, yes. However, there's also a huge rift developing in the village between the majority, who still believe that Charlotte is just a harmless old woman, and those who think she's some sort of baby-eating Satan worshiper. Obviously, Iris sees herself in the former camp as, I have to say, do I.'

'I'm afraid nearly everyone at work is convinced Charlotte is guilty, and if I'm honest I'm being increasingly swayed that way myself.'

'In that case, I think this is where you need to hear about my own recent research efforts. After the success of discovering that eyewitness account from the start of the previous century regarding a sighting of the druids, I started rooting through other old newspaper articles. What I've unearthed in them is absolutely fascinating. Apparently, there were lots of run-ins between the two families going right back to the start of the twentieth century.'

'Any particular reason for the hostility?'

'It seems it had to do with a dispute over a patch of land that ran between the two farms. Any guess which specific field that might be?'

Joseph raised his eyebrows. 'The one with the Celtic temple that was once built on it?'

'In one. And that was just according to the old newspaper I was able to dig up. That naturally got me wondering just how far back this family feud ran. It was Iris who hit on the idea of checking the Domesday Book. I'm sure you remember it from your history lessons back at school.'

Joseph grimaced. 'Maybe give me a refresher. Back in the day, I was more interested in avoiding doing any actual work in history lessons. We used to get the teacher to talk about his experiences as a bomber navigator in the Second World War.'

Dylan shook his head, and steepled his fingers like a master getting ready to give a class. 'Well, let me continue your education then. After his conquest of England, William the Conqueror commissioned the Domesday Book. Basically, he wanted a comprehensive survey of landholdings and all the resources of the country he'd just won.'

'I still don't understand how this is of any relevance to our investigation?'

'Just give me a chance and I'll tell you. It turns out that both the Trelawney and Harris families are listed in the Domesday Book as owning the adjacent farms near Fernbridge, but the ownership of the field with the temple wasn't confirmed at that time, possibly because it was still viewed as a sacred space. However, several centuries later, it seems the Harris family claimed it as their own, something the Trelawneys seemed less than thrilled about.'

'Are you suggesting that Charlotte and Margaret's less-than-cosy relationship could still be due to this disagreement over a piece of land?'

'That's certainly what it seems like to me. We already know that their respective fathers weren't exactly the best of friends.'

Pieces of the puzzle started to slot together in Joseph's mind. 'So, how would the ritualistic angle to the Cloaked Reaper killings be connected to this?'

'Now, this is where it gets really fascinating,' Dylan replied. 'From what I can tell from the records, it was the Trelawneys who were directly descended from the Celts who once lived there.'

Joseph's eyes widened. 'Not the Harris family, then?'

'No, they arrived relatively late in Fernbridge, somewhere around 800 AD. Certainly, you would have thought it was Charlotte, considering her beliefs, who might be able to trace her family roots back to the Celts, especially with the temple on her land. But no, it appears her own Pagan-derived practices are just something that developed separately by chance.'

'So, you're saying any continuing rituals are more likely to have something to do with the Trelawneys?'

'Well, it's not beyond the realm of possibility that knowledge of the temple might have been handed down from generation to generation within their family. And if you want further evidence of which family knew about the temple, I also managed to dig up another fascinating fact. You know we came across a Celtic triskelion symbol at the local church, the same symbol we discovered at the temple site?'

'Yes, what about it?'

'Guess which family paid to build the porch, including the floor with that particular stone design?'

Joseph narrowed his eyes. 'The Trelawneys?'

Dylan nodded. 'So, with that in mind...' The professor deliberately let his words trail away.

'You're not seriously suggesting that Margaret Trelawney was our murderer?'

'I don't think that's likely, especially in light of her recent death.'

'In that case, who killed her and all the others, if not Charlotte?'

Dylan spread his hands. 'I've honestly no idea right now. Maybe there is another surviving Trelawney family member out there, or someone close to them who knew the story. Whatever the truth is, me and Iris aren't giving up. As for you, you're nothing if not tenacious. I'm confident that you'll get to the bottom of this with or without our help. Anyway, how did I do?'

'As a research assistant, you are second to none.'

'No, I didn't mean that, although I will take the compliment. What I actually meant was, have I managed to distract you from those thoughts rattling around in your head?'

'If you mean the bank robbery and all that implies for me personally, then let's just say I'll try to put that on hold until I get the results back from Amy's ink tests.'

Dylan smiled. 'Then my work here is done.'

'Hello,' Iris's cheery voice said from outside *Avalon's* door.

'Do please let yourself in, and perfect timing—I've got Joseph with me,' Dylan replied.

Iris bustled into the cabin, shaking down an umbrella beaded with rain, before slipping her coat off. After nodding to Joseph and kissing Dylan on the cheek, she took a seat and sniffed the air.

'Something smells rather delicious in here,' Iris said.

Joseph gestured to the cake. 'The good professor here has been baking up a storm.'

'Have you now?' Iris said, giving the professor an impressed look.

'Would you like a slice? I did make it especially.'

Joseph looked between the two of them, wondering suddenly if he had inadvertently crashed a romantic liaison. But before he could say anything, Iris was placing a very old leather-bound book down on the table.

'Well, actually I'm very pleased you are here, Joseph, as I have this for you,' she said.

'And that is?'

'A fascinating tome I borrowed from the Bodleian Library. It's a bound thesis written in 1897 by a Master of Arts student who studied anthropology at Christ Church. He was specifically researching oral history throughout Oxfordshire. I have to say, typical of a more worthy academic piece, it's a bit stuffy in places. However, it's still filled with some fascinating insights that otherwise would have been lost over time, and this one entry in particular.' She started thumbing through the pages until she arrived at one with a white feather stuck between them, Dylan's preferred bookmark.

Joseph realised his friend must have given it to her. If that wasn't a show of affection, he didn't know what was. He tried to suppress a smile as Iris started to read from the page.

'"The Trelawney family of Oxfordshire, believed to be of ancient Celtic descent, offers a unique example of cultural persistence through their continuation of pre-Roman religious rituals into the 18th century. Residing near the site believed once, according to local oral history, to be a Celtic temple, the family maintained practices centred around agricultural deities, notably during Lughnasadh, the harvest festival. Their rituals, specifically animal sacrifices, were aimed at ensuring agricultural success and were performed at the Fernbridge Celtic temple site, somewhere considered spiritually significant among the Celts."'

Dylan traded a look with Joseph. 'There we go then, confirmation that we're absolutely on the right trail with the Trelawneys.'

Joseph smiled. 'I agree.'

'Trust me, it gets even better,' Iris said, clearing her throat. '"One notable event occurred in 1742 during a severe drought when the family conducted a sacrificial rite involving a prized bull. The subsequent return of rain, attributed to this ritual, bolstered the family's reputation for possessing powerful, albeit arcane, knowledge. The Trelawneys, known for their expertise in herbal medicine and divination, occupied a complex social position. They were both revered for their healing abilities and feared for their pagan practices."'

Dylan clapped his hands together. 'And there we have it—confirmation that Margaret Trelawney's ancestors, at least, knew about the temple and were also involved in practicing some sort of pagan magic. That can't be a coincidence.'

Joseph turned all this new information over in his mind as things started to come into focus. 'Aye, it can't. Even if we still don't know who the murderer is, this will definitely put us on the right path to help us track them down.'

'Then I'm happy to have been of some assistance,' Iris added.

Dylan nodded, beaming at her. 'Indeed. Would you like any more cake, Joseph?'

The DI glanced down at his empty plate, not even realising he'd been eating it as the two professors had been speaking. 'Good God, yes, and this time I intend to appreciate every bite before I go back to St Aldates with all this new intelligence.'

The words had barely left his mouth when his mobile rang. He glanced at the screen to see Chris's name on the display.

With a sense of wariness, he took the call.

'Joseph, I thought you'd like to join me at Ms Trelawney's autopsy. It turns out Doctor Jacobs has found something rather interesting about that glittering dust you noticed on her neck. I've already called Megan, and she's going to swing past to pick you up.'

'Some sort of fertiliser then?'

'No, and that's why I want you both there, because what they found has nothing at all to do with farming.'

'Okay, and I have some rather interesting information of my own.' He raised his eyebrows at Dylan and Iris who both smiled back at him. 'See you soon.'

As he ended the call, Joseph gave Dylan and Iris a thoughtful look. 'Seems like what might have been our first real evidence to link Charlotte to Margaret Trelawney's death is anything but.'

'Surely that's an interesting fact in itself,' Iris said.

'Oh, don't I know it,' Joseph replied.

'Then you'd better get over there and find out who this evidence *does* point to.' Dylan said. 'But first, let me wrap up some pieces of that cake for you and Megan, knowing what a sweet tooth she has.'

'That would be grand, and thank you.'

A few moments later, provisions secured, the DI left Iris and Dylan to enjoy their cake, and whatever else was going on between them.

CHAPTER TWENTY-THREE

Despite his considerable animosity towards his boss, the DI had wasted no time bringing Chris, and Megan, up to speed with what he'd learned about the historical aspect of the ritualistic sacrifices at the old temple site. But working out the implications of it all would have to wait because, suited up, they'd just entered the autopsy lab.

Rob and Claire were both sitting at a workbench next to the autopsy table with a sheet draped over it. More incongruously, they were both tucking into a box of Celebrations' chocolates.

Doctor Rob Jacob's gaze, as always, focused first on Megan, and he gave her a cheery wave, before nodding to Joseph and Chris, making it clear who his favourite detective was. That was underlined when he jumped up, grabbed the box of Celebrations, and headed over to her with it.

'They were on special offer at the supermarket, and Claire, in her infinite wisdom, thought it would be a good idea to buy three of them for work.'

Doctor Claire Reece nodded. 'Basically, both of us have zero willpower when it comes to chocolate, so please help yourself, if only for the sake of our waistlines.'

Megan didn't need to be asked twice, and considering she had already eaten three slices of Dylan's spiced cake, she took a *fill-your-boots* handful and stuffed them into her pocket.

'I'll have these later,' she said, beaming at him.

Joseph caught the slight scowl on Chris's face before it vanished again. The DI had long suspected the DCI also had a soft spot for Megan, but as of yet had done nothing about it.

Meanwhile, his romantic competition used every opportunity he could to charm the DC. Certainly, giving the woman chocolate was one very direct way to her heart. And that was fine in Joseph's book right now. If Megan swerved a bullet with the SIO, a man who'd obviously flushed his moral compass down the jacks, that was fine with him. Who knew how the boss would try to leverage Megan into doing the Night Watchmen's bidding? And that absolutely wasn't going to ever happen on Joseph's watch.

Rob belatedly offered the Celebrations first to Joseph and then Chris, but both detectives waved him away. The ever-present smell of formaldehyde in the lab meant that food was the last thing ever on either detective's mind when they were there.

'So what is it exactly you found for us, Rob?' Chris asked.

'Well, to start with, it wasn't actually me this time. Doctor Reece took it upon herself to take a sample of the glittering dust I believe you first noticed on the victim's neck, Joseph?'

'Aye, and the assumption is it had something to do with her assailant grabbing her when they pushed her down the stairs?' the DI replied.

Rob nodded as he headed over to the slab and pulled the cloth down to the top of the woman's hips.

Ms Trelawney, her eyes closed, lay on her back. Even in death, her lips were pinched together in permanent disapproval. But what turned Joseph's stomach and made him reach for his

Silvermints was that the top of the woman's skull had been removed to expose the brain. Even Chris paled. Megan, stoic as always, barely batted an eyelid, a look of fascination filling her face instead.

Doctor Reece, who'd just finished eating a mini Bounty, popped her gloves on and pointed. 'If you look closely you can see the damage to the frontal lobe, as well as secondary tissue damage to the right hemisphere. There are abrasions on the forehead, consistent with impact injuries. You'll see there is also a laceration on the bridge of the nose, along with swelling and contusions around the mouth and jaw. Additionally, there are multiple contusions and abrasions on the chest. When taken all together, this suggests the victim had multiple contact points with the steps as she fell down them. Additionally, the top of the spine around vertebrae C_5 through C_7 displayed multiple fractures on the X-rays.'

'So the short version is she died by breaking her neck?' Chris asked.

Doctor Reece smiled. 'That's another way of putting it.'

'Out of interest, how can you rule out that these injuries weren't from a weapon of some sort?' Megan asked.

'Fractures from a fall down a flight of stairs usually result with multiple impact sites such as we see here,' Rob replied. 'A single blow with a weapon might cause a more isolated and concentrated fracture of the cranium.'

Claire nodded. 'Also, the presence of subgaleal hematomas and the patterns of brain injury, along with the scalp lacerations, showed a more diffused pattern. If they were a weapon-inflicted injury, we would expect to see a specific direction of force and a particular type of damage. All the victim's injuries are consistent with her tumbling and hitting her head on the right-hand side, before slamming her head, presumably on a step, which broke her neck on the way down.'

'So, how can we rule this out as a simple accident?' Megan asked.

'Based on the trauma to the brain alone, the victim was hurled with considerable force into the wall,' Rob replied. 'That's consistent with the bruising from a grab mark on her right shoulder.'

Megan gave Joseph an impressed look. 'Which is exactly what you said at the scene.'

The DI nodded at Rob and Claire. 'Well, you can't hang around with these two, without some of it rubbing off on you.'

Rob chuckled. 'Perhaps, in that case, I should be asking you to join our team rather than Megan.'

Joseph held up both palms. 'That will be a hard no from me. Anyway, what about all that pixie dust on the victim's neck?'

With a flourish, Rob gestured towards his colleague. 'Over to you, Doctor Reece.'

Claire picked up a tablet and powered it on. 'Yes, the lab results were very interesting. The substance we retrieved from the skin was unlike anything we'd ever seen before. Here, let me show you a microscope view of the first thing we discovered when we took a closer look at it.'

The doctor turned her tablet around to show a highly magnified view of fragments with a distinctive layered structure in semi-transparent strata. But even more significant was the distinctive shimmering, iridescent sheen to all of the layers.

'What is it we're looking at here?' Joseph asked.

'According to the lab analysis we got back, these are mica-based pearl lustre pigments. Apart from that, there were traces of human DNA other than the victim's in the sample taken. We think, because of that, it's safe to assume the murderer was wearing gloves. Those must have been impregnated with this substance previously and left trace amounts behind when they seized her by the neck.'

'That we already guessed,' Chris replied. 'But the question we're all keen to know now is, what is this mica substance used for? You said on the phone it was nothing to do with farming.'

Doctor Reece nodded. 'Basically, because of its pearlescent effect, mica is often used in cosmetics, plastics, textiles, and sometimes in ceramics.'

Joseph's eyes widened as something came into focus in his mind—the expensive pot he'd seen on display in the village hall in Fernbridge. The same pot that was up for auction the night that Ms Trelawney had been murdered.

'Could this mica substance be used in a ceramic glaze?' he asked.

'Almost certainly,' Rob replied. 'Why, you look like you might have an idea where this came from?'

'Well, unless it's one hell of a coincidence, I ran into a man called Arthur Cleaves in Fernbridge. He just happens to make pots with glazes that are worth a lot of money.'

'You're suggesting this potter could have murdered Ms Trelawney?' Chris asked.

'Well, it's certainly worth having a serious look at him—specifically, whether he has an alibi for the time of her death,' Joseph replied.

'And what about a motive?' Megan asked.

'Well, he did have that argument with her during the meeting she was chairing about Charlotte Harris,' Joseph said. 'Don't forget, Arthur was one of the few people who stood up for her. Maybe he felt angry enough with the way Ms Trelawney treated Charlotte to do something about it. Perhaps he went to her and they argued, and it escalated into a violent exchange where he ended up throwing her down the stairs.'

'You're forgetting that the killer was wearing gloves, not to mention the Druid robe,' Megan said.

'Also taking into account they came tooled up and took Charlie Pankhurst down with a cosh,' Chris added.

'Aye, all good points,' Joseph replied, trying to avoid looking at Ms Trelawney's exposed brain on the slab before them.

'This is certainly the first piece of solid evidence we have to pursue,' Chris said. 'To start with we need to take a long, hard look at this Arthur Cleaves character. The question is, is he also our serial killer?'

Turning the thought over, Joseph stared off into the middle distance. 'The man must be in his early seventies. That makes him old enough to have been around when the first victim disappeared in 1966, even if he was only in his late teens.'

'Still old enough to murder someone,' Megan said.

'Just so.'

'Okay, I've heard enough,' Chris said. 'I want you both to start digging into Arthur Cleaves's background to see what you can find that might single him out as a potential serial killer. Once you've done that, armed with that information, I think you should pay him a little visit.'

Even as Joseph nodded, there were still things that didn't make sense to him. The potter had seemed the very definition of a kindly older man. But there again, it wouldn't be the first time someone, who'd been considered above suspicion, had turned out to be the killer in a murder investigation.

As Clare covered Ms Trelawney again, Rob was heading towards them with the box of Celebrations.

'It seems you have your work cut out for you, Detectives,' the senior pathologist said. Then he held up the chocolates. 'Here, you better take some more for the road.'

Joseph wasn't surprised when Megan stuck her hand in again and took another massive handful, which she stuck in her other pocket.

The DI caught the amused look on Chris's face. 'I don't know where you put it all, Megan.'

'Trust me, I always find a way.'

Far from being amused, Joseph felt a spark of irritation at the SIO. In what parallel universe did the fecking man live in where he believed it was okay to carry on with light-hearted banter when he was rotten to the core of his being? In his opinion, the man wasn't worthy to lick Megan's shoes. But as the SIO's attention turned to Joseph, the DI forced his expression into one of amusement.

'She has bottomless legs, apparently,' he said, which made Chris's smile widen.

Yes, Joseph could play this game just as well as his boss. But when this case was done, and he had the final piece of evidence linking him to the note, the gloves would well and truly be off. No fecker was going to threaten the life of his daughter and get away with it.

CHAPTER TWENTY-FOUR

A PILE of empty Celebration wrappers littered Megan's desk as Joseph placed a cup of coffee from the Roasted Bean in front of her. Grudgingly, and in an effort to keep up appearances, he'd also placed one on Chris's desk. He'd only just resisted the urge to spit in it first.

'You did want a cappuccino, right, boss?' he would have said, if he'd managed to work up enough saliva for the froth.

'What are you smiling about?' Megan asked, looking up from her screen.

'Nothing in particular,' Joseph said, making sure he looked anywhere but at Chris, hovering over at the incident board and tapping a pen against his lips as he looked at the information. On it was now a very large question mark next to Arthur Cleaves's name, which had joined Charlotte's as one of their chief suspects.

Megan took a sip of her coffee and pulled an appreciative face. 'That really hits the spot.'

'Don't I know it,' Joseph said, placing his cup down and drawing up a chair alongside hers. 'So, in my absence, what have you found out about Arthur with your research into his background?'

'He was born in 1949 in Fernbridge and has lived in the area ever since, working as a potter. His career took off right from the start, around 1967, when he was still a teenager. Arthur started using a unique glaze, which caught the attention of art critics, collectors, and galleries. He was eventually awarded the British Craft Council Award for Excellence, along with the Golden Clay Award at the National Pottery Exhibition.'

'And that's a big deal in the world of pottery, is it?' Joseph asked.

'Apparently. But it's the prices that are absolutely eye-watering. Normally, collectors hang on to the vases and they rarely come up for sale. That helps push up the price. At an auction at Sotheby's one recently went for two hundred thousand.'

Joseph almost spat out the coffee he'd just been sipping. 'How fecking much?'

'Tell me about it. Apparently, it's all about their pearlescent glaze.' She raised her eyebrows at him.

'Oh, you absolute star. Go on.'

'Apparently, the finishes are unique to Arthur's pots. And I'm quoting here from an art critic in the Sunday Times.' Megan cleared her throat. '"Arthur Cleaves's latest collection, showcased at the National Pottery Exhibition, exemplifies his mastery of glazes that bring a mystical depth to each piece he produces. They create a dynamic interplay of shifting hues—from deep blues to vibrant golds—captivating the viewer with every flicker of light. Cleaves's art invites exploration of the magical interplay of light, colour, and form, His vases are a journey into his enigmatic brilliance that defines his craft."'

'Jesus, it sounds like that art critic thinks Arthur is a regular Michelangelo.'

'Yes, albeit one who specialises in pots.'

'You'd certainly never know what a big deal he is in the art world, meeting him. At least on the surface, he's as modest as they come.'

'From what I've been able to dig up about him, Arthur's never loved being in the spotlight. He's also a bachelor, having never married or had a relationship of any sort. According to the electoral roll, he lives alone in a barn conversion. Apart from that, he seems to be a model citizen, never having so much as a parking ticket in his entire life. Oh, and get this—according to financial records I've been able to dig up, he's worth somewhere north of fifteen million.'

Joseph whistled. 'Now that's one well-paid artist. And all that from throwing pots. Maybe you and I are in the wrong game.'

'I do sometimes wonder,' Megan replied with a small smile, taking a long sip of her coffee.

Joseph did the same, and as he savoured the rich roast, he took a moment to focus his thoughts. 'So, what about a link to the Trelawney family, or indeed, Charlotte, for that matter?'

Megan sat back in her chair, a wide smile on her face, and beckoned Chris over. 'I think the boss is going to want to hear this as well.'

'What is it?' the SIO asked as he joined them.

'I was just looking into Arthur Cleaves and guess who he happens to be related to?'

'Well before I saw the cat-who-got-the-cream look on your face, I would have said Charlotte, based on the way he stood up for her,' Joseph replied.

'Believe it or not, it's the opposite. It seems that Arthur is actually a cousin of our latest victim. Trelawney was his mother's maiden name.'

'Bloody hell. So Arthur could know about the family secret about the temple?'

The DC smiled. 'That's certainly not beyond the realm of possibility.'

Joseph zeroed in on the man's name that was on the board as a candidate for prime suspect. But then he thought of the argument the potter had with Ms Trelawney at the village hall meeting.

'But you would never get the impression he was related to Ms Trelawney based on the way he laid into her,' Joseph said.

Chris shrugged. 'It wouldn't be the first family where members have fallen out. Blood isn't always thicker than water, you know.'

Joseph nodded. 'True. But what about Charlotte? Any explanation as to why he was so prepared to stick his neck out for her?'

'No idea. That's something we can ask Arthur when we talk to him.'

'Absolutely, I'd like the two of you to head out to his home right now. But it's still too soon to show our hand, so for now, you should restrict this to a fact-finding mission. Besides, I'm still not ruling Charlotte out just yet. For all we know someone in the Trelawney family talked and she found out about it.' Chris looked at Megan. 'Excellent work, Megan. This, and the discovery about the mica, feels like a significant step forward in our investigation.'

Joseph might have his issues with Chris, but at least he acknowledged his colleague's contribution.

'Yes, very well done indeed, Megan,' he added. 'I'm certainly looking forward to seeing the reaction on Arthur's face when we ask him if he uses that substance in his glazes. Not to mention asking him his whereabouts the night of his cousin's murder. I get the feeling this is going to be a very productive day indeed.'

'Here's hoping,' the DC replied as she grabbed her jacket.

CHAPTER TWENTY-FIVE

Joseph and Megan were driving through the afternoon rainstorm towards a barn conversion nestled in the nook of the valley. It was surrounded by trees with an expanse of gently rolling Chiltern hills stretching out all around it. The wasn't a sign of any other building for miles around.

'Now that's my idea of a dream place to retire to,' Joseph said as he pulled up in the gravel driveway.

'I thought you were wedded to the idea of living on *Tús Nua* forever?' Megan asked as they got out of the vehicle.

'Maybe, but this wouldn't be a bad alternative either. A bit of land to call my own and in the heart of the countryside. Although the real dream would be for it to be next to a river with its own quay where I could keep my boat moored.'

Megan smiled at him. 'Now that, I can definitely see. But isn't it a bit early for you to be thinking about retirement? Besides, wouldn't that particular lifestyle mean you'd have to start wearing tweeds and flat caps, and trade Tux in for a black Labrador?'

'I do worry about the mental stereotypes you have for people who live in the country,' Joseph said, shaking his head.

Megan grinned as they headed towards the house, their footsteps accompanied by the pattering drumbeat of rain on the gravel drive.

Joseph had already noticed there was no signage announcing the presence of a world-renowned potter living at the property. Arthur was obviously a man who very much liked to hide his light under a bushel. The only hint of something interesting was an adjacent narrow former stable block. On it, modern black-framed windows had replaced the wooden ones. Joseph could make out large skylights at one end of the building. Whatever was beneath them would certainly be flooded with light even on a grey day like this.

As for the main barn itself, it was a beautiful conversion, the middle section filled with vast floor-to-ceiling windows. A magnificent chandelier with blown globes of teal glass resembling oversized raindrops, was visible hanging in the entrance atrium. To Joseph's eye, it looked more like a sculpture than a light fitting. Behind it, an upper-storey walkway connected both sides of the house. The DI could easily imagine Arthur standing up there, perhaps with a whisky in hand, looking out at his kingdom. He knew he would if he owned this place.

'Isn't this place rather on the large side for someone who is living alone?' Megan asked.

'If you have the sort of money Arthur has, then apparently not.'

As they headed towards the front door, Joseph spotted two cameras mounted at either end of the building, along with a camera doorbell.

Megan had noticed them as well. 'Someone takes their security seriously.'

'Well, you would, living out in the middle of nowhere,' Joseph said as he was about to press the doorbell.

A cheery, 'Hello,' came from behind the detectives, and they turned to see Arthur Cleaves standing in the doorway of the converted stable block.

'What are you doing all the way out here, Detectives?' the potter asked, wiping his hands on the white clay-splattered overalls he was wearing.

Joseph wasn't in the mood for niceties and cut straight to the chase. 'We need to ask you some questions about Margaret Trelawney.'

Arthur's face registered surprise. 'Why would you want to do that? I barely knew the woman, other than that she was a cantankerous old fart who delighted in spreading gossip and making people's lives miserable. Surely, you're better off talking to people in Fernbridge if you want to know more about her.'

'You say that even though she was your cousin?' Megan asked as the rain began to fall harder.

Arthur clicked his tongue against the roof of his mouth with a tutting sound. 'Ah, so you know about that. That's not something I like to publicise. I've never liked the woman and never wanted to be associated with her in any way. You see, our respective parents were estranged, and for good reason. Let's just say the apple didn't fall far from the tree when it came to Margaret and her bully of a father. Of course, I'm as horrified as everyone else to hear about her murder.'

Before Joseph could reply, a clap of thunder split the sky and the rainstorm turned into a deluge.

'You'd better come in out of the rain before you get soaked through, if you want all the sordid details about the Trelawney family.' Arthur ushered them into the converted stable block.

Joseph took in the pristine gallery space. Glass display cases housed numerous ceramic vases, each one illuminated by spotlights, showing them off to their best effect.

It reminded him of the way the Ashmolean Museum liked to display its exhibits. But what really caught the DI's attention were the incredible glazes on Arthur's creations. In the village hall, the pot had certainly looked good, but here, lit as they were meant to be, the pots shimmered with iridescent light.

'No wonder these pots go for eye-watering prices; your glazes are absolutely stunning,' Megan said, taking in the kaleidoscopic play of light of the vase nearest her.

'You can blame the collectors for driving up the prices,' Arthur replied. 'They're always badgering me to create new pots but I haven't for years now. Of course, I only created twenty-two of these pots in my Ethereal Amphora range, which has also helped drive up their value.'

'Surely, that doesn't make much sense from a business point of view?' Megan said.

Arthur smiled at her. 'You sound just like my accountant. But I'm already comfortably well off, so I only create when the inspiration strikes me. Some might call me mad, but that's how I prefer to work, waiting for my muse to whisper in my ear. Sadly, she hasn't done so for a while now. I suppose that's just the fickle nature of inspiration for you. However, and you're the first people I've told this to, I've had an itch of an idea for a new creation bubbling up, and I've just thrown a practice pot, ready for when the real work begins.'

'Which is?' Joseph asked.

'The preparation of the glaze. As I hope you can tell by what's here, that's where the real magic happens. In many ways, the ceramic itself is the canvas on which my glaze is painted. Would you like to see the pottery design I've created so far?'

'We'd love to,' Megan replied as though they were regular, wealthy customers with a wad of cash to put down as a deposit.

'Then please follow me through into my studio.' Arthur led them towards a door at the far end of the gallery.

Joseph and Megan followed the potter through to the second half of the converted stable block.

In stark contrast to the moodily lit gallery, just as Joseph suspected it would be, the potter's studio was flooded with daylight from the skylights, despite the darkening storm clouds overhead.

A potter's wheel took pride of place near the middle of the room, directly beneath one of the skylights, and upon it was a white pot. Metal shelving lined the walls, filled with unglazed, fired white pots, and large drawings and paintings of designs adorned the walls.

But none of that held Joseph's eye. That was reserved for the well-ordered desk at the back, and specifically, the framed photo on it, of a beautiful raven-haired woman, whom he recognised as a much younger Charlotte Harris.

Did that mean she and Arthur had been romantically involved at some point? That could have all sorts of implications for their investigation into this mild-mannered man.

The potter headed over to the freshly created pot. 'There she is—my latest creation, although as I said, she's only a prototype.'

Even unglazed, the potter's skill was evident. The walls of the vase were so thin that the light from the skylight seemed to pour into the pot, making it glow like a pale light bulb had been mounted inside it.

'Okay, I think I'm starting to understand why people fight over the opportunity to own one of your pots,' Joseph said. 'Even unfinished, they're impressive.'

Arthur gave the DI a warm look. 'Thank you for saying that. Despite my success, I grapple with a lack of confidence sometimes. I spend so much time wrapped up in my head, trying out different designs and rejecting them, until I finally arrive at something that really speaks to me as an artist. And that doesn't always happen. Intuition is everything in my line of work. So for someone else to pick up on what I've been feeling my way towards, means a lot. But of course, there's still the glaze to come, and that will take months of experimenting and test firings until I find a finish that complements and elevates it to what I've been striving towards.' He gestured towards a series of glazed test tiles arranged in a line on the wall, covering the colour spectrum.

'That's actually what we want to talk to you about,' Joseph said. 'Do you happen to use mica in any of your glazes?'

Arthur blinked several times before his expression settled into one of confusion. 'I'm afraid the ingredients of my glazes are a closely guarded trade secret. You'll understand if I don't want other potters replicating my work.' His face grew serious. 'What's this visit about exactly, Detectives?'

'Please, just answer the question,' Joseph replied, not wanting to give anything away.

The potter's gentle demeanour vanished, his eyes hardening as he crossed his arms. 'I'm afraid that without a court order, I'm not going to reveal the contents of my glazes to anyone.'

Megan already had her notebook out as the initially friendly atmosphere quickly became frosty.

'Look, we're not asking for your secret recipe—just a piece of information that would be a great help in our inquiries,' Joseph replied.

Arthur's expression softened slightly. 'Oh, I see. You should have led with that. Okay, I don't suppose telling you a single ingredient will hurt, but the simple answer is no. I don't use mica. Why are you asking?'

Joseph needed to say just enough to keep the potter on-side, without tipping his entire hand. 'It may be relevant to Margaret Trelawney's death.'

Arthur gasped, his eyes widening. 'So that's why you're here. You thought I used mica in my glazes, which would put me in the frame for my cousin's murder?' He nodded. 'Yes, I see your thinking very clearly now, Detectives.'

Joseph realised there was no point in beating around the bush any longer, but he could still play this as though the spotlight hadn't fallen on the potter himself. 'I'm sure you understand we need to follow up every lead, however minor.'

The anger that had been flickering in the potter's eyes, died away as his brow smoothed out. 'Of course you do.' Then he nodded. 'But there's something you may not have considered about the mica. Isn't it something usually found in plasterboard? If this has something to do with Margaret's death, maybe you should be looking for a builder instead?'

Megan gave Joseph a sideways glance, her eyes widening slightly. They both knew what she was thinking—they were going to have to look at Charlie Pankhurst, who would certainly have access to a material like that.

'As I said, we're looking at all possibilities right now,' Joseph said, feeling like kicking himself for not even considering an alternative explanation for where the mica might have come from.

'But of course, I suppose the most likely suspect is still Charlotte,' Arthur said. 'I mean, who else could it be? It's no secret that my cousin made it her personal crusade to make Charlotte's life hell. It would be understandable if that poor woman finally cracked and decided to take matters into her own hands.'

'I see,' Joseph replied. Then he gestured towards the photo on Arthur's desk. 'I'm sure you understand that I have to ask this, but were you, or are you, romantically involved with Charlotte?'

For the first time, a slightly broken look filled the potter's face. 'Sadly not. You see, my timing was always off. Mike Clifford swept her off her feet before I'd even plucked up the courage to ask her out. But even though Mike ended up marrying Charlotte, he was never good enough for her. After all, he had that affair with Sally Blanchard even though he'd just married Charlotte, not to mention all the other women he dated later. The best thing that happened to her was him leaving.'

'Yes, we know all about that,' Megan replied. 'But you two never dated after Mike left?'

Arthur shook his head. 'Not for the want of asking. Unfortunately, Charlotte is happy living at Shadowbrook alone and with only her dog for company.'

That explained the photo of the farmer on his desk—unrequited love, a tale as old as the hills.

'In light of that, can you tell us where you were around nine on the night of Ms Trelawney's murder?' he asked.

The potter peered at him. 'You're not seriously suggesting I'm a suspect just because I happened to be related to that Gorgon of a woman?'

Megan gave the potter her best winning smile. 'As my colleague already said, we have to follow every lead, however implausible.' The DC's softly softly approach seemed to reap immediate dividends.

Arthur's shoulders dropped and he nodded. 'You need to be thorough. Well, your question is thankfully easy for me to answer. The night my cousin died, I was at the charity auction dinner in the village hall. You may have heard I donated one of my pots. It alone raised about half of what they needed to repair the church roof. I'm sure you already know this, but Margaret was there too. However, she left early, complaining of a stomach ache just before the auction began.'

Megan looked up from her notes. 'And you remained behind?'

'If you mean, did I walk my cousin home because she had a tummy ache? Then, absolutely not. As I'm sure you've already gathered, I couldn't stand the woman. But before you get any ideas about me being involved, there are plenty who attended the auction who will confirm I didn't follow her home to do the wicked deed. Look, I don't want to tell you how to do your jobs, but shouldn't you be concentrating your efforts on tracking down Charlotte? Surely, just based on the fact she's on the run, isn't exactly a great look for someone who's meant to be innocent?'

'Let's just say we're very keen to speak to her,' Joseph replied. 'Talking of which, I don't suppose you have any idea where she might be hiding?'

'I'm afraid I have as much of an idea as you do regarding that. Charlotte knows the countryside around Fernbridge better than anyone. She's also highly resourceful and could hide out for years if she put her mind to it.'

Joseph traded a frown with Megan. 'Well, if you think of anywhere she might have gone, please let us know at once.'

'Of course I will.'

Megan arranged her face into an innocent expression. 'Oh, out of interest, where's your kiln, Arthur?'

Joseph barely managed to stop himself from gawping at her. He'd been on the brink of writing him off as a suspect as soon as his story checked out for the time of Ms Trelawney's death. But of course, the man standing before them had access to an intense heat source.

'Just through that door, out the back, why?' Arthur replied, looking none the wiser.

Megan smiled. 'I'd love to see it. You see, I used to do a bit of pot-throwing when I was studying A-level art. Unfortunately, my exam piece exploded in the kiln.'

Arthur grimaced. 'Ah yes, that can happen if the kiln is heated too quickly or there are air bubbles trapped in the clay. You also have to be careful how the kiln is stacked. Even with all my experience, I've still had the odd mishap. But if you really want to see it, I can show you. Although, I warn you, there's not exactly a lot to see.'

'It's just that I've been thinking about getting a small kiln for myself.'

'In that case, we artists need to encourage each other when we can.' The potter beamed at her and led them through the door into a small room. Inside it was a large steel box about three metres across and with, in Joseph's opinion at least, more than a passing resemblance to a bank safe. However, instead of a numbered dial, there was a temperature gauge on the front. When he spotted the chimney leading up through the roof, his heart rate quickened. Could this really be it? Were they on the verge of solving the case?

Megan made an appreciative cooing noise as she gazed at the kiln. 'I know this sounds geeky, but can I look inside?'

Oh, you little beauty, Joseph thought. Of course, if there was anything that looked like human ashes there, he'd be giving the potter a caution faster than he could spit.

'No problem,' Arthur replied, oblivious to how close to being arrested he was. He undid the catches and swung the heavy door open.

Both detectives took in the pale brick-lined interior. It was filled with horizontal plinths, presumably where pots were stacked when the kiln was in operation.

Joseph's eyes scanned the floor for any ash deposits, but there was absolutely nothing. He felt a surge of disappointment wash over him as the prospect of an imminent arrest faded away. Certainly, the kiln looked immaculate. If this amiable man was their serial killer, he made sure to tidy up after himself.

Megan gave Arthur a wide-eyed look. 'The number of pots you must be able to fire in a kiln this big!'

'Yes, it's certainly overkill for my needs, but I've always fantasised about creating a six-foot pot but never got round to it.'

But still big enough for a human victim, hey? Joseph thought.

'Well, if it's anything like your latest creation, I'm sure it's going to be stunning,' Megan replied without missing a beat.

'We'll have to see,' the potter replied with a warm smile as he closed the kiln door.

As Arthur escorted them back to his studio, Joseph cast a sideways glance at his colleague.

'*What are you up to?*' he mouthed.

'*Trust me,*' she mouthed back.

Once they were back in the studio, Megan crossed over to the line of glazed tiles on the wall and leaned in for a closer look. 'Any idea which glaze you'll use for your latest pot?'

'None of those, actually. I'm thinking of creating a new glaze for this one. We'll just have to see where my muse leads me for this, my grand finale.'

'Based on your previous work, I'm sure she won't lead you astray,' Joseph said, getting into the spirit of things.

Arthur turned to him. 'I certainly hope not, although she can be a fickle mistress sometimes.'

'No doubt.'

'Anyway, I think we've taken up enough of your valuable time,' Megan said, glancing at Joseph.

Whatever her scheme was, Joseph trusted her enough to let her run with it. 'Thank you, Arthur, for being so cooperative,' he added.

'I hope you discover who murdered my cousin, whether it turns out to be Charlotte or someone else,' Arthur said.

'We certainly intend to do our best,' Megan replied as though she was now the senior detective on the case.

With a nod to the potter, they showed themselves out.

As Joseph headed towards the Volvo, he cast a look at Megan. 'A-level pottery, my arse.'

Megan smirked at him. 'Well, I needed to win him over so

he wouldn't suspect anything. And what about that kiln? Suddenly, we don't just have our mild-mannered potter in the frame for Trelawney's murder, but also potentially for all the others found in the field.'

'Oh, I know. But taking a dislike to his cousin is one thing, even if he is sweet on Charlotte, but a serial killer? What's his motive? Unless Arthur is a bit insane… Then again, I suppose he wouldn't be the first artist to go a bit loopy.'

'Well, clear motive or not, we should have hard proof one way or another very soon,' Megan replied.

'You mean we should get a warrant so Amy and her team can make a thorough search of his property, specifically his kiln?'

'Why wait?' Megan opened her pocket and took out one of the glazed ceramic test tiles. She grinned at it. 'Now, how did that get there?'

'So that's why you wanted to get out of there so fast. And don't tell me it just fell into your pocket.'

Megan's grin widened. 'Whoops.'

Joseph shook his head as he unlocked their car. 'You really are picking up all my worst habits.'

The DC shrugged. 'It certainly seems that way.' As they reached the Volvo, she hurried around it and jumped into the driver's seat before Joseph could. 'Anyway, I can't wait to hand this over to Amy to see what she finds out when she analyses it.'

'That makes two of us,' Joseph replied. Unable to suppress a smile at the DC's ingenuity, he handed her the keys.

CHAPTER TWENTY-SIX

JOSEPH HAD WASTED no time dropping the tile off with Amy, to hopefully discover if it contained mica. After that, they'd been en route to report back at St Aldates when Megan had insisted on stopping off at McDonald's just off the ring road for a loo stop.

The DI sat alone in the Volvo, rocked by the ever-increasing wind as rain pelted it in a fair imitation of hailstones. Half the carpark was flooded; ripples like waves against the beach ran across the surface, splashing on the pavement that wasn't yet underwater.

As Joseph waited for his colleague to appear, by all rights his mind should have well and truly been on the case, especially with the potential breakthrough they were on the cusp of. Instead, his thoughts were focused on the text Amy had just sent. The DI had opened it straight away, thinking that somehow she'd managed a rush job on the analysis of the glaze's contents. It turned out to have nothing to do with that. But what it said felt like a metaphorical earthquake had just ripped through his entire world.

In the text, Amy had simply written, *'No DNA found on the note, but the two ink samples are a match. So what's this all about, Joseph? I haven't entered an official log file but you definitely owe me an explanation for this.'*

This was the evidence he'd dreaded getting about Chris. The note might not have his boss's DNA on it, but it proved that his pen had been used to write the note Joseph had found at St Barnabas.

How could you betray us like this, Chris? Joseph thought, typing out a quick thank you and a promise to fill her in later.

A matching ink sample might not be a smoking gun, but for the DI it was the confirmation of guilt he'd been waiting for. The question now was what should his next step be? Ellie's safety took priority. The time had come to have another meeting with Kate and Derrick, with advice from Dylan on the sidelines. Then, collectively, they would decide what to do next.

Megan emerged from the restaurant, and Joseph wasn't surprised to see the DC had seized the opportunity to grab some food. But far from looking pleased with herself, she looked troubled as she ran through the rain, avoiding the numerous puddles.

'What's with the expression?' he asked, as she got into the car, already half soaked through. 'You look like someone who's just been told Maccy D's was out of grub.'

Megan shook her head as she took three boxes out of the soaked brown bag and opened them to reveal they each held a cheeseburger.

Joseph shook his head. 'Ah, you shouldn't have bothered. Not really in the mood for one of those.'

'Don't worry, these are all for me.' She stuck her hand into the bottom of the bag, and like a magician pulling a rabbit out of a top hat, took out a cup of coffee and handed it to the DI. 'I know it's not the Roasted Bean, but the coffee from these places isn't bad.'

'Aye, you're not wrong. Maccy D's uses Arabica beans for their coffee. Thanks,' he said, but wasn't going to be distracted. 'So that aside, why the face like a smacked arse?'

That raised a smile as Megan took her phone out and turned it to show him an article about a kiln. 'I used my time in the loo to do a bit of research. It turns out that it couldn't have been used to reduce the bone to ash.'

'But surely it gets hot enough?'

'Yes, but it's not the right sort of heat. Certainly the flesh and fat would have melted away from the bones, but it couldn't have reduced them to ash. Apparently, the sort of incinerator they use in crematoriums utilise exposed gas jets to burn the body with a controlled supply of oxygen. A kiln simply isn't up to the task.'

'Feck, and there was me thinking we'd made a major breakthrough.'

'You weren't the only one. It seems we got a bit ahead of ourselves.'

Joseph blew out a puff of air. 'Aye, it does, doesn't it? I really should have known better after all my years on the force. Just because a theory has a nice ring to it doesn't mean it's correct. And like Arthur said, mica comes from other places like plasterboard.'

'You're saying we developed tunnel vision?'

'I think so. Albeit for good reason, since that's where the historical evidence was pointing. But it seems we need to pull Charlie Pankhurst in for questioning. But maybe, as Arthur said, we shouldn't forget that Charlotte Harris is still the most likely suspect.'

'But doesn't it seem a little odd that he suggested Charlotte was the murderer when he was obviously in love with her?' Megan said.

'Aye, I did find it unusual that he still had a picture of her on his desk,' Joseph admitted. 'But we can't allow ourselves to get hung up on Arthur again, especially considering what you found out about the kiln. Perhaps this is all just what it first seemed, Megan. That the murders are part of an occult ritual she has practised on her land for years, starting back when she was a teenager in the sixties. Somehow she must have found out about what used to happen there and decided to pick up where the Trelawney family left off, but this time with human sacrifices. Of course, that's still conjecture at this stage. The one thing I know for certain is that Shadowbrook Farm is part of that woman's soul.'

'That's rather poetic for you,' Megan said, as she set to work on her first cheeseburger.

'You can rely on an Irishman to go misty-eyed occasionally when the occasion demands it.'

The DC snorted, and she gazed out of the window as the rain hammered down on the Volvo's roof. 'We better get a move on and give Chris the news. He's not going to be happy.'

'Aye, but those are the breaks—' Joseph's phone warbled and he glanced at the screen to see DCI Chris Faulkner's name on it. 'Oh, well, it seems we'll be telling the boss that news sooner than later,' he said, accepting the call.

'Sorry, Chris, but it looks like Arthur Cleaves is a bust.'

'Trust me, I already know,' Chris replied over the car's speaker system.

'Sorry, but how?'

'Someone just rang the investigation hotline. It seems Charlotte Harris was spotted less than thirty minutes ago heading through a small hamlet called Willowcombe.'

'Hang on, didn't we pass through there on the way to Arthur's place,' Megan said.

'Precisely, and that's why I'm ringing. Our eye witness said they saw Charlotte turn down the track that heads to Arthur's house. That makes me think she can't be headed anywhere else.'

'You think she's going after Arthur now?' Joseph asked.

'That's my guess, and certainly based on the note she left us about tracking down the murderer, it appears Charlotte has the potter in her sights.'

'Sorry, boss, when you say "has him in her sights"—'

'We have to assume she's going to murder Arthur,' Chris interrupted. 'I certainly don't want to take any chances. And if Charlotte isn't going there to kill him, at least we'll have an opportunity to arrest her and bring her in for questioning.'

'Surely, there must be other officers who are nearer to Arthur's home than we are,' Megan said. 'The Wallingford team to start with.'

'Normally, yes, but this bloody storm has brought trees down right across the county. Half the roads are impassable. Looking at the vehicle tracker it appears you're the closest team available. I'm heading there now with backup, but you should be able to make it there ahead of us. Just make sure Arthur is okay and guard him until we arrive.'

'And if he isn't, and Charlotte is standing over his dead body?' Joseph asked.

'Do your best to keep her there until we get there, but no bloody heroics. You hear me, Joseph?'

'Aye, I do. Besides, I have Megan to keep me in check this time round.'

'I'll do my best, boss,' the DC said through a mouthful of her second burger.

'Make sure you do,' Chris said. 'I'll see you both soon.' The line clicked off.

Joseph started the engine, flicking on the blues and twos as another gust of wind sideswiped the vehicle, making it sway.

'I can already tell this is going to be a *fun* trip,' Joseph said, the irony rolling off his tongue, as he accelerated through the puddles. He had no idea just how right he was about to be.

CHAPTER TWENTY-SEVEN

THE WINDSCREEN WIPERS whipped back and forth at their most demented high-speed setting to fight the growing deluge. As Joseph drove through the storm towards Arthur's home, lightning lit up the surrounding landscape in abrupt black and white.

Once, driving through treacherous conditions like this, the DI would have broken out in a cold sweat. It certainly wasn't lost on him that this felt painfully close to the weather on the awful night his baby boy, Eoin, had died after he'd lost control of the family's SUV on a flooded road. For years afterward, he'd been plagued by a phobia of driving. But Chris, the same man who he felt had betrayed him, had stepped in and helped him through his fear of vehicles on, of all places, a race track. The DCI had been nothing but supportive, and from that, their friendship had grown. That was, until now. The part of the DI's mind that wasn't wrapped up in this case kept returning to the matching ink. Even now, part of him still couldn't—or more accurately, didn't want to—believe it.

Ahead, the Volvo's headlights picked out a large shape sprawled across the road. With an awful feeling of déjà vu from the night of the crash that had killed his son, the DI hit the brakes hard. The vehicle's ABS did a sterling job, bringing it to a shuddering stop in the rain, which was turning the tarmac into a shallow river.

'Feck, this is all we need,' Joseph said, looking out at the downed tree blocking the entire lane from hedgerow to hedgerow. 'Is there another track we can take that will get us to Arthur's house?'

Megan was already checking the satnav and shaking her head. 'No, I'm afraid this is it. We could fit the tow rope from the emergency kit to the tree and try pulling it out of the way?'

The DI looked at the broad bough of the tree and shook his head. 'The only way that thing is going to be shifted is when the fire brigade chops it up into small pieces with a chainsaw. We'd better ring Chris to let him know this route is blocked.'

Megan nodded and took her phone out. Chris picked up in two rings.

'Are you there yet?' he asked over the car's speaker system.

'No. We've just come across a tree blocking the road,' Joseph replied.

'Not another bloody one. We've been running into the same problem on our way to you. I can try to get the fire brigade to your location but they're going to be flat-out busy in this weather. We managed to squeeze past two downed trees already in the Land Rover, but only just. The patrol cars with me didn't manage to get past, but at least I have Ian and Sue with me.'

'What about the police helicopter?' Megan asked.

'Not a chance in this storm. How far out are you from Arthur Cleaves's place now?'

'Still a few miles to go, boss,' Megan replied. 'We could abandon the vehicle and try to make it in on foot?'

Joseph pulled a face. 'Every minute counts if Harris is on her way to settle some score with Arthur. And the fact that there's no sign of her vehicle in front of that tree suggests she may already be there.' A surge of frustration coursed through him. He felt like thumping the steering wheel and was just resigning himself to walking the rest of the way when he spotted the gate just to their right.

'Hey, Megan, have you got that walking app you showed me when we were on the dig? You know, the one detailed enough to show all the field boundaries?'

'Yes. Why?'

'I want you to see where that leads, and if there's a way back onto this lane further along.'

'You're going to try to get past the downed tree by driving through an adjacent field?' Chris asked over the phone.

'That's the general idea.' Joseph reached over, took the high-powered torch from the glove box, and wound the window down, letting a squall of rain into the vehicle. Beyond the gate, in the torch's beam, glistening pools of water dotted the grassy field. 'Okay, it looks passable if we're careful. So what's the verdict, Megan?'

She gave him a thumbs-up. 'It looks like there's a second gate at the bottom corner of that field. It's about two hundred metres further along. The good news is there's no fence between us and it. The bad news is that the field already looks really waterlogged to me.'

'Just as well that we have four-wheel-drive, then.'

'The V90 may be four-wheel-drive, but don't forget it's not a Land Rover,' Chris said over the phone. 'If you get bogged down in soft ground, you'll get as stuck as any regular two-wheel-drive vehicle.'

'Understood, but it's still worth giving it a go. If we get stuck, we'll revert to plan A and walk there instead,' Joseph replied.

'Okay, then let's do this,' Megan said. She opened her door and rushed to the gate, the wind whipping her hair up in a fair impression of a banshee as she unlatched it and swung it outwards.

'We'll be in contact to let you know how we get on, Chris,' Joseph said, as he backed up the lane a little bit.

'Okay, but you should know that Sue and Ian are in the back, betting on whether your driving skills are up to it.'

'Don't tell me, Ian is betting against me.'

'How did you guess?' he heard the DI's voice call out in the background.

'Just a hunch. Anyway, I'll ring back soon to let you know you've lost your money, Ian.'

'Counting on you,' Sue replied.

Smiling, Joseph ended the call, closed his window, and stuffed the torch into the door-side bin. Trying not to imagine the smug look on Ian's face if this attempt went sideways, he turned the Volvo into the gateway.

Painfully aware the vehicle didn't have off-road tyres fitted with a deeper tread, Joseph kept his speed down as he crept through the gate. As soon as the vehicle was clear, he brought the Volvo to a stop while his colleague threw the gate closed, assisted by the gale, and came running back to the car.

Water dripping from her hair despite her raised hood, Megan slammed the door and turned to him. 'Be careful, that grass is an absolute quagmire.'

'I'll try my best,' Joseph replied.

Slowly he drove forward again, turning the wheel until they were parallel to the hedge running along the side of the lane.

A crackle of lightning struck a hilltop less than two miles away with a deafening boom, lighting up the landscape in monochrome tones.

Joseph couldn't help wondering whether Charlotte was still somewhere out there in the storm, maybe delayed by the tree as they had been. Or had she found another way to the barn thanks to the advantage her Land Rover had given her?

With a dozen similar scenarios filling his head, the DI drove the Volvo down the gentle slope towards the bottom corner of the field, where hopefully there would be a gate waiting for them. He was keeping their speed down to ten miles an hour, but the wheels were beginning to spin. The floodwater was flowing down the hill with them in a growing, impromptu river.

It was thanks to that, that Joseph spotted the ragged peaks of a well-grooved muddy track hidden just beneath the surface a moment too late. With a bump, the Volvo dropped into it like a train settling onto rails. Moments later, a graunching sound came from the bottom of the vehicle as it scraped over rocks buried in the track. They shuddered to a stop.

Joseph hit the throttle, and a shower of floodwater sprayed up from all four wheels as they spun freely. Then, like an animal pulling itself free from a bog, the Volvo shuddered as one of its wheels finally found purchase and it pulled itself out of the hidden depression.

Based on how the wheels kept spinning, the soft muddy surface was a considerable challenge for the V90, all-wheel drive or not. Joseph increasingly felt like he was sailing rather than driving the vehicle as the water deepened around them.

Megan cast Joseph a frown. 'I think you might need to pick up a bit more speed if we're not going to end up getting permanently stuck in this lot.'

Joseph gestured to the steepening descent ahead. 'Aye, but the faster we go, the less control I'll have if things start to run away from us.'

'I know, but I don't think we have much choice, unless we want to wade the rest of the way to the road.'

The words had barely left the DC's mouth when the vehicle

lurched down again and an even louder scraping sound came from the vehicle's floor and it shuddered to a stop.

'Feck!' This time, Joseph didn't wait, and gunned the engine. The Volvo twitched left and right as individual wheels briefly found traction before losing it again.

A loud bang, followed by a bellow from the engine, made it sound as though the car had been transformed into some sort of super truck.

'I think that was the exhaust being torn free,' Joseph said grimly.

'The fleet manager at St Aldates is going to love you when we return this to the car pool.'

'Don't I know it,' Joseph replied, keeping the engine revs high. The V90, doing a reasonable impression of a V12, continued to claw its way along the hidden track.

The DI felt the tension across his shoulders let go a fraction as the headlights picked out the dull metal bars of a gate only about ten metres ahead. Even more importantly, he could see that it led back onto the relative safety of the hard-surfaced road. But as the DI tried to apply the brakes, the brake pedal vibrated beneath his foot, and the ABS kicked in. It had absolutely no effect on slowing the Volvo as it continued to slide through the soft mud towards the shut gate.

'Joseph!' Megan said with a squeal, grabbing the handle and pushing herself back into her seat.

'I'm fecking trying!' The DI stamped harder, to no avail. In a split second, he made a decision and lifted his foot off the brake, stamping instead on the accelerator.

Like a dog let off its leash, the Volvo surged forward, working with the growing torrent rather than against it. They hurtled towards the gate, which Joseph could see was already partially open thanks to the floodwater running through it.

Joseph just prayed the impact wouldn't be enough to trigger

the airbags, which would automatically shut the V90 down as a safety measure.

The vehicle half-sailed, half-drove into the gate with a resounding clang, sending it flying open. The detectives lurched in their seats, but Joseph let out a long sigh of relief when the airbags didn't deploy. Then, just like that, they were back out on the road, fishtailing slightly as Joseph fought to control the vehicle.

With solid tarmac beneath its wheels, even with the floodwater running over the surface, the V90 was back on its territory. Like a dog shaking off water, the Volvo roared forward out of the floodwater and onto a clear stretch of road.

'Shit me sideways!' Megan exclaimed, looking at Joseph.

The DI grinned at her as they roared away down the lane. 'I couldn't have put it better myself.'

Joseph and Megan pulled up outside Arthur's barn conversion just as the rainstorm intensified even more, making the water falling from the eaves resemble a waterfall rather than rain. The rumbles of thunder had been growing steadily more intense as the storm drew closer, bathing the horizon in almost continual flashes of brilliant white light. The wind screamed around the vehicle as the two detectives got out into the stinging, biblical rain.

Megan headed around to the front of the vehicle and shook her head.

'Ouch,' she shouted over the tumult.

Joseph joined her to see the front wing scratched and slightly dented, and one of the running lights hanging off by its wires. He pulled a face in response, but was already scanning the surrounding valley.

There was no sign of anyone or anything—or specifically, an old Land Rover—in the yard, or anywhere else for that matter.

The DI felt a huge surge of relief. 'It looks like we're in time after all. Maybe Charlotte tried another route and got held up.'

'Alternatively, she's parked it round the back and is already here.'

'Oh, you're just a bunch of fecking rainbows today, aren't you?'

Megan smirked and she took out her baton, extending it.

Together, they raced towards the barn conversion, its huge picture windows lit up like a department store in the darkness.

They reached the oversized front door, large enough to drive a small tractor through, when it swung open, and Arthur himself stood there, looking out at them, once again sporting a surprised expression.

'I saw your car pull up on the security cameras. But why on earth are you out in this awful storm?'

'Because your life may be in danger,' Joseph replied. 'We believe there's a strong possibility Charlotte Harris is on her way here—if she's not already somewhere on your property.'

'Don't be ridiculous. Apart from anything else, my cameras haven't picked up anything. Besides, why would Charlotte hurt me? I've been nothing but supportive.'

'We don't know for certain that she does, but we're not taking any chances,' Megan said. 'We need to get you out of here.'

Joseph gestured back towards the road. 'I don't think we'll get very far, thanks to that tree being down. I also don't fancy our chances trying to go up that field through the mud again.'

Megan thinned her lips. 'So, in other words, we sit tight until the cavalry gets here?'

'I don't think we have any choice. But at least if Chris comes the same way we did, the Land Rover will do a lot better than the Volvo did at off-roading.' The DI examined the very thick front door and the substantial locks built into its frame. 'Is the rest of the house as secure as this, Arthur?'

'Very. And like I told you, I've got security cameras covering every angle of the barn and the studio.' He gestured behind him at a small display mounted on the wall, showing numerous camera feeds.

'Good. Then you lock yourself in here with DC Anderson.'

Megan stared at the DI. 'What about you?'

'I'll keep guard outside and patrol the perimeter, ready to intercept Charlotte if she turns up. So sit tight, and don't open that door to anyone until our backup arrives.'

Megan nodded. 'Just tell me you've got a baton on you?'

Joseph pulled a face, then grinned as he took one from his pocket. 'It seems I'm picking up a few tricks from my younger colleague.'

'Thank God for small mercies,' Megan replied, then nodded to him as she closed the door.

Joseph heard the locks click into place. The metaphorical drawbridge had been raised.

He peered into the raging maelstrom, his hand tightening on the baton, before pulling up his hood and striding off into the swirling storm.

CHAPTER TWENTY-EIGHT

Rain slammed in Joseph's face as the wind roared around the buildings. The conditions only helped increase his sense of isolation as he headed away from the welcoming lights of the barn.

When the DI had first seen this place he could almost imagine himself living here. But right then, in the middle of a huge storm with a murderer possibly closing on their location, he was painfully aware of just how isolated it was.

As the darkness deepened around him, he took the LED flashlight from his pocket and turned it on. A beam lanced through the maelstrom, creating a pool of light that caught the sheets of rain slanting down in front of him and making it almost impossible to see anything beyond twenty metres.

The DI walked along the back of the building, using the torch to flush away darkness, in case Charlotte had already reached the property and was hiding somewhere. As he walked along the side of the studio he heard the distant rushing of a stream in full flood. He rounded the edge of the stable block and directed his torch towards the source of the sound.

Through the haze of rain, Jospeh could just make out a dark

line next to an old disused track, running down from the top of the hill to where it passed through the property, and specifically past a building he hadn't noticed before.

The small dilapidated garage was set back from the studio. The structure was made from sheets of rusting corrugated sheet and looked at odds with the pristine nature of the rest of the property.

Joseph figured Arthur had probably inherited the building when he'd bought the property and hadn't got around to renovating it yet. It certainly looked like the sort of place that someone might be hiding.

Joseph headed toward it for a closer look, but the wind drove into him, a snarling fist of nature trying to drive him backwards. The DI bent his head into the gale, the rain slanting almost horizontally as he reached the garage. As he swept his torch's beam over the structure he caught a flash of light reflecting back at him through a gap in the dilapidated wooden doors. He put his eye to the gap for a closer look.

The first thing Joseph registered was that the glint of light had been from a headlight of an old green Land Rover. The next thing his brain registered was that it was a flatbed version, just like...

Right on cue, a crackle of thunder split the sky, leaving his ears ringing as a lightning bolt struck a lone tree at the top of the hill in a dazzling blast of energy, almost as though the big man upstairs was throwing a metaphorical exclamation mark into the moment.

Not that Joseph needed any more prompting. His thoughts were already racing ahead as he checked for a lock on the door. After seeing none, he slid his fingers through the gap in between and heaved. With a groan, followed by the squeal of rusty hinges, the door juddered open.

Illuminated by his torch, Joseph fully took in the vehicle

before him. A quick check of the plates confirmed what he'd already suspected. It was Charlotte's vehicle. It was a bold move for her to hide it here. Maybe she'd kept her lights off as she'd approached the farm so Arthur wouldn't spot her.

Then, another more likely explanation struck him. Being sweet on her, could he have offered her sanctuary? Perhaps, even now, she was hiding in the house.

He was just turning to run back to the house when his phone rang. But when he took it from his pocket, rather than seeing Chris's name on the screen, he saw Amy's.

'Look, I'm in the middle of something, can it wait?' he asked as he took the call.

'We've just had a major breakthrough,' Amy replied. 'That tile you gave me for analysis, just came back from the lab. To start with, the ceramic itself was actually bone china.'

'Hang on, bone as in—'

Amy cut him off. 'Yes, as in bone ash mixed into the clay. According to the lab tech guys, the bone enhances its whiteness, translucency, and durability.'

'Shite. Specifically human bone ash in this instance?' Joseph asked, but already knowing the answer.

'You've got it. And it gets better. It's also been used in the glaze, along with traces of mica matching what we found on Ms Trelawney's neck. The lab team believes that's what helps give Arthur's glazes their iridescent quality.'

All the fragments of information came flying together in Joseph's mind. Perhaps the potter had even murdered Charlotte and stored her Land Rover in the garage until he could get rid of it.

'So, Arthur Cleaves has been turning his victims into pots?' he asked.

'As surreal as it sounds, that's certainly what the evidence is pointing towards.'

'Shite on a fecking bike. I've just left Megan alone with that psychopath to supposedly guard him from Charlotte. Do me a favour and let Chris know what you've found out.'

'Leave it to me, and get back to Megan before that murderer does anything to her.'

Joseph was already running as he hit the end call button. With the wind now on his back as though the big man upstairs was giving him a helping hand to get him there in double quick time, Joseph rounded the corner of the studio and skidded to a halt. His heart leapt into to his mouth at the sight of the front door standing open and light spilling out.

No, no, no!

Joseph raced towards it with an effort that would have made an Olympic sprinter proud.

He practically flew inside, calling out as he slid to a halt.

'Megan! Arthur! Where are you?' he shouted. Just as he'd dreaded, there wasn't a response. Was he already too late?

Joseph's thoughts were spinning as he rushed into the atrium. A glance left and right along the open-plan living area and kitchen, revealed no one. His gaze tore to the stair case to the upper floor and bedrooms.

The DI had taken three steps towards it, when something caught his eye outside through the atrium window. The skylights in the studio were lit up. As far as he could remember they hadn't been when they'd first arrived. Maybe on some pretence Arthur had lured Megan over there with him.

The detective raced back out into the storm, trying to ignore the nightmare images competing for space in his imagination.

The DI didn't so much as open the door as shoulder charge it, which sent it flying open and banging into the wall with a resounding thud. He raced into the gallery, but no one was there. The door swung shut behind him with a click, and the noise of the storm was instantly muffled, an almost eerie silence descending.

'Megan, Arthur, are you in here?' the DI called out. Once again there was no response.

But Joseph's instincts were already kicking in. Something told him he wasn't alone in this building. He took his telescopic baton out and flicked it to its full length.

The DI prowled through the gallery, threading his way through the display cases and the individual pots illuminated inside them. This time, Joseph felt a distinct sense of unease as he took in their shimmering glazes. What sort of sick mind would come up with something like using human remains in their art?

The DI reached the door to the studio and, baton ready to do its worst, opened the door with his free hand. The bright light after the relative darkness of the gallery was almost blinding, and it took a moment for his eyes to adjust. When they did, he realised the workshop was empty as well. The only sound was the relentless drumming of rain on the large skylights above. No, not the only sound...

Joseph could just hear a distant hissing coming from the open door leading into the kiln room.

He strode towards it, and the moment he stepped through, he spotted Megan lying on the floor. His stomach clenched, bitterness tanging the back of his throat, the DI raced over and squatted beside her. Pressing his fingers to her neck, he relaxed a fraction at the pulse he found there. Unconscious, not dead.

'Megan?' He gave her a gentle shake, but she didn't respond.

His eyes started to sting just as he noticed the smell of gas scratching at his nose.

What? he thought.

The hissing sound was much louder inside the room. He scanned the interior, and saw the source. A hose had been disconnected from the kiln and the end of it vibrated as the poisonous gas gushed out. Whatever was going on here, Joseph needed to get Megan out before it was too late for either of them.

Joseph dropped his baton, and scooped his hands under Megan's shoulders. Before he could lift her, the door slammed shut behind him, followed by the sound of bolts sliding into place.

He looked over his shoulder at his only escape route, his head swimming, realising too late what had just happened. He ran over to it, tried to turn the handle, but only confirmed what he'd already known. The door had been locked from the outside and he and Megan were trapped.

'Arthur, so help me God, open this fecking door before I tear you a second arsehole.'

'All in good time, my friend, but not quite yet,' Arthur's calm voice replied.

'For Christ's sake, man, don't do this. Backup is on the way. You haven't got a chance.'

'Maybe, but not before I start my final piece.'

'What? You're not...' Joseph's voice faltered as nausea filled his gut. 'Making any sense,' he managed to finish.

'It will, it will, and you'll both help me in the creation of my final masterpiece, even though it was meant to be Charlotte.'

Joseph felt his mind tilting and spots began to pop in front of his eyes. He knew he only had moments left before he passed out, and that he wasn't getting out through that door anytime soon. There had to be something else he could do.

The DI turned back to the room and fixed his wavering gaze on the gas hose. If he could reconnect it...

He half walked, half stumbled back towards the kiln. With his vision starting to blur, he reached out and grasped the end of the hose. His fingers fumbled as he tried to push the end of the hose onto the end of the ridged connector, but his grip kept slipping.

Once, twice, three times...

His lungs burned and he began violently coughing as he slouched sideways. Joseph thudded into the side of the kiln and slid down it. Darkness enveloped him, and he lost consciousness.

CHAPTER TWENTY-NINE

Joseph's head ached like he'd been struck with a sledgehammer, not once but twice. He was pretty sure his eyes were open even though all he could see was pitch blackness. A patter of rain was coming from somewhere overhead.

The DI heard someone groan next to him. He reached out towards the source of the sound and felt brick under his fingertips. Then they brushed someone else's hand.

'Megan, is that you?' he asked.

'Yes, but my head hurts like the worst hangover in the history of hangovers. What happened?'

'We both passed out after being gassed by Arthur in his kiln room.'

'Bloody hell, yes, it's all coming back now. He said he picked up someone on his cameras, heading into the studio. Before I could stop him, he rushed outside. Of course I went after him. I caught up with him in the kiln room. The next thing I knew, I smelled gas, and Arthur locked me in, then I passed out.'

'Which is eventually where I found you and where he pulled the same stunt on me.'

'So Arthur's been our man all along?'

'It's definitely looking that way, especially after what Amy discovered.'

'Which is?'

'Later. We have bigger problems right now.'

'Where are we?'

'Presumably, in the kiln, and I don't know about you, but I don't much fancy finding out what he has in mind for us next.'

Joseph dug into his pocket and pulled out his torch. Turning it on, he saw Megan's pale face.

'Shite, my phone's gone,' he said, checking his other pockets. 'How about you?'

'Same.' Megan scowled.

The detectives took in the confined space they were stuck inside. But rather than the pale brick they'd seen in the kiln, this space had a low, arched roof just above their heads, not leaving them enough room to stand. It was about two metres wide and four long and lined with darker, charred red brick. There were also two narrow slits in the walls on either side.

'Oh, double shite,' Joseph muttered.

Megan's forehead ridged. 'This isn't Cleaves's kiln, is it?'

'Aye, but that's something of a moot point. Based on those soot marks, this thing is definitely used for burning things. This is probably where Cleaves murdered his other victims.'

A slow handclap came from outside of wherever this was. 'Very well deduced,' the potter said.

'For feck's sake, let us out already,' Joseph replied.

'Sadly, we both know that's not going to happen. No, we're all on a journey together towards my final masterpiece.'

'What the hell do you mean by that?' Megan asked.

'I mean that as I have done with my other creations in my Ethereal Amphora vase range, I will use the bone ash left over from the two of you to create my final piece of work. I have to say the idea of two souls bound together for eternity in one of my creations, has rather an appeal to me.'

His voice had taken on a dreamy quality, but now it hardened. 'It was never meant to be like this. After getting rid of my cousin, I was going to set her twisted soul free in a vase for my penultimate creation. Then for my grand finale, something I'd been working towards my whole career, I was going to create a masterpiece from the ashes of my one and only true love, Charlotte Harris. What better way for me to go on worshipping her?

'But sadly, she allowed the archaeological dig to take place in her field where, unbeknownst to her, the Celtic temple was located. After that, all my carefully crafted plans began to unravel. Aided of course, in no small part by your tenacious investigation.

'But I'm nothing if not adaptable, Detectives. When Charlie interrupted me moving my cousin's body, and then Charlotte went on the run, I started to consider a new plan. So here we all are tonight. It's funny how things have a way of working themselves out.'

Although Joseph couldn't see him, he could easily imagine the madman smiling. Despite the precariousness of their situation, the detective part of Joseph's mind was still desperate for more answers.

'So that's why you killed all those people over the years, simply to turn them into fecking pots?'

'Not just pots,' Arthur corrected. 'They gave their lives for the pursuit of my creation of masterpieces.'

'Interesting use of the word *gave*,' Megan said. 'Don't you think *stolen* would be more appropriate?'

'Only if you think of it in a narrow-minded way, which seems to be a common problem among people today. Some of us are motivated by something much more profound in our lives. Make no mistake, I'm pursuing sacred work here.'

Joseph let out a hollow laugh. 'Right. But let's just suppose for a moment you're not stark raving mad, why scatter some of your other victim's ashes on Charlotte Harris's farm?'

'To frame her, of course. It was a well-known secret in my family about the old Celtic temple on the land her family stole. So, I thought, what better way to have an insurance policy than to scatter the ashes left over from my work? Everyone already knew about Charlotte's pagan beliefs, and if the ashes were ever discovered, they'd come to the conclusion she had been performing some sort of sacrificial ritual there. That would only be reinforced by the old rumours about what my ancestors got up to on that land. It's amazing what people will believe if you whisper the right thing into their ears.' He laughed.

'Especially my cousin,' he said after a moment. 'She was the most gullible of the lot. I knew the rumours I'd started would find their way back to her, like a spider sitting in the middle of a web of gossip. Particularly ironic, was that the more I argued that they were just stories, the more fervently Margaret believed them. Then again, my cousin was always gullible like that, always ready to believe the very worst in people. Especially when it came to Charlotte.'

'So why kill her as well?' Megan asked.

'Because I knew it would cast suspicion on Charlotte. That's why, as I had with all the other abductions, I used a Land Rover with cloned plates that matched hers. I also made sure I wore a hooded cloak for all of my abductions. Exactly the sort of thing that someone into paganism might wear for their little ceremonies. Of course, it also had the added benefit of hiding my identity. That way if my Land Rover or I were ever spotted when I abducted someone, suspicion would automatically fall on Charlotte.' He sighed.

'Unfortunately, the final part of my plan never came to pass, thanks to that dig. You see, I'd intended to make her write a confession before killing her. Then, as far as the world was concerned, racked with guilt, Charlotte would have taken herself off somewhere to commit suicide.'

'So is this where you burned all your victims' bodies?' Megan said.

Arthur chuckled. 'Don't you recognise where you are?'

Joseph realised he did, even if he'd only seen it from a distance. 'We're in the animal incinerator that Charlotte's father built, aren't we?'

'Once again, very well deduced, Detective Stone. You see, I burned my victims up here in the middle of the night so there was no danger of anyone spotting the smoke coming from the chimney, especially Charlotte. Then, back at my property, I had special grinding equipment installed to mill down the remains. Unfortunately, as you discovered, the odd tooth fragment would slip through during the process. However, since I'd had the foresight to scatter the remains on her land, all the evidence pointed towards Charlotte. You see, I really have thought of everything.'

'You must realise that the game is up,' Megan said. 'It's only a matter of time before our colleagues catch up with you.'

'Not tonight they won't, which is all that really matters to me now. Don't forget that they're on their way to my home, believing, as you yourselves told me, that a crazed farmer was going there to kill me.'

'How'd you get us here, anyway?' Joseph asked.

'I used an old track that runs from the back of my property over to the back of Charlotte's. So you see, right now, no one knows you're here. All I need is enough time to reduce your bodies to ash. Then, I will collect what I need before making my escape.'

'You know what the problem with that is, Arthur? For all your plotting, your pots have already given you away,' Joseph said.

'Please don't worry yourselves about that. I've had plenty of time to prepare for my exit from the world stage.' His voice had taken on that almost lyrical tone again, sending shivers up and down Joseph's spine. 'I have a humble French gite in Bordeaux with another studio waiting for me to create my magnum opus with the essence of your two souls. And, of course, I have a new alias all ready to go, as well. By the time anyone catches up with me, I will almost certainly be long dead of old age.'

His tone changed again, all business. 'Anyway, talking of dying, dear people, I need to press on. There are only so many hours of darkness left to hide the smoke from the chimney. Please don't take any of this personally. Take solace from the fact that it was because you have done your jobs so well that you're here at all. Besides, you will both live on in the ultimate expression of my art. What better way to be remembered?'

'Not as a fecking glorified ashtray, it bloody isn't!' Joseph said.

'There, we'll have to agree to disagree,' Arthur replied. 'Now, if you'll excuse me, I need to turn on the fuel supply and fire up this old incinerator one last time. Farewell, and thank you for your selfless sacrifice to the fine arts.'

'I'll give you a bloody *sacrifice*,' Joseph shouted.

Megan exchanged a look with Joseph. 'Of all the ways I thought I might die—a car crash at high speed, shot in the line of duty, that sort of thing—I never imagined it would be barbecued alive.'

'And it won't be. We're not done yet. There has to be a way out of this fecking thing, some way to stop this thing from burning us alive.'

Megan pointed to the two holes in the walls on either side of them. 'That has to be where the flames will be coming from.'

'So, we need to block it with something, so the flames can't reach us,' Joseph said.

He pulled off his cagoule, and Megan quickly followed his lead, stuffing both garments into the parallel slots.

'I know my waterproof is pretty good at keeping out the rain, but it's not exactly fire retardant,' Megan said. 'At best, it will take the fire a minute to burn through it.'

'I know, but a minute is better than nothing.' Joseph's mind was racing. There had to be a way out of this hellhole.

He looked at a closed inspection hatch built in the end wall, but it was far too small to get through. Regardless, he tried pushing at it, but rather than move the hatch, the floor beneath them shifted a fraction. Looking down, he could see slight gaps on either side of the floor they were on.

'Hang on, if this is an animal incinerator, how did they load something as big as a cow into it?' Joseph said.

'A forklift?' Megan suggested.

'It would still be tricky to get a cow's carcass into this relatively confined space. But I have a hunch.' Joseph sat and braced his feet against a pillar in the wall and pushed. There was a loud squeal of rusty metal rubbing on rusty metal as the floor beneath them shifted a fraction. Joseph immediately realised what was probably happening. One more heave with his feet confirmed his theory. The platform moved a few centimetres before jamming into the far end of the chamber. 'Okay, I think I've got it. I think this floor we're on is actually a platform mounted on rollers. It can probably be pulled out so animal carcasses can be loaded onto it, before being slid back into the incinerator. That means I expect there's a door at the end the platform is jamming into with some sort of catch.'

Megan quickly nodded. 'That makes sense. So free that, and we can open the door?'

'It's certainly worth a shot.' Joseph began directing his torch's beam around the edges of the square door an he spotted a slight crack near the top. When he directed the light directly into the fissure, he could make out the dull surface of a metal rod just beneath the surface.

'Okay, this looks promising. But we need something thin and strong enough to excavate the brick with. I don't suppose you have a multi-tool on you?'

'Sadly not, but I do have this.' Megan handed her trusty baton to the DI. 'Guess Cleaves didn't think it was important.'

Joseph set to work, using its tip to chip away at the gap and showering him with fine brick dust.

They heard a clicking, followed by a whooshing. A second later, their two cagoules started to smoulder, and choking smoke rapidly filled the chamber.

Joseph exchanged a grim look with his colleague as they heard chanting coming from outside. Even now, Arthur was keeping up the pretence of this being part of a Pagan ritual. Maybe in the madman's mind, it was, but rather than securing a bumper crop, it was a sacrifice to the gods of creativity.

Trying to ignore the sense of dread coiling in his gut, the DI redoubled his efforts, driving the baton up harder and harder like a chisel into the brickwork. Ever-increasing lumps of brick broke free around the edges of the crack. Within thirty seconds, he'd done enough to reveal the metal rod linked to a hooked piece of metal in the growing fissure. The catch, it had to be. He just needed a bit longer to work it free. A glance at the cagoules starting to glow red in the flame-slits told him time was an asset in terribly short supply.

'Okay, let's try something else,' Joseph said. He shoved the end of Megan's baton into the hole again, but this time he used it like a lever. The DC quickly grabbed hold as well and together they heaved.

Just when Joseph was convinced the end of the baton was going to break clean off, there was a cracking sound and a much larger chunk of brick broke free, easily doubling the size of the hole. Joseph tried to reach the rod again, but couldn't quite get his fingers on either side of it.

'Let me try,' Megan said.

Joseph nodded and quickly made room for the DC.

Megan slid her slim fingers into the hole they'd opened up. Teeth clenched, she managed to grip the rod between her fingers. Then, millimetre by millimetre, she edged it forward.

The DI could just see the catch starting to rotate. 'You've got this. Keep going, Megan.'

With a roar, a spout of flame burst from the right-hand slot and Megan's cagoule gave up the uneven task of keeping the fire at bay.

Both of the detectives moved as close as they could to the door as the blue flames blazed into the chamber and the temperature soared. Megan didn't waste any time. She turned and stuck her fingers back into the hole, working hard at the metal rod, her hands trembling.

Joseph pressed his back against the door, bracing his legs against a brick column in the side wall, ready to push with all he had the moment the catch was released.

A bellow came from the second fire slot as Joseph's cagoule gave up as well, and a second jet of blue flame joined the first. The heat soared even higher, quickly burning away the oxygen in the chamber.

Joseph was already light-headed, mind becoming numb. *This is it,* he thought.

'Yes!' Megan's voice shouted. Then her face loomed over his as she shook his shoulders. 'Fucking push!'

The DI gritted his teeth, then, with his feet still jammed against the pillar, his muscles quivering, he pushed his back hard into the door. Megan added her strength to his and together, they pushed.

With a squeal, a crack of light emerged. It was followed by a glorious deluge of rain hitting the tops of their heads. They continued to push the trolley open centimetre by centimetre.

Just when a spark of hope had filled Joseph's heart, and he'd redoubled his efforts, a pair of gloved hands appeared at the lip of the door and the platform came to a shuddering stop.

'Literally, over my dead body,' Joseph called out, lifting the baton and smashing it hard onto the exposed fingertips. They heard a strangled cry as the hand was snatched away. Moments later, they heard a second shout followed by a loud thud.

That was all the encouragement the detectives needed. Working together, before the potter had a chance to try to stop them again, they pushed the trolley out into the thunderstorm. The cold air rushed in, sucking some of the heat from the furnace with a blast of winter air.

Charlotte stood over them, her hand outstretched, first helping Megan and then Joseph off the furnace trolley.

The DI took in Arthur's crumpled form lying at the farmer's feet, a discarded shovel next to his body. Then, for just a moment, he thought he was seeing double. Two nearly identical Land Rovers were parked side by side a short distance away. Then his brain caught up. One was Arthur's doppelgänger version of the farmer's actual vehicle.

Megan knelt beside Arthur, checking his pulse.

'Don't worry, he'll live,' Charlotte said, looking down at the prone man with anger in her eyes. 'I only hit him hard enough to knock him out, although he deserves far worse, considering what he was trying to do to you.' She looked at each of them. 'Are you both okay?'

Joseph nodded. 'As good as can be expected almost being turned into an overdone roast.'

Megan nodded, 'All things considered, fine, apart from the fact I just lost a brand new cagoule.'

Joseph gave her a sardonic smile. 'I'll get you a new one, my shout.'

The farmer gave them a confused look just as pulsing blue lights came from the hillside below them. Joseph glanced down to see yet another Land Rover, albeit a police one this time, race around the side of Shadowbrook Farm and head straight up the hill towards them.

'I thought you might appreciate some backup,' Charlotte said, gesturing towards the fast-approaching vehicle. 'Luckily for you, I've been keeping an eye on our mutual friend here. I had my suspicions about him after I heard Margaret was murdered. I parked out at the top of the hill and was keeping an eye on his place when you two turned up. After he loaded you into the back of his Land Rover, I followed him back here to the old incinerator. It seems just as well I did.'

'We owe you our lives,' Megan said.

Charlotte shook her head as the police Land Rover skidded to a stop. 'No, I think you had the situation pretty much in hand, although I'd like to think I helped a bit in the end.'

'Aye, the fact we got out of there without suffering any burns is testimony to that,' Joseph said, looking at the flames still flickering in the furnace.

'Then I'm glad to be of service,' Charlotte said, as Chris, Ian, and Sue rushed over.

Chris gave the other Land Rovers a confused look. 'What the hell has been going on here?'

'A Land Rover meet-up, boss,' Megan replied, giving Joseph a look.

He laughed, drawing in big lungfuls of the sweetest air he'd ever tasted in his life.

CHAPTER THIRTY

Chris looked out at the investigation team gathered in the incident room. 'Just to let you know, Cleaves's vase collection has now been seized for evidence.'

'What's going to happen to them, considering they contain human remains?' Ian asked.

'Apart from taking samples for analysis, I suspect they'll end up being destroyed out of respect for the families. In total, there are twenty-two victims, the same number as the Ethereal Amphora vase range, each one containing an individual's remains. Thankfully, Arthur kept all the news clippings about his victim's disappearances in his desk drawer, which has made our lives considerably easier.'

Sue shook her head. 'So much for the sum of a supposed great artist's life's work.'

'Yes, Arthur wasn't exactly thrilled to hear the fate of his vases when we interviewed him in hospital,' Joseph said.

'I bet he wasn't. That aside, was he cooperative?'

Joseph nodded. 'Very. He's still deluded enough to believe, at least in his mind, that he was doing the right thing in the pursuit of creating great art.'

'In what universe is murdering someone just so they can end up in a pot, ever the right thing?' John asked.

'That's insanity for you,' Megan replied.

'At least we did learn one other thing from him, and that was about the disappearance of Mike Clifford,' Chris said. 'Cleaves admitted to murdering Charlotte's husband. Said he forced him to write a letter, saying he was leaving her, then he killed him. Cleaves even temporarily moved into the boardinghouse Mike supposedly gave Charlotte the address for, pretending to be Mike, before pulling his final vanishing act. That way, there wasn't any suspicion of him being murdered.'

'Why did Cleaves kill Mike in the first place?' one of the other detectives asked.

'When Arthur discovered Mike was having an affair with Sally Blanchard behind Charlotte's back, he took matters into his own hands. He abducted Sally, murdered her, and then burned her body. Initially, he gave Mike the benefit of the doubt, but when he continued to have a string of affairs, Arthur finally decided enough was enough and murdered him.'

'What about the ritualistic aspect of the murders?' John asked.

'That was purely subterfuge, even down to wearing druid-type robes,' Chris replied. 'It was all playacting to make sure Charlotte would take the fall if the remains were ever discovered.'

'So you've got a signed confession for all of this, then?' Derrick asked from the back of the room, where he'd materialised out of nowhere. Joseph sometimes wondered if the DSU had been a magician in a former life.

'Just a recording for now, but we don't anticipate any trouble getting a formal confession when he's eventually released into our custody from hospital,' Chris replied.

'Then a job very well done indeed, even if the wild goose

chase for Charlotte Harris seriously dented my budget and wasted resources,' Derrick replied.

'We didn't know she was innocent at the time,' Joseph said before Chris had a chance to reply.

'Maybe, but if you had managed to bring her into custody in the first place, we would have worked that out sooner rather than later.' Derrick gave Joseph a pointed look.

Even though Joseph knew that the DSU was actually an ally, he still had a knack for being a right royal pain in the arse sometimes.

'Anyway, that aside, you all did a good day's work and you should all call it a night,' Derrick continued. 'Then I expect you all to meet me at Wallace's for an early morning breakfast; on me. It might have taken us a while to get there, but ultimately this is a good result and a serial killer will be locked away for a very long time indeed. So let's celebrate the moment whilst we can. See you first thing tomorrow, ladies and gentlemen.'

Several officers in the room were trading surprised looks, especially Megan, who was giving Joseph a wide-eyed—*what the hell just happened*—look.

But the DI was distracted, considering how the big man had changed. Maybe, out of all this Night Watchmen mess, Derrick was finally starting to remember that he was a good copper at heart and his sharp edges were softening.

Then the DSU locked eyes with Joseph. 'Of course, there's always going to be an exception. Somehow you managed to put yourself and your colleague in harm's way.' Just like that, all attention was back on the DI.

Megan shook her head, 'It wasn't like that, sir—'

Derrick made a chopping movement with his hand. 'I don't want to hear you making excuses for him.'

Chris scowled. 'No, Megan's right. Joseph believed he was

protecting Arthur Cleaves from Charlotte Harris. Not the other way—'

The superintendent made the chopping motion again and glared at him. 'I don't want to hear your excuses for him, either. Stone, follow me.'

Joseph did as he was told, shrugging to the others as he followed the big man out of the room. So, it seemed a leopard couldn't change his spots after all.

He followed Derrick into his office like a disobedient dog, and waited while he closed the door behind him.

Joseph stood tall, hands clasped behind his back. 'Look, before you break my balls again...' But his words trailed away as Derrick raised his palms.

'Sorry about that, Joseph, but we do need to keep up the charade.'

The DI dragged his hand through his hair. 'Aye, I suppose we do. So what's this really about?'

'I just had a very interesting chat with Chief Superintendent Kennan. It turns out she wants our investigation notes on a number of small local drug gangs. I'm guessing that she's checking whether I'm still loyal to the cause. I've been instructed to drop off a memory stick with the information at the old Blake's Brewery on the outskirts of Banbury. No doubt they'll use this as further leverage to keep me in line.'

'As though threatening your wife's life isn't enough.'

Derrick sighed. 'I know, but maybe they've heard about our separation and just want to make sure I keep behaving myself. Anyway, your rather misguided attempt to gather video evidence actually gave me an idea.'

Joseph was already shaking his head. 'It's not worth the risk of planting another trail cam. You know the hot water that landed me in.'

'Yes, but there's more than one way to crack an egg. I was

looking at a satellite map view of the brewery. There's a nearby wood on a hill that overlooks it. Say, someone was up there with a camera and a powerful telephoto lens borrowed from the equipment store...'

'Whoa, there. I've already put my neck on the line, not to mention my daughter's, with my own foolhardy attempt to gather evidence.'

'I know, but this could be the breakthrough we've been looking for. After all, if Chris picked up the last drop, there's every chance he could do it again. Don't you want to be able to get hold of the evidence that confirms once and for all that he's working for the Night Watchmen?'

Joseph stared mutely back at the DSU. It was a good question, because even now he felt conflicted about the man's guilt. But this way, he might get the evidence to prove it.

'Okay, I'll ask Kate to take herself and Ellie off on a weekend retreat. Something like a spa experience. That way we can get them both safely out of the picture until we know how this pans out.'

'Good man. Look, I know how risky this is, but I wouldn't even be suggesting it if I didn't think it was worth it.'

Joseph blew out his cheeks. 'I just pray you're right about that.'

Joseph's old cagoule he'd been forced to wear after he'd lost his last one in the incinerator, was anything but waterproof. In the rain dripping down from the branches of the tree he was crouched beneath on the edge of the wood, it was almost like the damned garment was acting like a sponge, making his clothes even wetter. A trip to an outdoor shop was going to be at the top of his to-do list after he was done with this.

The DI had wrapped a plastic bag around the super-sized lens he'd picked up from the equipment locker at work, along with the large frame format SLR camera. He peered through its viewfinder down the slope at the abandoned brewery below him. Derrick, true to his word, had already been and gone. Joseph had watched the big man drop the memory stick off under an upturned bucket near the broken-down entrance to the brewery as he'd been instructed, before heading away again in his car. That had been two hours ago.

After everything that had happened, Joseph was exhausted, but he was determined to stay the course and wait for whoever would show up. Under any other circumstances, the DI would have collapsed happily into his bed. But this was far too important to give in to the fatigue.

With the view of the brewery framed in the viewfinder, he panned the camera over the ruined building below him, bounded by a security fence.

The large red brick building would certainly have been imposing back in the day with its towering arched windows. Now, most of the brewery had been swallowed by ivy and half of its walls were missing. However, the most significant damage was to what had been a tall chimney at the back. It had collapsed into a line of rubble stretching out from where it had once stood. Just to finish off the general look of the ruins, small waterfalls of rainwater were emptying from broken guttering into the yard in front of the building. They had created deep puddles that, over the course of the DI's surveillance, had run together to form a small lake.

He didn't doubt that, with its proximity to Banbury, what remained of this building would be restored to its former glory and converted into flats at some point. But today certainly wasn't that day, and the building's former elegance was rapidly becoming a distant memory.

Another shiver ran through Joseph as he heard the distant sound of a car approaching down the same track that Derrick had used earlier. Half expecting to see Chris's TR4 come into view, the DI's heart rate quickened. But what he saw instead was a black Audi A4 with low-profile wheels. Probably the performance S model, based on the distinctive growl of its engine.

So, if it isn't Chris... he thought, as the vehicle pulled up to the gate.

Joseph kept the lens trained on it, finger poised above the shutter release. Then the passenger door opened, and a man got out, jogging through the rain and up to the gate, dragging it open.

The DI managed to get several clear shots of the broad-shouldered figure, zooming in on his face as he turned around.

The air caught in Joseph's throat. He was as sure as he could be that it was Greg Carlton, a DCI from the Cowley station on the other side of Oxford.

So he's one of the Night Watchmen's inside men? Joseph thought. *But who's driving the vehicle, then? Chris?*

Greg pushed the gate open and waved the vehicle through. As the Audi drove past, Joseph watched through the camera lens as the man raised what looked like some sort of telescope to his eye.

'Get your head down!' a voice growled from behind him.

Joseph turned to see Chris crouched just behind him, a camera clutched in his hands.

'What the feck?' the DI replied, shock surging through him.

'I said, get bloody down or you'll blow this whole operation.' Chris shoved Joseph hard in the back, pushing him prone onto the wet ground, and hurling himself flat as well.

Joseph turned his head and watched as Chris crawled up alongside him.

'I don't understand. What the hell is going on here?' he whispered.

'I'll explain everything later, but right now, the priority is for us not to get spotted. That's an image intensifier Carlton is using. Even in the shadows of these woods, he would have spotted you standing there as though you hadn't a bloody care in the world. So if you want an explanation, don't move a muscle and just watch how this all unfolds.'

The DI, his mind a storm of confusion, did as he was told, keeping himself pressed to the ground. But, mentally, he sighed with relief. Whatever Chris was, he wasn't a bent copper. His sense of relief was so palpable he felt the weight dissolve.

The DCI had his own camera pointed down at the scene below them, and Joseph cautiously followed his boss's lead. Carlton was sweeping his scope along the tree line but thankfully didn't stop when he pointed it toward the spot where the two officers were hiding at the edge of the woods.

Behind him, the Audi had stopped inside the yard. Joseph zoomed in on the driver's door as it opened.

His mind locked up as he saw the person who got out. It couldn't be. But there she was, striding straight towards the bucket and turning it over.

Amy.

'No...' he whispered to himself.

'I'm so sorry you had to find out this way, Joseph,' Chris said.

Joseph barely heard the words as he watched her brandish the memory stick at Carlton, before heading back to the car, grinning widely.

Joseph took several photos before turning towards his colleague. 'You're telling me that Amy is working for the Night Watchmen?'

'There's a lot I'm going to need to debrief you on.'

'And what about you?'

'Like I said, there's a lot to tell you.'

They watched Amy drive back through the gate and Carlton close it behind her, before climbing into the vehicle.

Chris continued to take photos as the vehicle drove away and Joseph tried to come to terms with this new reality. His boss hadn't been the one to betray him, but his girlfriend had.

CHAPTER THIRTY-ONE

After Joseph had dropped the Peugeot that Derrick had signed out for him back at St Aldates, Chris had joined him on *Tús Nua*. Having given them both up as a bad job when it came to getting any attention, Tux had taken himself off to the DI's bed to sleep.

Joseph held his almost cold mug of coffee he'd barely taken a sip from. 'So let me get this right. Amy, the woman who I have been dating and thought I knew, is actually working for the Night Watchmen?'

'I'm afraid so and, as far as we can tell, she has been for a long time.'

'We?'

'I suppose there's no point in not telling you now. I'm NCA. I've been working undercover at St Aldates.'

'Shite on a fecking bike. Seriously?'

'Seriously. The NCA became aware of some of the Night Watchmen's activities a number of years ago. At first, we thought they were just another crime syndicate. But the more we looked into them, the more we realised they were a lot more than just another professional gang. Money is simply a means to an end for them.'

'That end being?'

'In a word, power. Their ambition is to become untouchable, taking out any rival gangs that get in their way.'

'Like the Shotgun Raiders?'

'Exactly. And it seems, they're moving on to the small-fry drug gangs. If they don't bend the knee and become part of the Night Watchman's distribution network, they'll be eliminated. Faced with that choice, especially when no one will question what they're capable of after how they dealt with the Shotgun Raiders, they'll all fall into line soon enough.'

'In other words, they want to become the biggest bully on the block.'

'I'm afraid it's far more than that, Joseph. When I said it was all about power, I really meant it. The Night Watchmen already have a number of senior judges in their pocket, and several politicians, too. There are even hints that some elements of our armed forces may even be compromised as well.'

'Fecking hell. What are we talking about here, a coup?'

'Maybe not quite as extreme as that, but enough real influence to make sure their crime syndicate is untouchable.'

'Jesus, and this is where Chief Superintendent Kennan's ascent must come in?'

Chris gave Joseph an impressed look. 'So you know about her involvement?'

'I've not exactly been sitting on my arse either. I followed a colleague to a clandestine meeting with her, and watched the woman offer them a bribe, which, I'm pleased to report, they refused.'

'By colleague, I assume you mean Derrick Walker?'

Joseph did his best to give the DCI a blank look. 'Sorry?'

A smile curled the corners of Chris's mouth. 'Don't worry, I know all about our DSU's involvement and how the Night Watchmen have manipulated him. We also know it was Derrick who handed over the information to them about the Darryl Manning prisoner transfer. And before you ask, we only found out about that after the event. Our intelligence indicated he was one of the senior officers in the Thames Valley Police who had been corrupted.'

'Okay, there's obviously no point in denying it. But you do know he was blackmailed, right? They threatened Kate's life.'

'Yes, we're well familiar with the Night Watchmen's coercion techniques, just as they did with you and your daughter.'

'For feck's sake, you knew about that and didn't do anything?'

'I didn't say that. We have had officers keeping an eye on your daughter for a while now; ever since you received that threat.'

'You mean the man Ellie spotted following her was one of yours?'

'Yes, although he realised she'd clocked him and his cover had been blown.'

Joseph couldn't help but smile at hearing that. 'Once a policeman's daughter, always a policeman's daughter. She has a good instinct on her.'

'Maybe she should consider working for the NCA.'

'No disrespect, but over my fecking dead body, boss.'

Chris chuckled. 'Point taken. Anyway, am I right in thinking that you and Derrick have been working together to expose what the Night Watchmen have been up to?'

'That's about the measure of it. But you should also know that Kate and Dylan have been helping out, too.'

The DCI simply nodded. 'That doesn't surprise me. Not Megan, then?'

Joseph shrugged. 'I didn't want to compromise what I'm sure is going to be a meteoric career.'

'I agree, she's destined for great things, so keeping her out of it makes sense. But what I'm intrigued about is not once did you place your trust in me. I thought we were mates?'

Joseph grimaced. 'How could I, when I thought you might be working for them? I spotted you staking out St Barnabas Church where I did the drop. If you're going to arrest Derrick, you might as well arrest me too. I was the one who handed over sensitive material about the Shotgun Raiders gang to them.'

Chris raised his eyebrows at him. 'I don't think so, especially when you have gone out of your way to try and build a case on them.'

'But surely your superiors will insist on heads rolling once your investigation is completed?'

'Who says they need to know anything about you and the memory stick?'

'Sorry, you're saying you haven't reported it to them?'

'Other than that they were trying to coerce you, no. Apart from anything else, I defy anyone to not act like you did when being blackmailed with their daughter's life. A court of law might have eventually reached the same conclusion. But why take the chance of throwing away the career of one of the finest officers I've ever had the honour of working with?'

Joseph looked at the man to check he wasn't taking the piss, but his expression seemed genuine enough. 'Bad habits and all, hey?'

A smile cracked Chris's face. 'Bad habits and all. But I'm afraid I won't be able to offer the same level of protection to Derrick. The NCA was already well aware that he'd been compromised.'

'But I literally have evidence of him refusing a bribe, not to mention the fact he alerted me about tonight's drop so I could capture photographic evidence of it.'

'Which will all count in his favour. But at best, it will result in a plea bargain, especially if he's prepared to give evidence against the Night Watchmen. However it goes, I'm afraid we're still looking at the end of his career here, even if he's just forced to take early retirement.'

'There's really nothing else you can do?'

'I'll certainly do everything in my power to protect him, but I'm afraid that boat has already sailed.'

'Well, if it helps, I'm more than happy to stand as a character witness for the man.'

'Despite the very obvious grudge he's held against you at work?'

Joseph shrugged. 'What can I say? Times have changed.'

'Well, you're a bigger man than I am. Anyway, time to discuss another subject.' Chris took out Joseph's trail cam and handed it back to him. 'I can't believe the risk you took trying to use this. If they had spotted it, you would probably be in a shallow grave by now.'

Joseph gave the DCI a dumbfounded look. 'You did a sweep of the church before they arrived?'

'Afterwards, I'm afraid. Luckily for you, they weren't quite as thorough as I was. But knowing you, I suspected you'd try something, and it seems I was right. That's why I left you a note warning you to stay in your lane. I needed you to believe the crime syndicate had left it for you.' He took out his phone and clicked on the screen. 'Would you like to see the footage?'

Even as Joseph nodded, he already knew what he was about to see. Sure enough, when Chris turned the phone's screen towards him, Joseph's stomach clenched. There was Amy, heading up the stairs into the pulpit and reaching under the lectern. She withdrew the memory stick from its hiding place and slipped it into her pocket, before heading away again.

Joseph felt the back of his eyes stinging and had to squeeze the bridge of his nose to prevent the tears from spilling. 'How could she do this to me?'

Chris patted him on the shoulder. 'What I'm about to tell you is going to be difficult to hear, Joseph, but you need to hear it anyway. I'm afraid Amy has been corrupt for some time. It seems she has expensive tastes and her head was easily turned by the Night Watchmen when they first approached her.'

'Sorry, but I don't understand. Why would the Night Watchman want a scene of crime officer on their payroll?'

'Really? Just think about it.'

Joseph turned the idea over in his mind, and then he sighed. 'Because she'd be the right person in the right place to make sure that any incriminating evidence disappeared.'

Chris nodded. 'Correct. We have a number of suspicions surrounding specific cases where Amy was involved. Crime scenes we believe had a connection to the Night Watchman, including most recently the Shotgun Raiders' ambush in the Abingdon Bank job. DNA evidence from their man who was wounded mysteriously went missing in the lab.'

Joseph felt like his grip on what he thought was reality, was starting to slip away. 'So you're saying they paid Amy to make sure key evidence from crime scenes went missing?'

'That's the measure of it. Missing DNA evidence and a whole lot more besides.'

The DI clenched his fists, nails pressing into his palms just enough to ground himself. His thoughts became sharper, more focused. Then he took a slow, deep breath, trying to steady the growing tension within him. How could Amy have betrayed them all, let alone him, like that?

'Jesus H. Christ. I would be arguing with you tooth and nail that you'd got your facts mixed up, if I hadn't witnessed Amy picking up the memory stick tonight,' he finally said.

'At least you know the truth now, Joseph. But we've come to maybe the most uncomfortable aspect of this investigation...'

There was something in the DCI's tone that raised the hairs on the back of Joseph's neck. 'Go on?'

'I'm afraid your relationship with her is not what it seems. You see, you're not the first detective Amy has dated. It's something of a honey trap. Once she was convinced you were really onboard and could be manipulated to join their ranks, any pretence of a relationship with you almost certainly would have been dropped.'

A deep chill settled in Joseph's chest and spread like ice water through his veins. 'Shite, you're saying she was sleeping with me just to recruit me?'

'We can't be totally sure of that, but it's kind of her MO.'

Joseph blinked, trying to process the words, each one cutting like a blade into his soul. Then the DI's mind returned to what they'd both witnessed outside the abandoned brewery. 'Was DCI Carlton one of her conquests?'

'Yes, and he's a married man, but she still managed to lure him into an affair that I'm afraid to tell you is still very much alive and flourishing.'

Joseph slowly shook his head as he stared at his knuckles. 'I've been played, haven't I?'

'As I said, we can't be sure, but it's hard not to reach that conclusion. There's something else you need to know, and that's about Carlton. We have intelligence to indicate he was one of the men who ambushed your prisoner convoy with Daryl Manning.'

A tidal wave of memories hit Joseph—one of the masked men spraying the cab of the police van with bullets, followed by the prisoner compartment of the vehicle. Then the broad-shouldered guy, who he now knew had to have been Carlton, wagged his finger at him and Megan, admonishing them to keep down or risk being shot.

A knot of fury blazed in his gut and the DI's eyes narrowed to slits.

'And you haven't fecking arrested him?'

'It would have compromised a Night Watchmen informant we recruited from the Met. If we had, it would have tipped them off about our source. Not only would our informant have been murdered, but our whole investigation would have been blown. As difficult as this situation is, we still need more time to gather intelligence so we can be sure to root out everything the crime syndicate is involved in once and for all. From police officers to judges, and everything in between.'

'So that includes letting me, like a right eejit, hand over intelligence that Amy then scooped up? Evidence that led directly to the slaughter of the Shotgun Raiders gang on the high street in Abingdon?'

Chris's shoulders sagged. 'Our intelligence indicated they would just be recruited into the Night Watchman, just another cog in their machine. We found out too late that the gang had already rejected them. That's why the Night Watchmen decided to eliminate them and make it look like part of a turf war. Please believe me, if I'd had any idea about what really was going to happen, I would have done everything I could to stop it.'

Joseph remembered the haunted look the DCI had at the bank robbery crime scene. In hindsight, he realised just how traumatic it must have been for the man.

His gaze softened on Chris. 'Carrying all this on your shoulders must be one hell of a burden, especially with how things ended up unfolding.'

'It is, and it keeps me up at night, Joseph. I keep second-guessing myself, how we might have avoided such a monumental screw-up like that, just like I felt when Manning was killed and we had two officers injured. That's why I'm determined to make sure everyone in that organisation pays. The question is, do you want to help me?'

'How exactly?'

'Specifically, you need to keep up the pretence of being in a relationship with Amy, so she doesn't think you're onto her.'

'Hang on, are you seriously suggesting I keep sleeping with her so she doesn't get suspicious?'

'I can't tell you what to do, but if you can't bear to be with her any longer, then for God's sake, come up with a convincing reason to leave her, like still being in love with Kate.'

'Right...'

Chris held up his hands. 'This is your decision and no one else's. The most important thing is that Amy is kept in the dark about what you know.'

'I'll certainly do my best,' Joseph replied, with absolutely no idea what he was going to do. It was all too startling, too raw, to fully process yet.

'So how am I meant to play this with Derrick, Kate, and Dylan?' the DI asked next.

'You need to keep our conversation to yourself for now. When the time is right, we can bring them in, but this isn't that moment. Kate, specifically, really does need to back off. Whatever influence you have with her, use it, because make no mistake, she is putting herself in very real danger.'

'Which is easier said than done. My ex-wife is a force of nature, especially after Ellie's life was threatened.'

'Just do what you can, for Kate's sake.'

'I'll try. But what about me? What do you expect me to do? Sit on my hands pretending we never had this meeting, and play nice with the likes of Chief Kennan and DCI Carlton?'

Chris tilted his head to one side as he gave Joseph an appraising look. 'That's the real question, isn't it? Do you want to be a bystander in this, watching how things play out from the sidelines, Joseph? Or do you want to be actively involved in the investigation?'

'How exactly?'

'By working with me. I couldn't think of another officer I'd rather have by my side. Besides, could you really stand not knowing what was going on with my investigation?'

For the first time, a real smile cracked the DI's face. 'Aye, you might have a point there. Count me in. After all, this all got very personal for me a while back, and I want to see it through.'

'Good man, although I had more than a hunch you'd say that.'

Joseph looked at the DCI appraisingly. 'I do have one question, though. I know you said that Amy played me, but what about you, Chris? Was this whole business of getting me to help you restore your car simply a way of finding out if I was on the level?'

'At first, maybe. I knew what my instinct said about you, but I needed to be sure. For what it's worth, I do actually consider you a mate now.'

'That's good to know because the feeling's mutual.'

This time the DCI smiled. 'If it wasn't the middle of the night I'd suggest a toast, but I need to get back to my bed. We'll both be expected to attend Derrick's breakfast celebration at Wallace's.'

'Aye, I suppose we do have something to celebrate.'

'We do.' As Chris stood and slipped on his jacket, he reached out his hand. 'Here's to bringing those Night Watchman bastards down, not to mention catching a major serial killer.'

Joseph shook the proffered hand. 'Amen to that, my friend.'

With a nod, Chris headed out and closed the cabin door behind him.

As Joseph sat back in his seat, his gaze fell upon a photo of him and Amy she'd stuck on the wall behind the sink. It was all he could do not to march over and rip it into tiny pieces. Of all the revelations, it was her betrayal that hurt the most. Joseph already knew, whatever happened, he was never going to be able to forgive her for that.

CHAPTER THIRTY-TWO

It had been a surreal day at work for Joseph. Everyone was in a celebratory mood about Arthur Cleaves finally being brought to justice. The DI had done his best to look upbeat and join in, but the revelation about Amy was still sitting heavily on his shoulders. Even more so since they were meant to be going to the Dancing Frog Thai restaurant for their regular date night later. The fact that it was still on after she'd barged in on him and Kate would have come as a surprise. But after what Chris had told him, he'd been less than surprised to receive her text saying she was looking forward to seeing him later at the restaurant.

Of course you fecking are, he'd thought.

That was why he was sitting opposite Amy as she ate her starter, a green papaya salad, and he pushed his steamed prawn dumplings around on his plate. So far he'd only managed to eat a single dumpling. He felt physically sick sitting opposite a woman he found almost impossible to maintain eye contact with.

Despite what he'd promised Chris, he wasn't sure he was going to be able to play along, especially since he now knew that

Greg Carlton's bed would be waiting for his girlfriend. Maybe that was the real reason that they'd had so few date nights. Joseph had thought it was just because their work schedules had always clashed. Now he wasn't so sure.

'So, great news about the Cleaves case,' Amy said, trying to get a conversation going for the third time.

Joseph continued to push the dumplings around his plate with his chopsticks. 'Yes, we got there in the end.'

'Thank God for that. From what I've been hearing on the grapevine, Cleaves was deranged enough to believe he was actually doing his victims a favour by immortalising them in his pots. How sick must someone be to believe that could ever justify murder?'

'Aye...'

Amy dropped her fork onto the plate. 'Oh, for God's sake! Will you please look at me, Joseph?'

With a major mental effort, he raised his gaze to hers, fighting hard to keep the ember of anger burning in his chest from engulfing him. He shrugged. 'Sorry, it's been a long, long week.'

'Is that all?'

Joseph's guard went up. 'What do you mean?'

'For goodness sake, stop with all the play-acting.'

Joseph literally felt his stomach plummeting towards the ground until the next words came out of her mouth.

Her eyes bored into his. 'This is all about Kate, isn't it? Look, we need to talk about what happened.'

Under other circumstances, Joseph would have been filled with a sense of guilt, but he wasn't living in that world anymore.

When Joseph didn't say anything, Amy pushed on. 'I know there will always be a thing between you two, and I have to learn to accept that. Maybe I overreacted, but I love you so much. I know we can put this behind us.'

Love, there's a joke if I ever heard it, he thought bitterly. This was obviously all part of her play to reel him back in.

He stared across the table at the woman who was increasingly becoming a stranger to him by the minute. The same woman he'd laughed with more times than he could count, a woman he thought he would always be able to rely on, a woman he'd even made love to under the light of the stars on a hot summer's night. All of it lies, a mirage that Amy had conjured to make him think they could have a life together, all the while playing him for a fool.

When Joseph still didn't respond, Amy frowned and reached across the table towards him. Any pretence that things were even vaguely okay was washed away when he flinched away from her touch.

Amy stared at him open-mouthed as though he'd just physically slapped her. 'I see,' she whispered, the tears of an actor filling the eyes of someone Joseph had never seen cry before.

She withdrew her hand, eyes blinking. 'Please, Joseph, we can get past this.'

Normally the DI would have melted seeing Amy's distress, but he knew this was all part of the act, too. He could barely look at her now without feeling his skin crawl. The problem was he needed to keep his word to Chris and not jeopardise the entire NCA investigation. Thankfully, he already had an out.

Now it was his turn to put on a performance. 'I'm sorry, Amy, but I realise now I'm still very much in love with Kate. You know as much already.'

She nodded slowly. 'But that doesn't mean there isn't room for me in your life.'

'I wish that were the case, I haven't got room in my heart for a new relationship. I'm sorry, Amy, but we're going to have to end it.'

It was Amy's turn to stare mutely back at him before finally finding her voice. 'Please don't do this, Joseph.'

Even though he knew the truth about the SOCO, he found himself wavering for a moment when he saw the pleading look in her eyes. But then his resolve hardened. No, it had to be this way.

'Sorry, this way will be easier for both of us in the long run. I'm just trying to be honest with you.'

Amy's nostrils flared as a single tear ran down her cheek. Without saying another word, she put her napkin down on the table and stood. She held his gaze for a moment and then, shaking her head, walked straight out of the restaurant.

Joseph could easily imagine that once Amy was far enough away from the restaurant, her expression would morph from one of heartbreak to one of anger that a man she'd used, had just rejected her. He hung onto that mental image, because it was a lot easier to deal with than the face of the woman who'd looked broken to her core.

A waiter materialised before Joseph. 'Is everything okay, sir?'

'Grand. Can I have the bill please?' Joseph replied.

The waiter pointed to the almost full bamboo box of dumplings still on the table. 'Would you like those to go?'

When the DI looked at them he had to swallow down the bile rising in his throat. 'No, I'm grand. Thanks all the same.'

Joseph sat back in his chair as the waiter headed away, feeling like all the other diners' eyes were on him.

Dylan was just fixing up a new caged bird feeder when Joseph appeared, heading towards *Tús Nua*.

After the confrontation with Amy, Joseph was doing his best

not to draw his friend's attention and just slip into his boat to escape the world. However, Max and White Fang had a different idea. They sped towards him, barking their greeting as they came, seemingly oblivious to the fact that the approaching human was carrying the weight of the world on his shoulders.

But their owner was far more astute than his two canine charges, who sat before Joseph, looking up at him expectantly.

'What's wrong?' Dylan asked.

Joseph briefly toyed with the idea of his go-to, *I've got a migraine coming on,* excuse. But the professor's eyes were searching his face, and he knew from experience his friend would see straight through that explanation. He might not be able to tell Dylan about Chris being an NCA agent, but he could share part of what had just happened.'

He took a mental breath and met his friend's expectant gaze. 'It seems I've just broken up with Amy.'

Dylan put down the bird feeder that Raffles was watching from a nearby tree, with what probably amounted to an amused expression for a squirrel.

'I'm so sorry, Joseph.'

'Aye, that makes two of us.'

'You better tell me all about it over a glass of something,' Dylan said.

Joseph raised his shoulders. 'I'm not sure I'd be great company at the moment.'

'Don't worry, you don't need to be. However, if I have any skill, it's that I'm a good listener. Besides, I have just the gin to help with a broken heart.'

Joseph gave his friend a skeptical look. 'What, it's so strong I'll pass out and forget all my troubles?'

'That sounds more the remit of moonshine. No. I was thinking of the bottle of Monkey 47 gin, distilled in no less a place than the Black Forest in Germany.'

'And exactly what secret ingredient does it have for it to be the perfect pairing for a man who feels like his soul has been ground down into the ground?'

Without missing a beat, Dylan smiled. 'The forty-seven botanicals are such a complicated, nuanced flavour you will be too busy thinking about them to wallow in your own pit of despair.'

The corners of the DI's mouth turned upwards. '*Wallowing,* now is it?'

'Well, you do have a face like someone who's been slapped with a wet fish.'

Joseph snorted. 'Fair play to you and your colourful metaphor, Dylan. But I think, in this instance, I do have a good reason, wallowing and all.'

Dylan nodded. ' Yes, I suppose you do. Certainly, you and Amy seemed really good together.'

'That's what I thought, too,' Joseph replied with a flat tone.

'Okay, let's get some good quality gin down you and talk this all through.'

Joseph nodded, realising he really did need the company of a good friend right then.

Dylan gave a sharp whistle and both dogs, along with Tux, who emerged from behind the tree where he'd been keeping a beady eye on Raffles, all fell in behind him as they headed into *Avalon's* cabin.

For the first time, Dylan had been proved wrong. Joseph had barely registered the taste of the Monkey 47 as the professor gave him the space to talk. Throughout his monologue, Joseph's gaze had been fixed firmly on the flames flickering in the professor's stove as he recounted what had happened in the restaurant.

For once, probably sensing his human needed a bit of moral support, Tux had chosen his lap over the professor's as Joseph had talked.

The DI had recounted a highly edited version of events, with any mention of Amy's connection to the Night Watchmen left out, not to mention Chris being an undercover NCA agent. However, he did tell the professor that he'd come across information that proved the DCI hadn't been compromised after all. That gem had been met with some considerable relief from this friend. So for a straight thirty minutes, the focus of the words spilling out of his mouth had been about Amy, until finally, he had run out of things to say and finished the last of his untasted gin.

The silence lingered between the two men as the professor kept his gaze on the flames, before he finally lifted his eyes to Joseph.

'So did Amy confirm she'd been sleeping with this DCI Carlton chap from the Cowley station?'

'I didn't actually bring it up, but trust me that information comes from a very reliable source.'

'I see. But you haven't given Amy a chance to defend herself from this accusation?'

'It's not an accusation, it's a fact, Dylan.'

The professor took a sip of his gin as he gave Joseph a thoughtful look over the brim of the glass. 'Even so, based on what you haven't actually said, I get the impression you were more than ready to throw the towel in. Why is that exactly, Joseph?'

Just like that, the DI realised this amateur detective had got to the meat in the sandwich and there was no way he could duck the question.

'It's like this. You see, Amy, wasn't the only one who was being unfaithful, although, in my defence, it was never physical.'

Dylan narrowed his gaze on his friend. 'We're talking about Kate here, aren't we?'

Joseph nodded. 'Of course we are. I know this won't be news to you, even after the heartbreak of Eoin's death and then the divorce, I've never stopped loving her.'

'And she, you,' Dylan replied, as though it was a fact that everyone knew.

Joseph sat forward in his chair. 'You really believe that?'

'Have you ever seen you two together? The ease and the warmth you still have is undeniable. The way you still look at each other when you think the other one isn't looking. It's as deep a love as I've ever seen between two people. There's a thread that seems to always draw you back to each other however hard you try to lead separate lives. As far as I'm concerned, that's the real definition of love. What you have now are the embers that remain after that first flush of a relationship. For some lucky people, like you two, that deepens into something so much more. The only reason you're not still together is because of the aftermath of losing Eoin. Then Kate found some form of healing in Derrick's arms, and you, until recently, in the solitude of your boat.'

'Bloody hell, have you been rehearsing this speech?'

Dylan smiled. 'Maybe for a while. I notice you're not denying it either?'

'How could I? We both know it's the truth. Also, and I haven't told you this yet, but when Kate was over here we almost had a moment.'

'What do you mean by *a moment*?'

'I mean, I think we were about to fall into each other's arms when Amy walked in on us. Although nothing had actually happened at that point, she was more than able to sense what might have given more time.'

'I see. And was that why you broke up with her?'

Joseph paused before answering, looking down at Tux as he stroked the back of the cat's head. He needed a moment to compose a watered-down version of what really happened. But that was the thing. Maybe after that moment with Kate, there was no chance of a future with Amy. The truth was, his love for his ex-wife was as strong today as it had been when they'd first dated, stronger even, than the heartbreak over Eoin and all.

But rather than trying to explain that to Dylan, he came up with a one-word answer.

'Aye.' That was all he could tell Dylan—at least for now.

The professor gave him a quizzical look. 'You are a man of few words when you want to be, Joseph.'

'Maybe I missed out on the gift of the gab when they were handing them out.'

The professor chuckled. 'That, my friend, is as far from the truth as it's possible to get. Anyway, if this means you and Kate have a chance to find your way back to each other, then I'm all for it. Some relationships are only meant to be for a short time, a brief spark of warmth on a winter's night and companionship that enriches each other's lives. However, some, and I'm obviously talking about you and Kate here, are a story that lasts forever.'

'Good God, man, have you been reading romance books on the sly?'

Dylan let out a real belly laugh. 'No, but just because I'm a bachelor doesn't mean I don't know a thing or two about love.' The professor's gaze settled back on the fire and he didn't elaborate any further.

But Joseph knew his friend well enough to know he was holding something back and he had a good idea what it was.

'You're talking about Iris, aren't you?'

Dylan shot him a look. 'I didn't say anything of the sort.'

'Then look me in the eye and deny there isn't something

between you two. Or are you going to accuse me of being an Irish romantic now?'

The professor opened his mouth to say something, his expression indignant. But then his shoulders dropped and his expression softened. 'I should have known you'd be able to see straight through me.'

'Aye, much like you can with me. So tell me, my friend, why aren't you two together? What's the story there?'

'I missed my chance far too many years ago, Joseph. You see, a fellow academic swept Iris off her feet and married her before I could even pluck up the courage to ask her out. Sadly, he eventually died from lung cancer. Theirs was a relationship that was meant to last, just like yours and Kate's. The problem is, even though I've always had feelings for Iris... What's the modern vernacular the students use? Oh, yes, unfortunately, she always had me in the friend's zone.' Dylan fell silent.

The DI could almost see the play of painful memories in the man's eyes.

Dylan blinked, surfacing from wherever he'd been in his mind. 'However, this conversation isn't about me, it's about you and Kate. So take it from me, now that you both have the opportunity to let each other fully back into your lives, please grab it with both hands. Don't live a life of regret like I have, Joseph.'

'Seriously, you think I should give it a second whirl with Kate?'

'To be honest, I'm surprised you didn't years ago. Don't spend your life pining away for the love of a woman you know you're meant to be with.'

Just like a switch had been thrown, the DI felt he was able to really breathe again. He also knew in that moment, with every fibre of his being, that Dylan was right.

'Okay, but I'm going to blame you if this all blows up in my face,' he said.

'Trust me, it won't. Now, what do you say to another glass of Monkey 47? Maybe it will touch the sides this time so you can actually taste it.'

Joseph laughed. 'Now that sounds like a plan.'

It was as Dylan was refilling his glass that Joseph's phone pinged. When he glanced at the screen his heart leapt. It was from Kate.

'Ellie heard from John that you've finally solved the Hooded Reaper case. What do you say to that delayed family and friends Sunday meal tomorrow at mine to celebrate? Obviously bring Dylan and Amy. Also, it will give us a chance to discreetly catch up.'

Joseph looked across at the professor as he started to pour the tonic into their glasses. 'Are you up for a Sunday lunch over at Kate's? She's in the mood to celebrate the end of our investigation.'

'Absolutely, and tell her I will join her in the kitchen to help.'

'I think that was part of her cunning plan all along.'

Joseph started to compose his reply to Kate. *'Count Dylan and me in, but Amy won't be coming...'* But how to handle the crime syndicate situation. *'I'm afraid everything has gone quiet on the other front, apart from the fact I now know for certain that Chris is innocent.'* He hit send.

Her reply came back less than ten seconds later. Kate had always been a fast typer. *'Bad news about NW, but thank god about Chris. Is everything okay with Amy?'*

'We'll talk about that tomorrow, x,' Joseph replied.

'Okay. x'

Joseph gazed at Kate's reply, easily imagining what would be going through her mind right now—whether Amy not coming had anything to do with the incident on the boat.

Dylan handed the refilled glass to Joseph. 'Now this time, try to appreciate it, my friend.'

'Oh, trust me, I will,' Joseph said, breathing in the scent of fruit, warm spices, and a subtle woody fragrance in the background. 'If it tastes half as good as it smells, I'm in for a treat.'

'You are, my friend, you are,' Dylan said, clinking his glass against Joseph's.

Joseph gave his friend a thoughtful look. 'How about inviting Iris to join us tomorrow?'

The professor narrowed his gaze. 'Have you got an ulterior motive for suggesting that?'

'Of course I have. And you can expect a lot more of that sort of thing in the future as well. At least until you sort it out. Advice can go both ways when it comes to matters of the heart, you know.'

'So it would seem,' Dylan said, looking at his friend and chuckling.

CHAPTER THIRTY-THREE

They were all gathered around the table in Kate's house. It put Joseph in mind of the good old days when their family meals had always been like this. Plenty of laughter, warmth, and enough love to fill your boots many times over.

Ellie and John were on great form, and generally keeping everyone laughing in something of a double act. But Iris often held the stage as well with old anecdotes about when she and Dylan had both been lecturing, leaving everyone in tears.

More than once Kate had caught Joseph's eye with a look that said, *God, I've missed this.*

She wasn't the only one.

For Joseph, this key equation of life—family—had been absent from his life for far too long. Now, here among the people he cared most about in the world, he felt a real sense of peace. Yes, this was what life was all about. Precious moments exactly like this one.

John pushed his empty plate away. 'Kate, that roast was absolutely amazing. Your potatoes were fantastic.'

'Ah, that will be down to my secret ingredient, namely

Dylan, who insisted on dealing with all of the veg, although I will take credit for the chicken.'

Dylan raised his glass to her. 'Well, your chicken was a triumph, and stuffing it with that orange made the meat beautifully moist. As far as my veg go, I do have a few tricks up my sleeve. A bit of honey added at the end of roasting them, along with a hint of rosemary, makes all the difference. As for the potatoes, goose fat of course, but also squashing the potatoes halfway through, creates lots of crispy edges.'

'Which is obviously the best bit,' Ellie said, finishing off the last one on her plate, before John beat her to it.

'Even I'm impressed,' Iris said. 'Your cauliflower cheese was simply'—she kissed her fingertips—'divine.'

Dylan couldn't help smiling at her. 'Using Gruyère in the sauce is the secret there.'

'Well, I had no idea you were such an exceptional cook. First baking, and now this latest revelation.'

Everyone gathered around the table gawped first at her, and then at Dylan.

'You've never cooked for Iris before?' Kate asked the professor, voicing what everyone was thinking.

Dylan shrugged. 'A bit of baking, but I suppose I never got round to a proper meal.'

'Then you owe it to her to start, so she knows what she's been missing,' Ellie said.

Joseph nodded. 'Yes, absolutely. It seems you've been hiding your light under a bushel all these years.'

'We'll have to sort something out,' Iris said, pointedly ignoring the grin Joseph was sporting.

Kate stood. 'Now I doubt anyone has any room, but who's up for a good old-fashioned trifle?'

'Count me in. Yours have always been the best,' Joseph said.

Ellie nodded enthusiastically.

'Okay. Maybe you can give me a hand, Joseph?' Kate said, tugging her ear—the old family code for *we need to talk*.

Joseph collected plates before finally heading to the kitchen. He found Kate leaning against the sink with an expectant look on her face.

'So?' she asked.

'So...' Joseph replied, deciding to kick off with the easier of the subjects. 'It seems that the Night Watchmen believe I'm fully onboard now, so it looks like Ellie is going to be safe.' Of course, in reality, he knew nothing of the sort for certain. But with knowing that one of the NCA team was keeping an eye out for her, gave him confidence she was in good hands.

Kate shut her eyes for a moment before opening them again. 'I can't tell you what a relief it is to hear that. But what about our investigation?'

'I know how hard this is going to be for you to hear, but I think we need to back off for now, Kate. At the moment they think they have me and Derrick under their thumb, so let's not rock the boat any more than we have to.'

Rather than the storm of protests he'd been expecting, Kate just nodded. 'I don't think my heart could handle it if Ellie's life was threatened again by anything that we did. Is Derrick on board with this as well?'

'I haven't actually spoken to him about it, but I doubt he'll disagree considering the stakes.'

'Okay. Just promise me we're not going to let them get away with all of this.'

'Don't worry, we won't. And when the right moment comes, we'll strike and they won't know what's hit them.'

'Then that certainly sounds okay to me.' She raised her chin a fraction towards him. 'So tell me about Amy?'

Joseph held her gaze for a moment. 'Basically, it's over between us.'

Her hands flew to her mouth. 'Please tell me this doesn't have anything to do with the other day on your boat?'

'Not entirely, but that was the straw that broke the camel's back. But before you get the wrong idea, I was the one who ended it.'

Her eyes searched his. 'But why, Joseph?'

'Why do you think?'

There was no need for any more words. An invisible magnetic force drew the two of them together until mere centimetres separated them.

Joseph reached out slowly and held Kate's face between his hands. 'I love you so much,' he finally whispered.

Kate opened her mouth, then closed it again, before doing a little nod. 'Me too,' she finally replied. Then, just like that, their lips found each other and the world melted away around them.

A cough came from behind them and they both turned to see Ellie standing in the doorway with her empty plate.

'Is this what it looks like?' she asked, looking between her parents.

Kate held out her hand to her daughter. 'I'm not sure, but I certainly hope so.'

'And I intend to have a lot of fun finding out,' Joseph added, beaming at the woman who had taken up permanent residence in his heart long ago.

Ellie rushed over, tears in her eyes, as she took her mum's hand and was drawn into a family hug. They all stood like that for a while, no one speaking, but hanging onto each other, because what else needed to be said?

JOIN THE J.R. SINCLAIR VIP CLUB

To get instant access to exclusive photos of locations used from the series, and the latest news from J.R. Sinclair, just subscribe here to start receiving your free content: https://www.subscribepage.com/n4zom8

ORDER SHADOWS OF THE MIND

DI Joseph Stone will return in
Shadows of the Mind

Order now: https://geni.us/ShadowsoftheMind

Printed in Great Britain
by Amazon